Little Kiss of Snow

A CREATURE CAFE CHRISTMAS ANTHOLOGY

CLIO EVANS

Contents

The Barista

"'T was the night before Christmas...."

"Don't you fucking start," I grumbled, giving Lucy a look that made him laugh.

Trixie snorted as she handed me a box of ornaments, raising a pink brow. "Hang the ornaments and then let's get out of here," she said, her voice lingering with want.

I narrowed my eyes but didn't disagree with her command. Plus, she'd spent a long time making these ornaments, and I was happy to see what they'd look like.

"Your hot chocolate, little angel," Lucy chimed, setting down the mugs on the table.

Trixie winked at me, leaning up to kiss my bearded cheek before going to our mate and sitting next to him. The devil himself was jollier than fucking St. Nick, but I couldn't complain.

It was the first night in a while that we were away from the twins, and I was nervous. I'd already checked my phone five times before Lucy had taken it from me, hiding it somewhere in the Cafe despite my threats.

We had a daughter and a son— Layla and Luca. Our

daughter took after me, and to our happy surprise, our son took after Lucy.

I smiled to myself as I turned, looking down at the ornaments. We had picked up a massive Christmas tree for the corner of the Cafe, fitting it in just barely. It was covered in garland, ornaments of all kinds, and twinkling lights.

There was only one thing missing. Well... ten things missing.

I reached into the box Trixie had given me and pulled out the first ornament. It was a little frame with a picture of Dante and Peter. Warmth spread through my chest, and I stared at it for a moment.

It had been about five years since I had matched these two, and they were happy. They had Inferna and Archie, their friends, and their pets. I'd seen a hardened demon turn into someone that loved his human more than anyone else in the world.

We'd formed a family, a tight network of friends that had only grown over the years. My daughter and son played with their kids, growing up alongside the children that came from the matches I'd made.

I still made matches, although it wasn't quite as swamped as that period of time had been.

"I wonder what they're up to tonight," Lucy chuckled.

I looked back over my shoulder at him, bringing a laugh from him and Trixie.

"I think we all know," I snorted, hanging the ornament on the tree.

"Should we expect another demon baby?"

"You tell me, little devil," I said.

"I think they're done," Trixie giggled. "Peter swore up and down that they were happy with two."

"Two is a lot," I said, thinking about ours.

Fucking hell, they were the most amazing and scariest thing that had happened to me. Every day, I wondered if immortality was really a thing when you had children.

I picked up the next ornament. Kat, Dracon, and Dell all grinned back at me, their names written in my mate's lovely handwriting.

"These are lovely, baby," I said.

"Thank you," Trixie sighed happily. "I thought it would be nice. I know the tree won't be up too much longer, but... it'll be nice for them to see once we're all around this week."

"Plus, the kids will like it," Lucy said. "Also... how much are we paying the babysitter?"

"Enough," I said, paling some.

We had plenty of money, but that had been a hefty bill. Understandable. Christmas Eve and...

"How many kids did we send them again?" I asked, turning to look at my mates.

"Eleven," Trixie said. "Our twins, Dante and Peter's two, the wolf trio, and then Jasper and Alex's four."

That had been a surprise to me, a happy one. Alex and Jasper had adopted orcs that needed parents, building a happy home for all of them. They had three sons and a daughter, all of them of different ages. The oldest was in his teens and a bit reckless sometimes, but they were working on that.

Then there were the wolf boys. Quinn, Luna, and Al had their hands full almost all of the time with those three. They were a wild bunch, and I could only laugh when my dear friends had to drag them by the scruffs out of the Cafe.

Raising werewolves wasn't easy.

Then, of course, there was Inferna and Archie. Inferna was independent and knew what she wanted— she looked like Dante. And then Archie looked more like Peter and preferred to keep to himself.

The babysitter was someone that I'd known for a couple thousand years, a Kraken woman that could handle eleven monster children with ease for one night.

Well, hopefully.

I picked up the next ornament and hung it up. Rum and Penny grinned back at me, happy as can be. Rum was covered in paint, as always.

Next was Meduso and Noah. I wasn't sure how Trixie had talked Meduso into a picture, but even my evil friend was smiling.

Al, Luna, and Quinn were next— Quinn's cheeks bright pink from being sandwiched between her mates.

Melody, Icarus, and Dalus grinned back at me next. I smiled, raising a brow.

"Did they send you a picture from the road?" I asked.

"Yeah," Trixie said, sipping her hot chocolate.

Dalus' music had taken off, and the three of them were out in the world a lot of the time now, coming back to the Cafe here and there and to visit Ella and Naomi.

"They look happy," I said, smiling.

"They are because of you," Trixie chimed.

Lucy chuckled, leaning back in his chair to sip his hot chocolate. I heard a little gasp and looked back, not surprised to see that his tail was now wrapped around Trixie's thighs.

"No games until I'm finished," I said. "And then we'll go home, and you'll find out what I have planned."

Both of their faces lit up with curiosity as I turned back to our tree.

The seventh ornament was Ella and Naomi, both gorgeous and smirking. The eighth was Jasper and Alex, both making silly faces. The ninth was Cam, Gabe, and Seth.

I smiled, lingering on theirs for a moment.

Gabe, surprisingly, had become a very good half-brother to

my kids— acting like an uncle most of the time. The three of them had become close, and I was happy to know that, over time, he and Lucy had healed some of their issues.

Lucy was still a jackass sometimes, but that was his nature and it was different now.

"They'll be over tomorrow," Trixie said, knowing that I was looking at their picture. "Gabe said that they had gifts for Luca and Layla."

"Oh gods," I sighed.

"I told them no pets this year," Lucy said, knowing what I was thinking about.

"Good," I said.

Last year, Gabe had shown up with a puppy *from hell*. By the time I'd opened my mouth to argue, Luca and Layla had run off in the yard with the puppy and Lucy and Trixie with them.

"Bean is a good dog," Trixie laughed. "Even if he had three eyes."

"He's not a dog," I sighed. "He's literally from hell."

"He's good," Lucy chuckled. "And you like him."

I refused to admit that.

But it was true.

I hung up the ornaments, saving ours for last. I pulled it out of the box, grinning.

We'd taken a picture last month— a full family one. Lucy, Trixie, Luca, Layla, Bean, and me.

Never in a million fucking years would I have believed I'd wear matching clothes with my family, but this photo was living proof that even the Grim Reaper could fall in love and have fun.

I hung it up, taking a step back with a grin.

Our tree was the best, casting warmth over the rest of Creature Cafe.

I turned around, giving Lucy and Trixie a look. The look.

"'Twas the night before Christmas...."

"If you say it again, I'm going to flay you without fucking you."

Lucy barked out a laugh, but my threat shut him up.

"Time to go," I said. "We have things to do, *mates*. And we will be back in the morning to celebrate with everyone."

Trixie stood up, her cheeks rosy with excitement. "Am I going to get devoured by my monsters?"

"More like fucked by them, but yes."

"Well, then," she said. "Let's go. Merry Christmas to me."

With that, the three of us turned off the lights of the Cafe and went out into the snowy night, knowing that we weren't the only creatures about to do some naughty things on this Christmas Eve night.

Jingle Balls

DANTE AND PETER

'Twas the Night before Christmas,
In a warm cozy cabin,
Where an incubus longed
to give in to his passion...

In this Holiday Tale,
you will find the following:

PIERCINGS

BONDAGE

DEGRADATION

COMPLETE SUBMISSION,

SPANKING

BALL GAGS

COCK CAGES

TAIL FUCKING

AND MORE.

CHAPTER 1

Peter

I plopped on the couch with a groan, closing my eyes for just a moment.

It was Christmas Eve and Dante and I had just dropped off Inferna and Archie at the babysitter. I almost felt bad for them, but they had agreed to watch all the children tonight for a very large amount of money that all of us adults had pooled together over the past year.

This was the first holiday in five years where I would be with just Dante. We were both excited, nervous, apprehensive, and doing our best to not feel any guilt. But, Inferna and Archie had been more than excited to go over to the babysitter and play with all of the other kids.

Plus, we all had a fun surprise for them in the morning at the cafe when they woke up.

"Still thinking about the kids?" Dante chuckled as he locked the front door.

We had booked a small cabin outside of town, one that was small and out of earshot of monsters and humans alike. It was quaint and cozy, the wooden walls keeping the warmth from the fireplace from escaping out into the snowy night. There was a couch and also a couple of chairs, both draped with soft flannel blankets.

We were completely alone.

I opened my eyes and lifted my head, smiling at him. Dante was still sexier than sin, the entire room filled up with his presence. He had become a little softer since we'd started to build a life together, the two of us growing closer with every year that had passed.

I loved my possessive, cranky, and exceptionally sexy incubus with every part of my soul.

I let out a breath, letting my worries go with it. "Yes," I said. "But... I think I might be able to forget for awhile."

"Oh, you will, my little pet," he purred. "I have plans."

"Plans?" I asked, raising a brow.

"Yes," he said, coming to me.

He knelt down next to the couch, holding my face with his clawed crimson hands. He planted a kiss on my lips and I parted them, deepening it with a soft moan.

Fuck, it had been too long. Having two very curious children meant that we'd had to lock all of our toys up and only bring them out when we were absolutely sure the two of them wouldn't wake up. Inferna in particular had a habit of finding things she shouldn't, going as far as running through the house waving a dildo around like a sword and chasing her brother.

Dante let out a low growl, drawing back for a moment. "I love you," he whispered, his breath tickling my ear. "And I'm going to destroy you tonight."

"Please," I whispered, my heart skipping a beat. "I want you to."

"Safeword?" he murmured.

"Pie," I said, swallowing hard.

"Good boy," he praised softly.

He gave me a gentle kiss and I knew it was going to be the last one I would get until he was done with me tonight.

The thought already had my cock hardening against my jeans.

He hissed, his hand curling around my throat. I sucked in a breath just as he squeezed, the pressure on the sides of my neck making my vision dot.

"Dante," I whimpered.

The air sizzled with heat as his tail wound up my leg, tugging at my waistband. He let go and I dragged in a breath, blinking quickly. He pulled me to standing, gripping my hair and keeping our bodies pressed together.

Over the last few years, his black hair had developed a small strip of gray. He blamed it entirely on having children, although he enjoyed everything about our two little monsters.

I reached up, curling my finger through the strand. He let out a soft growl, his cock hardening in his pants. I swallowed hard as it lengthened against my own.

"I think that we need to celebrate, pet," he whispered, his thumb slipping into the corner of my mouth. I bit him gently, heat spearing through me.

My mouth went dry, my heart pounding. All of the wicked things that came through my head left me wondering what devious activities he had planned.

"Strip," Dante commanded, taking a step back from me. He licked his lips, his gaze turning hungry. "We're going to celebrate by turning you into my little Christmas whore."

I let out a groan, already pulling off my clothes. They fell to the floor, gathering in a pile.

Our cabin was already toasty from the fire, but now it was turning into an inferno. Warm light spread over us from the Christmas tree and from the hearth, his shadow dancing behind him as he began to circle me. His tail traced my taut muscles as he walked, his growl becoming louder as the last of my clothing fell.

I was all too eager to be taken by him. I craved to be commanded, to be fucked. I was his human pet, and my body and soul belonged to him and him alone.

"You've been bad," he growled, his voice dropping low. "A naughty little pet. A little dirty whore that deserves to have his hole punished."

"Yes," I whispered. "Please, Dante. Punish me."

His laughter surrounded me. "Remember that you asked for it, pet."

I watched as he turned and went to a bag set on the floor by the door. He reached into it, pulling out a wrapped box. He took it to the small tree and put it beneath it, a smirk tugging at his lips.

"Crawl to me," he said, placing his arms behind his back.

It had been five years since this incubus had swept me off to a gothic manor, had tail fucked me in the park, and had made me his. Five years, but his commands still sent a shiver straight down my spine.

My cock was standing straight up now, but I didn't dare touch it yet. I fell to my hands and knees, still looking up at him as I crawled across the floor.

I stopped when I got to him, looking down at his feet. His tail slid around, the tip pushing my head back.

I gasped as I looked at him, my neck straining.

"Little pet," he said, giving me a benevolently evil grin. "There's a blue present beneath this little tree with your name on it. Open it."

Shadows lapped at his crimson skin, the golden glow of the tree giving his black eyes smiling crescent reflections.

My heart continued to pound as I picked up my present. There was a gift tag that said 'Peter, my soul mate'.

My eyes teared up for a moment as I untied the ribbon and tore back the paper, revealing a black box. I pulled off the lid, peeking inside.

A black blindfold, a ball gag, a red diamond cock piercing, and a new cock cage.

"Fuck," I wheezed. My blood rushed in my ears, a moan escaping me.

Dante tipped my face up with his tail again, lowering his face to mine. "I will be back in five minutes. I expect you to have fitted the cock cage on and the ball gag," he said, grinning as he let go of me.

He moved past me briskly and I turned to gape at him, but he'd already disappeared.

"Fuck," I mumbled.

I spread all of the items out, staring at the cock cage.

He'd given me an impossible command. I let out a soft groan, reaching down to stroke my cock. The only way I was getting that cage on was if I could make my erection disappear, which was damn near impossible unless I was able to cum.

I moved across the living room floor, and grabbed the clothing I had stripped out of. I balled it all up, placing it under my cock. Then, I began to hump it as hard as possible, attempting to drive myself to cum.

I let out a soft pant, desperate. I was desperate to obey him, but there was no way I would cum so fast without his tail inside of me.

"One minute!" Dante called.

Fuck.

"'Twas the night before Christmas...."

I let out a gasp as his voice echoed around me. I humped harder, wishing it was his hand wrapped around me instead of my own. Wishing his tail was fucking me, that his ridged cock was breeding me.

"And all through the house...."

Fuck. I moaned, my hips moving with desperation.

"Your creature was watching...."

I *could* feel him watching me now.

I was so close to cumming. All the pent-up desire from the last couple of days unfurled, pleasure swirling through me.

"The way you squirm like a trapped mouse."

The back of my head was suddenly yanked back, my eyes flying open.

Dante stared down at me, his black eyes burning a hole into my soul.

"I was going to be nice, but you couldn't obey me, Peter," he whispered gleefully. "Now, you're on my naughty list."

He dragged me back by my hair, making me cry out as he took me to the presents I had left sprawled out. Dante leaned forward and snatched the blindfold from the floor.

His tail curled around my neck, restricting my air. I choked as he tied the silken fabric around my face, bathing me in darkness.

I heard the jingling of metal and sucked in a breath as his tail loosened.

"Open up," he grunted.

I obeyed with a moan.

A ball was popped between my lips, forcing my mouth to stay open. He buckled the straps, fastening them tightly to my head.

His tail slipped down to my cock, and I immediately bucked my hips. Saliva was already starting to drip down my chin as I started to pant from his touch.

"Hands behind your back, Peter."

I moved them behind me, listening to his shuffling intensely. The tip of his tail lifted my chin up, and I heard his growl turn into a dark purr.

"Such a dirty little pet," he chuckled. "Can't even put a cock cage on right. Stay still. I'm going to tie you up."

He began to bind me, knotting the ropes around my body—around my chest, thighs, hips, legs, and arms.

The silence made my cock even harder, the sounds of the crackling firewood and the rope sliding over my skin the only thing I could hear.

He was taking his time, making sure that his fingertips lingered as they brushed my muscles. There was something still tender in his touch, but it was like being kissed by a flame. I was on fire, and he was just adding drops of gasoline to me.

I wanted whatever punishment he would give me. Whatever he did to me, whatever he decided I was worthy of.

His tail played with me while he tied me up, teasing my cock before sliding up to my nipples. I moaned as it eased back down, testing my entrance.

I wasn't able to move now, the ropes keeping me in position. I heard the clip and found myself wondering when a rig had been installed in the living room of this rural cabin.

Dante really had planned this out, all the way down to even this detail.

I should have known when he told me he would take care of booking the right place if I arranged the babysitter.

"Awww, my poor little pet. What are we going to do about this?" Dante taunted.

I felt his fingertips trace my hard shaft, dragging the tip of a nail over the pulsing veins. I shuddered as he paused and tugged the piercing he'd given me. I tried to shift my body, but the bindings wouldn't allow it.

I felt his hot breath against my chest. I groaned as his tongue flicked over one of my nipples, teasing me. He then circled around it, sending little shocks of pleasure through me. "Mmmm... you taste good, pet."

His dark laugh floated around me again, followed by silence. My ears strained as I tried to listen for his movement. I moaned around the ball in my mouth, letting my head fall forward.

Out of nowhere, pain cracked across my ass, his palm striking me. I yelped, tears springing to my eyes.

Another slap, harder than the first. Pain lashed through me again, my skin bursting with heat from the impact.

"Not red enough," Dante murmured. "I think it's time to decorate you. I think a new piercing would be good too, one with an ornament hanging from it. But we'll save that for last."

Fuck. I heard him move now, heard the soft clinks of ornaments hitting each other. Bells jingled, and I scowled as Dante tied them around my neck. He slapped my face playfully, and the bells sang in unison.

"We'll start with your nipples," he whispered gleefully. "And I want you to watch."

I dragged in a breath, groaning as the blindfold was ripped free. My vision was swamped with blinking red and green lights, and I realized that it was coming from me.

I dropped my head, looking down at my body in awe. He had tied me in ropes, but some of the ropes were intertwined with Christmas lights.

I was brighter than a damn Christmas tree.

Dante was kneeling beneath me, and I realized he was holding an ornament and a very sharp needle in his hand. He craned his neck back, meeting my gaze for a moment.

"I'm going to decorate you and then fuck you," he promised happily. "And then after I fuck you, I'm going to fuck you again. I'm going to fuck you until I think you've been bred, and then I'm going to make you clean my balls with your tongue. Then, we'll have some hot chocolate and a nice cuddle and sleep through the night."

My mouth would have fallen open, but it was already as wide as it would go around the ball wedged there.

He winked at me, and then in a flash, the needle was going straight through my nipple, then replaced by the twinkling ornament.

The pain made me scream, but it was soon turned into a helpless cry as Dante took my cock between his lips and sucked. His tail wound up around him, moving up my body and then stroking my ass. Pleasure bloomed, even though tears were rolling down my cheeks.

He continued to suck my aching cock, taking me all the way into his throat. He dominated every part of me. He owned my cock, my soul, my heart, my body.

He drew back and kissed my skin, his tongue swirling up to find the freshly pierced nipple. The weight of the ornament pulled, and now that the pain was beginning to fade— I realized there was even more pleasure. It was like my nipple was being tugged.

The tip of his tongue flicked across the bud, sending another shiver down my spine. "You taste like salvation," he hummed.

My eyes widened, my cheeks flushing. He turned to look at me and leaned forward, licking my chin and around my mouth. He swallowed and then grinned as he moved out from beneath me.

My eyes followed him as he went to a pile of round ornaments. I watched as he picked one out, a silver ball with glitter. The light flashed across it as he turned it over, inspecting what he was about to add to me. He then grabbed the cock piercing that was on the floor next to the cage, coming back over to me.

He bumped the nipple ornament, and I groaned as it swung, pain and pleasure spearing through me.

His hot breath blew on my cock, and my hips tried to move,

desperate for his touch. His tongue lapped out, circling just the tip. I watched the back of his head move, entranced.

His teeth gave the piercing there a small tug, drawing another sound out of me.

He was here to torture me. To drive me to the edge, to a place only he could take me to.

"Accept the pain, little pet," he commanded.

My heart began to beat faster as I anticipated what he was about to do. I felt the prick of the needle as he traced one of the veins bursting along my shaft, drawing in short breaths. He continued to flick his tongue across the tip as he tortured me, the pressure of the needle intensifying enough to bring forward the sensation of fire.

I squeezed my eyes shut, listening to the sound of his wet tongue lavishing.

He lifted my cock up, licking the underside of the head. I felt the needle shift down and made a noise.

No, I tried to moan, but my word was muffled entirely. It didn't matter if I said no.

I wanted this. I wanted this more than anything, and I trusted Dante.

I began to squirm, even though I knew it was pointless.

Dante's tail suddenly moved up my body, winding around my neck. I felt the buckles around my head loosen, the ball gag falling free.

I gagged and then coughed, testing my mouth to make sure it still worked.

"Dante," I gasped. "Dante —"

The tip of his tail forced its way into my mouth, drowning out the calling of his name.

"Relax," he purred, "Just the foreskin. If it's ever too much, you know our safe word and our signal."

It was quick and nearly painless, but I still choked on his tail as he pierced me. The tail began to move in and out, and I groaned as he took my entire cock back into his mouth, the piercing moving back and forth.

I was about to cum, I realized. I was about to cum, even though he had just pierced me, and I was deep throating his tail.

Fuck.

CHAPTER 2

Dante

Peter was writhing in his ropes, his cock hard in my mouth. I reached up and fingered him, listening for his moans as I sucked him. The bells around his neck jingled.

My chest burned with pride, with the undeniable bond I had to him. I knew how much he could take and how much he enjoyed the things that we did. I knew how far I could push him, how much I could break him.

Pleasure shot through me as he sucked the tip of my tail, his groans lost as it thrust in and out of his throat.

He was so close to cumming, and I knew it would only take a few more seconds before his cream would be spilling down my throat.

Then I'd be able to put that cage on him and get him hard all over again.

I bit down on his cock, just hard enough to make him scream but still gentle enough to bring him to another height of pleasure. His body was tugging at the ropes, his hips desperate to thrust.

I yanked my tail from his throat, allowing him to cry out as his cock began to pulse. His cum spilled into my mouth in spurts, the saltiness sitting on my tongue. I swallowed with a low growl and then drew back, watching him soften.

I licked my lips and leaned back, studying my work. Two piercings gleamed beneath the sparkling lights.

"Dante," he wheezed. "*Fuck.*"

I grinned to myself and leaned to the side, swiping the cock cage into my hands.

"Dante, I want you inside of me," he whispered.

My spine stiffened, and it took everything in me to ignore his quiet whimper.

"Dante, please," he said softly, breathless.

I still ignored him, studying the new cage. I began to fit it to his cock, still hiding my expressions from him.

"Please. Please," he gasped. "I need you to fuck me. *To breed me.*"

My head snapped around, and I looked at him, silencing him. "Did I not already tell you what I was going to do?" I sneered.

His bottom lip quivered, his breath leaving him.

"Since when did you start acting like such a brat?" I growled, raising a brow at him.

I watched his throat bob as he swallowed, and I turned back around, locking the cock cage. I grinned again, sitting on my haunches to study him. My mate was handsome, although definitely misbehaving.

I couldn't stand for that.

I moved out from beneath him and gathered up other ornaments. He stayed silent, aside from the soft breaths, as I began to decorate him— hanging ornaments from the ropes.

I picked up a round one made of glass and narrowed my eyes on Peter. I stepped in front of him, tipping his head up. His eyes widened, his skin beautifully flushed.

23

"Open," I commanded roughly.

His lips parted tentatively, his mouth widening.

"More," I growled.

He obeyed, opening as wide as possible.

I held up the glass ornament and popped it between his lips, watching it dawn on him what I was going to have him do.

"It's made of glass," I said softly, leaning in so that my nose was almost pressing against his. "If you drop it, this session will end. And make sure you don't crush it. I'd hate to see you hurt that way."

His breaths became erratic again, a moan escaping his throat.

I smirked and stepped back, admiring my mate again. His muscles were straining against the ropes, his skin red from the flush of pleasure. Tears were strolling down his cheeks, but there was still the gleam of dark desire burning in his eyes. The ornaments glinted in the light, the warmth of the living room surrounding us.

I had never been festive, but this would perhaps change my mind.

My cock was hard, aching to be buried inside of him. I wanted him to hold another child, another perfect outcome of our union. We had talked about it recently, and now the desire to breed him was burning in my soul.

I licked my lips and circled him slowly, tracing my fingertips along his back. His muscles shivered, his panting becoming louder. I gripped the rope and slowly spun him until his ass faced me.

"Mmm, you're such a treat," I whispered, swallowing back the dark part of me that wanted to rip into him.

I let my pants fall to the floor, stripping off all clothing. My cock sprang free, the ridges pulsing and eager. I gripped Peter's hips, moving closer to him. I held him in place, teasing him with just the tip of my cock.

He moaned, his body shivering. I knew he was fighting right now, fighting not to drop the ball and fighting not to crush it.

I stroked the curve of his ass lovingly, smiling to myself. "You can be such a good boy, Peter," I murmured. "My little pet. I've missed seeing you tied up and begging. Maybe the holidays aren't so bad."

He let out the softest noise, his head hanging down.

Without warning, I dug my fingertips into him and yanked him back— impaling him fully on my thirteen unforgiving inches. The ropes tightened as his body responded, his moan coming from deep within his throat. I began to thrust in and out of him, raking my nails down his back.

"Don't drop the ball, pet," I growled, pumping even harder. He felt like heaven, his hot body sheathing me with every pump. I lifted my tail, teasing his cock with it.

"*Mmmm*," Peter cried, his words gagged.

Pleasure burned through me, and I leaned closer to his body.

Fuck. I groaned loudly, tipping my head back as I continued to fuck him. I would make this last as long as possible— I wanted to know just how much he could take before dropping that damned ornament.

I slowed my thrusts, leaning forward to kiss his bare skin. "Nod if this is still good, pet," I whispered. "I want to know you're okay."

He lifted his head and nodded vigorously.

"You can drop the ball now," I said. "I want to hear your screams."

He immediately let it fall. I heard the glass shatter against the floor, and in the same moment, I pumped into him.

"Fuck!" he sobbed, dragging in ragged breaths. "Everything hurts, but everything feels so damn good."

"Good," I purred, "I love seeing you like this, pet. You're my perfect little present."

The lights that bound his body blinked as I started a brutal pace again, driving both of us to the edge. A cry ripped through me as I gave one last thrust, my cum spurting out of me and filling Peter. I held him close as I came, ensuring to keep every last drop inside of him.

I held him there for a while, floating in euphoria. I could feel our hearts fall into the same rhythm, our breathing slowing.

Finally, I pulled out of him, the cream spilling out of him and dripping to the floor. I spread his cheeks with my hands and leaned in, lapping at the mess.

"OH god," he gasped.

I looked up, licking my lips. "Yeah?"

"Please," he begged.

I grinned and then leaned back in, burying my tongue deep inside of him. I took my time cleaning him, listening to his whimpers.

Finally, I took a step back and went to the ropes that were attached to the rig, slowly lowering him until he almost touched the floor. I then went back to his body, scooping him up and then unclipping him. He was still bound in my arms, the perfect little present.

Peter's head immediately rested against my chest. "Fuck, that was amazing."

"We aren't done yet," I chuckled. "But I want to untie you."

I took him to the couch and laid him down, hovering over him as I began to loosen the knots and slowly untie him. He melted into the cushion, watching me with a loving gaze as I completely freed him. I unclipped the bells around his neck too, tossing them to the floor.

I was going to fuck him again, as I promised, but I would be more gentle. Somewhere in the the last few years, I had learned the true difference between making love and fucking.

I wanted to make love to him. To remind him that he was the center of my universe, the only reason I was whole. He had given me a family, given me a reason to try and be better.

I was still a monster, still a demon, but I was also Peter's mate— and that last part made me want to be better.

His arms immediately wound around my neck, and he drew me in for a kiss. Our tongues met, chased by the faint taste of blood. I drew back, scowling. "Did you get cut?"

Peter snorted, still kissing a trail from my jaw down my neck. He paused to suck, giving me a bite that I would call cute — especially for his very human teeth. "I'm fine," he murmured.

"Bite me again," I commanded. "As hard as you can."

He paused, letting out a breath. "You want me to bite you?"

I smirked, doing my best not to laugh. "Yes."

Peter's lips traced down my neck again, and then he paused, sucking hard. His teeth grazed me, hesitant.

"Are you scared you'll hurt me with your little teeth?" I teased, reaching down beneath us to play with his cock cage.

He groaned, arching beneath me. "I...I don't know," he gasped.

"Bite me, mate," I growled, gripping his balls.

He gave a yelp and then clamped his teeth down on my shoulder. His bite was soft at first, but then I gripped his cock harder, causing his teeth to bear down. Finally, he began to bite as hard as he could, drawing out a soft hiss from me.

The pain was refreshing, invigorating.

My cock sprang back to life, hardening against me. Peter let go with a gasp, his hand immediately finding my shaft and encircling it.

"You're so big," he groaned. "I want this inside of me again."

27

"You've become so demanding," I chuckled, but I didn't argue with him.

I lifted his legs, pulling them around my back. I drew back far enough, positioning my cock to push inside of him. I shifted forward, filling him up. He gasped beneath me, his hands fisting into the fabric of the couch.

The tip of my tail snaked forward, finding where my cock had entered him and joining. Peter's eyes flew open, his lips parting on a silent cry.

I stared down at him, cupping his face to look into his eyes. His cheeks were bright red, his eyes glazed over with lust.

I began to move, my cock and tail pistoning in and out in tandem.

"Look at me," I commanded, forcing his mouth open so that I could kiss him again.

I held his gaze for a moment before swallowing him up, our tongues meeting in heat. I gripped the cushion behind his head, ignoring the sound of it ripping beneath my talons. The couch began to screech, shifting as I fucked him harder. The sound of skin on skin echoed through the house, the fire crackling behind us.

Peter suddenly arched again, crying out. I felt his cum hit me, and I looked down, licking my lips as it leaked through the bars of his cage.

I sat back on my haunches, pulling his body closer. I gripped his thighs, watching my cock go in and out of him.

"Breed me," he gasped. "Please. *Fuck*."

Fuck, every time he begged to be bred, I couldn't control myself.

I growled, the primal part of me breaking free. I closed my eyes, my tail pulling out just as my cock went in, and I came again. I gasped, filling him up with everything I had.

I collapsed on top of him, laying my head on his chest and

listening to the pounding of his heart. His hands slid through my hair, playfully gripping my horns for just a moment.

"I love you," he murmured.

I smiled against him, breathing in his scent. "I love you too, Peter."

The two of us stayed like that for a while until, finally, I slowly pulled out of him. My cum spilled out of him again, leaking onto the couch.

I pressed my lips together. "Well. I guess I'm buying a couch for the hosts."

"Oh dear," Peter chuckled, moaning as he sat up. "Hmm... Perhaps we should make more use of the couch then, since it is damaged anyways."

He had a point.

Peter slid off the cushion, his knees hitting the floor. His eyes glinted with wickedness, his tongue darting out to wet his lips.

"You *are* naughty," I whispered. "My good little pet."

"I thought I was on clean up," he said, smirking as his hands ran up my thighs.

"Indeed," I grunted, sinking back into the couch. He spread my thighs, leaning in to swipe his tongue from the base of my shaft to the tip.

I groaned, closing my eyes. His tongue was pure bliss, and he was very detailed. He took my balls into his mouth, sucking gently before pausing on every ridge.

"You're hard again," Peter chuckled.

I opened my eyes, looking down at him. My cock was huge in his hands, dark red and throbbing. I could feel him smirking as he took one of my balls between his lips again. I narrowed my gaze. "And what are you going to do about it, *mate?*"

He sucked harder, and my cock jerked. Before he could

29

draw away, I reached forward and gripped his hair— forcing his mouth to the tip of my cock.

"Drink your milk, you naughty bastard," I growled, forcing his head down.

He choked on my cock, gagging around it. His nails dug into my thighs, leaving little half moon cuts. I let him go, and he drew back, gasping. But then, his hands wrapped around the base of my cock, and he began stroking, taking the tip back down his throat.

"Fuck!" I growled, my head falling back.

I hissed as pleasure speared me, forcing me to cum all over again. Peter swallowed quickly, doing his best to drink all of it. He licked up any droplets that escaped before cleaning his fingers, all the while watching me.

The bastard had me wrapped around his fingers, and he knew it.

Peter started to stand but then fell forward. I caught him, pulling him into my arms. "You idiot, you have to rest now. I'll clean everything up. Just stay here."

"On the cum stained couch?" he teased.

"Well, you said we should make use of it," I chuckled. "Stay here for now while I get some hot chocolate."

Peter nodded and relaxed, drawing one of the flannel blankets around his body as he curled up on the cushion. I paused for a moment, taking him in.

We had built such a beautiful life together.

"I'm not done with you for tonight," I said, smiling.

"I know," he chuckled, grinning. "I would expect nothing less."

I smirked and then leaned forward, kissing his forehead. I then rested mine against his for a moment, breathing in his scent. He wrapped his arms around me, holding me tight.

"I wonder how the others are doing," he said.

"Oh, I'm sure they're having fun. Dracon mentioned something about double knotting."

"Oh gods," Peter laughed.

I chuckled too and then stood. We still had the whole night ahead of us— one that would be filled with jingling balls, hot chocolate, and love.

O Cum, All Ye Faithful

KAT, DRACON, AND DELL

'Twas the Night before Christmas,
In their gothic home,
Two dragons eagerly await,
To make their kitten cum...

In this Holiday Tail,
you will find the following:

CUM INFLATION

DEGRADATION

COMPLETE SUBMISSION

TAIL FUCKING

BLOOD PLAY

BREEDING WITHOUT PREGNANCY

CUM EATING

SIZE DIFFERENCE

AND MORE.

CHAPTER 1

Kat

"We have the house to ourselves. No evil cat. No squalling children," Dracon said. "All for an entire night."

"Biscuit isn't evil," I snorted.

"I don't know. I think she's a demon," Dell chimed, shaking his head.

I grinned as Dell poured all three of us a glass of his finest wine, bringing it over to the kitchen island. It was a nice Dragonborn red, grown by some dragons and their mate in France.

It was wild how accustomed I had become to the world of monsters. Hearing about a winery in France owned by dragons no longer sounded like a fairytale and was something I'd come to enjoy.

It had been five years since the Barista paired the three of us. A weekend with two dragon shifters that would do anything to keep me by their side truly changed my life, and I loved everything about them.

Dell slid behind me after setting down the glasses, resting his chin on my shoulder. His face was freshly shaven, and he smelled amazing. Whatever cologne he had put on tonight made me want to kneel in front of him.

"Merry Christmas, kitten," he said softly.

A shiver of excitement worked up my spine, and I leaned into him, his warmth making my stomach flutter.

I caught my reflection in one of the windows in the living room across from the kitchen and studied us. I wore a silver dress with a sweetheart neck that glittered like crushed diamonds. My dragons loved things that sparkled, especially when they were on *me*. My blonde hair was swept back into a bun, and my lips were painted crimson red. My heels made me taller, although I was still shorter than Dell and Dracon.

Dell kissed my neck, drawing a moan from me. It was brief but enough to ignite a fire in my core.

Christmas Eve was upon us, and the three of us had decided that we would house sit. Rum and Penny had booked a place, as had Dante and Peter, and all the pets and children were with the babysitter.

"How much do you think this babysitter is making tonight?" Dracon asked, giving me a fanged grin.

His gaze raked over the two of us, burning with desire. I found myself staring at him, drinking in his appearance. He was wearing a steel gray button-down that hugged his muscles and slacks that made his ass look too damn good. His light brown skin was dusted with indigo scales, and his black hair swept back.

Dell nipped my ear lobe, jarring me from my daydream.

He stepped away with a devious little chuckle, leaving me hot and bothered.

"Uh. What?" I asked, clearing my throat.

Dracon only smiled, raising a brow. "How much do you think the babysitter is making tonight?"

His question damn near went in one ear and out the other.

His wings were tucked in behind him, the scales glistening in the lighting of our kitchen.

Five years together, and the two of them were still trouble. One dark look and I was putty in their clawed hands.

"Enough to live off for the rest of the year," Dell laughed. "Really though, it is nice to have some us time."

"It is," I said, letting out a pant.

I wasn't sure exactly what the two of them had planned for us, but I was excited. Dracon had been out and about more recently, going to 'get things for our time together'. Dell had been hoarding things in a closet that he had told me not to open, and I'd listened despite my curiosity.

I loved it when they surprised me.

"Well," Dracon said, his golden eyes twinkling with mischief. "A toast. To us."

"To us," I said, raising my wine glass.

"To us," Dell said, a grin spreading across his face.

We clinked them together, and I took a sip, letting out a happy sigh.

Dracon and Dell both sipped theirs, and then Dracon set his glass down.

I felt my pussy flutter now. He had that look, the dangerous one. The one that made me think he could swallow me up here and now.

"Come here, kitten," he said.

Dell smirked and moved aside, allowing me to go to our mate. In one swift motion, Dracon lifted me up onto the bar.

"Close your eyes," he said.

I listened to him, closing them. I heard the two of them shuffle, the sound of a box opening.

"Open your mouth."

I smiled a little and then listened, opening my mouth for them.

He held something to my lips, putting it in my mouth. I immediately groaned as the sweet and silky taste of chocolate met my tongue.

Oh fuck, it was glorious.

I opened my eyes as I chewed, the taste of dark chocolate and peppermint making me moan again.

Dracon held a little box of chocolates, each a piece of art. Artisanal Christmas chocolates.

"That's wonderful," I said. "Gods, they're gorgeous."

"Dell picked them out," Dracon said, giving him an appreciative look. "I picked out the flavors."

Oh, dear. I raised a brow, wondering if he'd put special ingredients in it....

"Dare I ask?" I asked.

Dell snorted. "You know the answer."

"Oh goodness," I said, but I still smiled. "So some of them have your cum in them?"

"Yep," Dracon said happily. "Not that you'd notice."

"I'll look for the extra creamy ones. You're both a little crazy sometimes."

It was true, but I had no complaints. Plus, dragon shifter cum was a lot tastier than it had a right to be.

Dracon leaned forward and stole a kiss, drawing out a moan from me as his fingers glided up my thighs. He set the chocolates to the side on the counter and pushed up the skirt of my dress, letting out a low growl.

"No underwear," he growled, shaking his head. "Such a naughty girl."

Ah fuck. My head tilted back in a gasp as he ran his fingers over my pussy.

"She's already wet for us, little dragon," he said, giving Dell a dark look.

I'd planned that, and it had been a good plan.

"She's a needy little slut," Dell said, the lilt of his accent making my heartbeat stumble.

Fuck, I was so lucky. Not only did I have two mates that were incredibly sexy, but both of them were also dragon shifters that loved turning me on.

My lips parted on a gasp as Dracon rubbed the pad of his thumb over my clit, humming deeply.

His other hand suddenly shot up, curling around my neck and drawing a groan from me. He squeezed, and I gasped, my blood rushing in my veins.

"Who's pussy is this?" he whispered, his thumb continuing to rub my clit.

Fuck. Heat rushed through me. He'd only just started touching me, and I was already close to the edge.

"Yours," I groaned. "Please. Please breed me."

"No," he growled. "Not yet, kitten. I want to hear you say it again."

"My pussy is yours," I rasped. "Yours to use however you want."

"Good girl," he praised, his grip easing on my throat.

He pulled his thumb away from my clit and offered it to me. I opened my mouth, sucking his thumb and tasting myself on it.

Fuck, I was so wet. So fucking wet.

"Keep sucking," he said.

I obeyed him, my eyes locked with his now.

"So obedient," he whispered.

I was lost in him already.

He pulled his thumb free and took a step back, looking at Dell. "Take her to our nest and get her ready."

"Yes," Dell said.

I looked down at both of their cocks as Dell came to me. They were both already hard, their cocks straining against their pants.

Dell picked me up with ease, carrying me out of the kitchen and down the hall to our nest.

Normally, we'd have all the magic barriers up around the rooms so that no one could hear anyone moaning or screaming, but they were down right now.

Whatever Dracon was doing, he wanted to be able to hear what Dell was going to do to me.

I wrapped my arm around his neck, pressing my lips against his ear.

"Are you going to breed me?" I whispered.

"Fuck," he mumbled. "Kitten, I'm going to do all sorts of things to you.

He kicked open the door to our nest and took me to the center of it, setting me down. He pulled me into a hungry kiss, his hands running down my body.

Fuck. I drank him in, reveling in his taste. His teeth pricked my bottom lip hard enough to draw blood, and he drew back— licking up the drops that were on his.

"I'm going to make you scream, kitten," he whispered.

My nipples hardened at his words. The way he said them, it was as if it was the only thing he cared about in the universe. Making me scream, making me cum for him.

Getting me ready for what our mate planned.

Anticipation and excitement ran through me, all mixed with heavy lust.

His claws curled into my hair and gripped while his other hand swiped down my dress, ripping the fabric. I gasped as he tore the dress away, tossing it to the floor.

"My dress!"

"I'll buy you a new one," he said, sending me to my knees. "I'll buy you twenty new ones. Suck my cock, kitten."

Fuck. I loved it when he was rough with me.

He gripped my hair harder, drawing a squeal from me. I reached up, unbuttoning his pants and freeing his hard cock.

I'd never get over his cock. It was beautiful, long and thick, and unlike anything that belonged to a regular human. It glistened in the warm lighting of our nest, precum dripping from the tip.

I leaned forward eagerly and licked the drop, groaning.

"You're taking both of our cocks tonight," he said.

"Both?" I gasped.

"Yes. Both."

Fuck. "How?"

"Suck my cock, kitten, like I told you to."

I groaned and took the head of his cock between my lips, enjoying the little gasp I got from him. My jaw stretched as I took as much as I could, gripping the base of his shaft.

He let out a little moan, his claws holding my head still as he began to pull his hips back and then thrust forward. He was gentle but still pushed me more than he ever had before. Tears filled my eyes, and I moaned, relaxing around him.

I wanted him to use me. To fuck me however he wanted. I gave into that wave of need, the one that dragged me down to a place I loved.

He let out a long grunt, fucking my face a little harder. "We're going to use our magic and stretch your little cunt," he growled. "Make it so you can fit our cocks together, kitten. And we're going to make you cum until you beg us to stop."

Together? They were going to take me together?

He pulled his cock free, and I gasped for air, tears streaming down my cheeks. He looked down at me, his lips curving into a devious smile.

"Oh, you little slut," he chuckled. "I love seeing your mascara run."

I couldn't help but grin. I'd worn the kind that ran on purpose.

I had known he would enjoy that, and seeing that he did made me feel good.

They were great at surprising me, but I had a few tricks up my sleeve too.

He wiped away one of the tears with a little *tsk* and then rolled me beneath him on our blankets. He pinned my arm over my head, a low growl leaving him.

Fuck, I loved it when he growled like that.

"Dell," I gasped. "Gods, I'm so turned on. I want you."

"I want you too," he chuckled. "And I will have you every single way possible."

He stole a kiss before stripping his clothes off and tossing them to the side. His iridescent wings spread behind him, his muscles rippling with a shimmer.

I wanted to run my fingers over each one of his rainbow scales, to trace the lines of his muscles with my tongue.

He leaned back down and kissed down my body, pausing to bite my nipples. I gasped at the flare of pain, but it quickly turned into heated pleasure.

I sucked in a breath as his tongue flicked out, tracing down my stomach, then down to my pussy. I spread my legs with a little moan, aching for his tongue. Desperate for him to taste me.

I looked down, my eyes locking with his as his tongue shoved inside of me. I gasped, my entire body bowing up. He growled, the sound vibrating through me as he fucked me with his tongue.

I gripped the blankets, letting out a scream. His tongue moved deeper, and I was reminded just how fucking great it was to have a mate that could shift certain parts when needed.

He thrust it in and out, making me writhe and pant. I was already getting so close to cumming, so fucking close–

He pulled back, leaving me with a sad moan.

"Such a needy little cunt," he whispered. "And all ours. You want to be fucked by your dragons, little kitten?"

"Yes," I rasped. "Please. I need you inside of me. Please!"

"Convince me, kitten," he said, licking his lips.

"Please," I whispered, sitting up. I slid my fingers down to my clit, rubbing myself with a groan. I was so wet for him. "Please. I want you to make me cum. I need you to breed me. I need you inside of me. It's all I want."

His eyes darkened, falling down to my fingers. I slid them inside my aching cunt, letting out a low moan. Goosebumps erupted over my skin, my nipples hard.

"Please," I rasped.

"Good little dragon," Dracon's voice came from the doorway.

I looked up at him, my eyes widening.

Dracon closed the door behind him. In his arms, he had a variety of things, but what jumped out to me first was the vibrator.

It was red and white like a candy cane.

Dracon stepped into our nest and arched a brow, setting the items down. He grabbed a spool of thick ribbon and tossed it to Dell.

Dell smiled, looking down at me. "You convinced me, kitten, but first, we have to do a couple of other things. Now, lay back and be a good girl for us."

CHAPTER 2

Dell

W ithin a few minutes, Dracon and I had Kat spread for us. We had bound her wrists together above her head and then had put a bar between her ankles that would keep her legs spread.

Her pussy was wet, her clit aching to be sucked and worshipped.

Fuck, my cock was so hard for her. For him.

Dracon and I had talked about this many times over the last month. In the spirit of holiday fun, we'd decided that giving her as many orgasms as possible and fucking her together would be memorable.

Kat's breasts rose as she took deep breaths, her skin flushed with a pink glow. Her scent had both Dracon and me on edge, our primal side getting closer and closer to breaking free.

Dracon knelt down next to her, dragging his claws down her stomach. She let out a little moan, her red lips parting. The mascara tears had dried, and her hair was now a mess from both of us pulling on it.

I knelt down on her other side, looking at Dracon.

"We need to make sure she can't close her legs," he said.

I couldn't help but smile. I leaned back and reached for the toy he had brought, the vibrator that he had bought just for this occasion. It looked like a candy cane.

I flicked the button on, and it came to life, the head of it humming with vibrations.

"Perfect," I said.

Kat moaned. "What are you going to do to me?"

"Make you scream," Dracon said. "Devour you. Use your pretty little pussy. And then fuck you and breed you together. How does that sound?"

"Good," she whispered, her bright blue eyes fixated on the toy.

I lowered it to her pussy, barely touching her clit with it. She cried out, her muscles squeezing together to no avail.

The bar between her feet kept her legs perfectly spread, and with her arms bound above— our little kitten was helpless.

"Perfect," Dracon said. "Keep it on her clit. Make her cum, little dragon."

"Yes, sir," I said, holding it down.

She screamed, her body straining as pleasure struck her. Every noise that fell from her perfect lips made my cock pulse, my entire body in tune with hers. Our bonds meant we could feel each other's pleasure, and in this instance, it was ecstasy.

"Dell!" she squealed.

Dracon grinned almost demonically. He leaned down, sinking his teeth into her nipple.

She cried out even louder, those tears returning. I knew the pain was sharp, but it was dull compared to the even sharper pleasure that was rolling through her.

Dracon groaned, drinking her blood. Feasting from her.

"Good girl," I praised, angling the vibrator differently.

This drew another scream from her, her eyes fluttering.

Oh, she was close. So, so close.

Dracon pulled back, licking up the bite he'd just made with a groan. His hand slid down between her legs, his fingers shifting so that he could plunge them inside of her.

"Fuck," he growled. "I can feel her about to cum."

Her body fought against the restraints, her orgasm crashing into her. I watched, cherishing and enjoying the way her expression changed as she came.

"Beautiful," I whispered, pulling the vibrator away.

She let out a moan, sinking back against the blankets. Dracon pulled his fingers free, holding them to my lips.

I sucked her essence from them, groaning. She tasted like heaven, our perfect little mate.

"Fuck," she whispered. "That was intense."

"Good," Dracon said, sinking down between her legs.

Her eyes flew open as she realized his tongue was about to be on her clit. She let out a little yelp as he began to lap at her, starting off gently before getting more and more intense.

"Oh— oh fuck!"

My hand fell down to my cock, unable to stop myself from stroking. I was so hard for her. So fucking hard.

Dracon paused for a moment, a little growl leaving him. "No, little dragon, don't you fucking dare. Did I give you permission to touch yourself right now?"

"No," I moaned, forcing my hand away. "I'm going to shift if I don't."

"Then shift some and be patient. But, worship her body, little dragon."

"Yes, sir," I said, leaning over her.

I was still painfully hard, but I would obey. I would wait until we were both buried in her hot cunt, fucking her together.

Kat whimpered, her hips bucking as Dracon began to feast on her pussy. I cupped her face, pulling her into a deep kiss. My tongue slid against hers, and then I moved it further.

Fuck. I was losing control. Seeing her like this, spread and helpless, made me want to devour her. To breed her for hours.

My body began to shift, and I didn't stop myself as my tongue lengthened. I didn't fully go, but it was enough for me to slowly take on the shape of a small dragon.

She gasped as I pulled my tongue from her mouth, her eyes widening. She let out a pant and then bowed up, a second orgasm crashing into her.

Fuck, it was so beautiful to see. My favorite thing in the world was watching her cum. Well, one of my favorite things.

The other was watching Dracon and her together.

She continued to pant, her cheeks flushed bright red.

Beautiful, I purred, knowing they could hear me.

She let out a helpless moan and surprised me by opening her mouth. I leaned down, letting my dragon's tongue fill her, sliding further until I hit the back of her throat.

I began to move it back and forth, fucking her like a cock. She made a noise, her eyes rolling back as I thrust it in and out.

I could hear Dracon's tongue in her pussy, doing the same. Within a few moments, the two of us found the same rhythm, moving in and out. Over and over again.

One of my claws curled around the ribbons that bound her hands, holding her there. I felt that cloud of desperation again, my cock now pulsing even more.

Fuck, there was no escape. I had always prided myself on self-control, but they both drove me insane.

I felt a hand curl around my cock and gasped, pulling my tongue free to look down. Dracon was still eating her out, but now his hand was stroking my cock.

Fuck, I growled. *Dracon, I can't.*

He pulled his tongue free for a moment, glowering. "If you want my cock later, you will not cum until I give you permission."

You bastard. I didn't mean it maliciously, even though it was a snarl.

He winked, going back to eating out our mate.

Fucking hell, they were truly going to drive me insane.

Kat gasped. "I am— ah fuck! I'm going to cum again."

I grunted, breathing in her scent as she came again. Her entire body vibrated under me, her muscles straining as she lost control.

"Please," she cried. "Fuck, I can't do more."

"You can," Dracon growled, gripping my cock harder. "Shift back, little dragon."

Fuck. I let out a low growl and shifted back into a more human form, only for him to grab me and shove my head down between her thighs.

"Little kitten, I'm going to take care of our impatient mate, and you're going to cum for us again. Understood?"

Her eyes widened, but she nodded, her lust apparent.

I breathed in the scent of her pussy with a moan, not hesitating to push my tongue inside.

Fuck, she was so tight. So tight and hot, I could feel her heartbeat through her pussy pulsing.

I groaned as Dracon moved down my body.

His tongue found my ass, and I damn near came immediately. He began to rim me, teasing me.

Kat and I both moaned together, lost to the pleasure that controlled us. She was a good little kitten, and I was a good little dragon— both of us slaves to whatever our mate wanted.

Dracon raked his claws down my spine, pain bursting.

He left me for a moment, and I heard the sound of a condom being ripped open. I closed my eyes, focusing on making Kat cum.

She let out a little moan, her body arching up. Another

orgasm washed over her, a slow one. An easy one that was long and had her walls clenching around me like a vice.

I pulled my tongue free, looking up at her.

"Four," she whispered brainlessly. "Fucking hell."

I felt the head of Dracon's cock against my ass and moaned, looking back at him. His golden eyes burned with need, his blue scales sparkling.

He arched a brow and thrust forward, filling me. I cried out as I took him, his massive cock spreading me only like he could.

"Good," he grunted. "Clean her up while I fuck you, little dragon."

I obeyed, even though I could barely think now. My cock pulsed as I reached up and untied her hands, moaning as Dracon gripped my hips and fucked me.

Kat watched us, a wicked little grin curving her crimson lips.

"Does he feel good?" she teased.

I narrowed my eyes, only to gasp as he slammed into me.

The moment her hands were free, she ran them up my chest, over my nipples and muscles, and down to my cock.

Her little hand gripped my shaft.

"Oh fuck," I gasped.

Dracon's grip on my hips tightened, the sound of his balls slapping against me echoing through our room. Kat started to stroke me quickly.

"Fuck both of you," I rasped, groaning.

Kat giggled as she kept going, the two of them sending me to the edge.

"Squeeze his knot," Dracon growled.

Kat reached down further, obeying him.

The moment she squeezed my knot, I let out a roar. I started to cum, sending streams of my hot seed all over her body.

Dracon growled, pulling out with a groan. He pulled the condom off, jerking his cock and then cumming all over me.

The three of us groaned together, and I relaxed, resting my head between Kat's breasts.

"We're not done yet," Dracon said, slapping my ass. "Not done at all."

CHAPTER 3

Dracon

Dell and I sat across from each other, our legs interwoven. Kat was between us, her body arched and moans driving me wild.

She was still covered in Dell's cum, and the two of us had spent the last few minutes licking up every drop. I ran my hands down her body, her skin soft to the touch.

I'd been thinking about this for weeks now. About her taking both of our cocks at the same time. We'd been together five years, and yet somehow, this thought hadn't occurred until Dell and I had been talking about knotting.

Then our plan came about.

I leaned forward, breathing in her scent. Our mating bonds shivered with delight.

She was excited, turned on, and a little nervous about taking both of us. She didn't believe that she could, but she would be able to.

"I can't take both," she rasped. "There's no way."

"Magic," Dell said, chuckling. "And lube."

He reached over, grabbing a bottle of lube that we had

bought just for this. He'd gotten it from another creature friend, one that often dealt with size difference problems.

Between our magic and this, she'd be able to take us.

"You will take both of our cocks, little kitten. Your cunt belongs to us, or have you forgotten?" I asked, reaching around to tweak one of her nipples.

She let out a little gasp and then a groan. I pinched her harder, finally pulling a little yelp from her.

"Dracon," she rasped. "Fuck. Both of you are going to destroy me."

She groaned, her hips moving. My cock was nestled against her lower back, hard all over again.

Dell poured some of the lube into his hands and stroked his cock, reaching around to do the same to mine. I grunted as his palms ran over the ridges.

"Is that candy cane lube?" Kat asked, letting out a little giggle.

It did smell like peppermint, and it was starting to tingle in a way that made me want to fuck her even more.

"Yes," Dell said, pouring a bit more into his hands and running his fingers over her pussy.

Kat gasped, her hips moving against his hand as he got her ready.

Her hair had unraveled from its bun in golden strands, her tan skin gleaming with cum and flushed from her orgasms. Fuck, she had been glorious. Seeing her wrapped up, her legs spread by that bar...

I looked to the side, giving it an appreciative look.

We'd be using that again, along with the vibrator.

"Say the spell," I commanded, giving Dell a nod.

Dell leaned forward, the words tumbling from his lips. Kat gasped as our dragon magic rushed over her, our bonds tightening as her body changed.

Her body would be made just for us, to take both of our dragon cocks at the same time. I wanted to see her belly full of our cum, her breasts bouncing as she rode us.

She began to moan again, and I knew she was even more turned on than before. Dell let out a dark chuckle, running his hands up her body.

I gripped her thighs and lifted her. Dell moved closer until our cocks were pressed against each other, our knots pulsing with heat.

Kat relaxed finally, fully trusting us.

"Do you want this?" I asked.

"Yes," she said. "Fuck, the magic feels good."

"Good," Dell said. "It should feel good, just like you'll feel good when you're full of our cocks."

Dell gripped both of our cocks, the ridges of mine rubbing against his. He let out a little breath as I began to lower our mate.

She groaned as we spread her, the heads slowly pushing inside of her. I could feel her pulsing already.

"Oh," she gasped. "Oh gods, that feels so good."

I sucked in a deep breath, my cock pulsing with need. I couldn't wait to be buried inside of her, to feel her warmth around me. I grunted, thrusting my hips up slightly, desperate to be inside. I loved the feeling of being next to Dell's cock, our shafts rubbing against each other.

"Who's pussy is this?" I growled.

She shivered, her breath hitching. "Yours. Dell's."

"Good girl. Are you going to take our dragon cocks?"

"Please," she whispered. "Yes. I want this more than anything."

"Good girl," I praised, grunting again.

Fuck, my control was getting closer to snapping.

She moaned, taking another couple of inches. Dell moaned, letting out a string of curses.

"Fucking five years, and we've never done this."

I grinned, my head tilting back. "Fuck, she feels good."

"She does," he moaned.

"Our good little kitten," I said, finally bringing her all the way down on our cocks.

The three of us cried out together, and she stilled as her body adjusted to us. I leaned forward, looking over her shoulder.

Fuck, I could damn near see the bulge of Dell's cock.

"Beautiful," I murmured.

I smiled to myself and then looked up at Dell, enjoying his lost expression. He was a slave to pleasure just like I was, just like Kat was.

With a soft groan, I lifted her and then brought her back down on our cocks.

She cried out, her head falling back onto my shoulder.

I did it again, sucking in a breath as she took us together. Over and over. I could feel her pussy against our knots as I bounced her up and down, drawing screams and gasps and cries from her.

Dell grunted, leaning forward and kissing her throat and breasts as we fucked her.

"You take them so well," I rasped.

Fuck, we weren't going to last long. She felt too good, and I was getting closer and closer to losing control.

"We're going to knot you," I said. "Knot you and breed your little cunt. You're ours, kitten."

"Yes," she cried. "Yes!"

The three of us continued to move, finding a carnal rhythm that had us each tumbling closer and closer to the edge. I was on the brink of cumming, my blood burning with the need to fill her. To push my knot inside her and hold her between us, pumping our cum into her.

"I'm close," Dell gasped.

Her pussy pulsed around the two of us, squeezing tighter as she let out a sharp yell. Her orgasm was beautiful, her muscles going taut as she came on our cocks.

Fuck. We gave one final thrust together, our knots pushing inside of her right as we both came together.

I gasped, my cock pulsing as I filled her. I could feel Dell cumming too, the three of us caught in the grips of blinding pleasure.

My knot swelled against his, locking her to us. We collapsed against each other, my chest heaving with breaths.

"Fuck," Dell rasped. He gave Kat a soft kiss and then reached around her, giving my hand a squeeze.

I nodded, a soft purr coming from my chest.

"I can feel both of you still cumming," Kat groaned.

I nodded, closing my eyes as more hot cum filled her. I looked over her shoulder again and groaned.

Her stomach was swollen with our cum.

The sight made me shoot even more into her.

"I love you," I said, nuzzling her. "Both of you."

"I love you too," Kat said, now fully relaxed.

"Was five enough, kitten?" Dell teased.

"Yes!" she laughed. "Gods."

I smirked, giving her shoulder a gentle kiss. "Merry Christmas, kitten."

"Merry Christmas," she giggled. "This was a good present."

"This is just the first one," Dell said, snorting. "You think this is all we're going to do?"

She groaned. "I can't take much more. You're already both knotted to me."

"Mmm, I think you'll like what we have later," I said. "But

of course, after this, I think a hot bubble bath and a massage would be nice, hmm?"

"Yes, please," she said, smiling.

I grinned. Both Dell and Kat were relaxed and happy, and I loved that more than anything.

I brought my wings around us, pulling us together.

It was Christmas Eve, and I couldn't think of a better way to spend it than in the arms of my little dragon and kitten.

Rum the Red Assed Minotaur

RUM AND PENNY

T'was the Night before Christmas,
In a cabin in the woods,
Where the Minotaur's Mistress,
Will make her creature be good...

*In this Holiday Tail,
you will find the following:*

Bull riding
Strap ons
Cum eating
Degradation
Submission
BDSM
Bridle and reins
And more

CHAPTER 1
Rum

I placed the last present on the floor, taking a step back and looking at all of them piled together.

I had spent the last few weeks shopping like a maniac. When I'd asked Penny what she wanted for Christmas, she had given me a cryptic answer as always, so I'd gotten her everything I saw that I thought she would like.

Plus, she deserved everything to make her happy. And 11 presents? That was the least I could do, especially for her.

We had rented a small cozy cabin, one that would offer us the peace and quiet that we both wanted.

Penny was still getting ready in the bedroom, planning something for me as well.

I felt my stomach flutter, the butterflies always there. Being with her was always a surprise, and this was no exception. Even after five years of being together, she was still my pretty Penny, and I loved all of the things that we got to do together.

It was Christmas Eve, and while I missed our ragtag family, having a night with my Mistress was the perfect way to celebrate the holiday. Plus, tomorrow, we would all get together for a big ass breakfast, and I'd crash Creature Cafe as Santa.

"Rum?"

"Yes, my love?" I asked, turning around.

The tips of my horns scraped the ceiling, drawing a curse from me. I hunched a little, giving it a dirty look.

"Close your eyes," she called, her voice muffled from the other room.

I thought about all of my instincts, the ones that made me want to run to her. The one that made me want to go and pick her up, and haul her to the bed and rut into her.

But no. Instead, I would listen to her command, and we'd save that for later.

"Yes, ma'am," I answered, closing my eyes.

I drew in a deep breath, the smell of chestnuts, marshmallows, and cinnamon filling the air. This cabin was small and cozy, and it somehow smelled exactly like Christmas. I loved it, but what I loved more was that above the homely scents, there was her. My mate, my goddess of a woman.

The floorboards creaked as she came into the living room, and I felt her come to me.

I sucked in a breath as her hand slid up my furred chest, her fingers intertwining with the strands. Her warmth enveloped me, the burning flame in our souls reaching for each other.

My cock was instantly hard. I felt a shiver work up my spine, and even though I was a monstrous Minotaur – I would always be weak for her.

"Oh goodness. What are all these gifts?" Penny asked.

"Surprise," I said, unable to hide my grin. I still held my eyes closed, though the anticipation was growing with each passing second.

"Oh my goddess, Rum," she laughed. "There are so many!"

"I couldn't help myself. Every shop that I went into, I always found something that I wanted to buy for you. And then somehow I ended up with 11 different things for you, but it was worth it."

Her little laugh floated through the room, music to my ears.

Tonight, I would submit to her. I would submit to my goddess, kneel to my Queen. And I couldn't wait to see what she had in store for me. Her punishments were always delicious, and the things she did to me were always exactly what we both needed.

"Mistress?" I whispered. "May I open my eyes?"

"Yes, pet," she said softly, her voice warm and lusty.

I opened my eyes, and the sight before me almost sent me to my knees.

Penny was wearing nothing but a red harness around her beautiful breasts and around her hips and thighs. Little crimson bows decorated it, the straps framing her body in a way that I would forever remember.

Fuck, this was my present. A present no one could beat.

I let out a loud groan. "Oh my gods," I said. "You're perfect, Mistress. Fucking hell."

Penny gave me a wicked smile, reaching up and grabbing my bull nose ring. She tugged me down into a kiss. I groaned as she parted her lips, allowing me to taste her.

Fuck, this woman was heaven.

"I want to open all of the presents," she said. "And I also have a present for you, pet."

"Yes, please," I rasped.

Some of the presents were for her, but some of the presents were things that I wanted her to use on me. I got a little carried away in a store that carried a whole bunch of kink items, finding a whole plethora of new torture devices for her to use on me. I'd gotten a custom paddle that said 'Penny's Pet', toys, and so many other things.

"May I taste you?" I asked. "Before presents."

"No," she said, arching a brow. "I want you to lust after me for a little bit."

"I'm already lusting, Mistress."

She leaned up and gave me another kiss and then sauntered over to the presents. She sat down on the floor, spreading her thighs so that I could see her pussy. My knees hit the floor, my cock throbbing against my gray sweatpants.

If she asked me to crawl to her, I would. If she asked me to bend over and take it, I would. I would do anything that my queen wanted, and I couldn't wait to see what we would do tonight to celebrate the holiday.

Penny swept her silky black hair back, giving me a little smile. "Like what you see, pet?"

"Yes," I whispered reverently.

I loved the way that the red straps tugged at her thighs, hugging her skin. Her sword tattoo winked at me, leading my gaze up to her pussy.

Penny winked at me and then picked up the first present, peeling open the wrapping paper. It was a small box, one that could fit in the palm of my hand. I grinned, knowing what was inside.

She opened it up, and her eyes widened. "Rum," she said softly, letting out a little breath.

The first present that she opened was one that had a lock and key inside. The key was for her and the lock for me, if she decided we would wear them.

"A reminder that I always belong to you," I whispered.

She made a little noise, her expression softening. "These are lovely. We will definitely wear them."

"Thank you, Mistress," I said, my cock pulsing from her words.

Pleasing her made me insanely happy.

She stroked them for a moment and then set them aside. "That's tough to beat."

"Keep going," I teased.

She picked up another present and began unwrapping it. This box was the one that had a new strap on, one that had a monster cock like mine.

She pulled it out of the box, her brows shooting up. "You think you can take this?"

"I will for you," I said, swallowing hard.

The cock was almost as thick as mine, with ridges that would be...fun to try.

"I'm going to breed you with this," she murmured, her words making me groan.

Fuck. I slid my hand down to my cock. Was I really going to get off to her opening the presents I'd bought her? Did pleasing her really turn me on this much?

The answer was yes.

She looked up at me, her eyes then falling to my cock. "Take it out."

Fuck. "Yes, Mistress," I said, sliding my sweatpants down.

My cock sprang free, precum glistening at the tip.

"Stroke it while I open these, but you aren't allowed to cum."

Oh fuck, I'd fucked myself.

I groaned but obeyed, taking my cock into my hands and stroking it. My hips bucked, pleasure drawing a little gasp out of me.

Penny spread her legs a little wider, her pussy glistening. I shook my head, unsure how I was going to make it.

She had nine presents left to open.

"You're so beautiful, Mistress," I whispered.

I stroked my cock, watching as she picked up the next

67

present. Penny held it up, tilting it to the side, taking her time teasing me. She set it down, peeling back the wrapping paper slowly. I let out a long moan, not sure how I was going to survive.

She opened up the box, pulling out the paddle that I had made for us. She grinned as she held it up in the light, almost like a trophy. She turned it over, letting out a little gasp.

"Penny's Pet," she said, smirking. "It's true. You are my good little pet."

"Yes, Mistress," I gasped.

"Stroke slower," she commanded. She ran her fingertips over the paddle wood, tracing the grains of it. "This is beautiful," she said.

I obeyed her command, even though all I wanted to do was cum now. I could feel my balls squeezing, the need to release getting closer and closer.

Penny carefully set the paddle to the side, lifting the next present. We still had eight more after this.

She opened it up, placing the wrapping paper to the side, in what was slowly becoming a little pile.

This was the one that had a dress that I had picked out for her, one that would hug her beautiful curves. It had a slit up the side, one that would reach her hips. It also had an open back and a neck that would dip down to her beautiful breasts.

She pulled it out of the box, holding it up. "Oh, this is beautiful," she said. "I can't wait to wear this. We'll have to go out on a date, so you can show me off."

I nodded, stroking my cock. Her pleasure was mine, her excitement making me excited. I loved watching her open the things that I had bought for her. I loved watching her expression change with happiness.

She carefully folded the dress, placing it to the side. The next present she opened quickly, pulling off the top of the box.

She laughed as she pulled out a new whip, one that had a

handle that had rainbow stitching. It was long, would hurt like a bitch, and would be a fun time for both of us.

"A whip?" She asked. "I think that your taste has gotten much darker, little pet."

"I want you to do whatever you want to me, and I want you to have the best equipment. You deserve the very best," I rasped, leaning forward.

I planted one hand against the floor, hunching over as I continued to stroke my cock and watch her. My muscles were getting more and more tense, and I was doing everything I could to hold onto my self-control.

"This will be perfect," she said, running her fingers over the leather. The next present was another toy, a vibrator. One that could be used for her or for me if she was feeling like torturing me some.

There had been times over the last few years that she had tied me down and had a vibrator pressed against my cock for hours on end. I had never cum so hard in my life, and I wanted to be able to do that again.

"Nice," she giggled. "So many new treats! We're going to have a lot of fun. It's too bad we only have one night here, but I promise we'll get to do all of the things soon. And tonight, we have a lot of things to do too."

I shivered with excitement, nodding with a grunt. I looked down at my cock, seeing it glistening with need, pre-cum dripping to the wooden floor. She set the vibrator to the side and opened the next present.

She hadn't told me or brought it up, but I had noticed that some of her hiking boots had become more and more worn out. So I went ahead and bought her some new ones, getting her some that would be the most comfortable for her work. The park where she worked had rough terrain, and I wanted her to be the best.

"Rum, these are perfect," she said. "I love you so much," she whispered. "How did you know that I needed new ones? I've been meaning to go shopping, but I just haven't had time."

"I've been keeping an eye on your boots," I admitted. "I just wanna make sure that your feet are comfortable when you're at work. For me, I just paint all day, but you're out in the wilderness, and I want you to be safe."

"I love you," she whispered, giving me a soft smile.

"I love you too," I whispered, letting out a long moan. Pleasure worked through my entire body, my cock aching harder and harder.

She set them to the side, bringing out the next present.

Four more. Four more presents, and then I would be able to cum at her command.

She opened up the next box, bringing out an entire kit filled with bath bombs. I had picked out scents that I knew that she would enjoy, ones that were her favorites. I wanted her to be pampered. I wanted her to feel loved.

"These look wonderful," she whispered. "We're going to have to take a bath together. And then maybe I can ride your cock while you wash my body."

"Yes, please," I moaned. "Mistress, I'm getting so close. I want to cum so badly," I begged.

"Soon, pet," she promised.

I gave her a little nod, stroking my cock faster.

The next present had candy inside, her favorite chocolates from the shop that was from a pixie and a leprechaun. They made the best chocolates in the world, and once Penny and I had discovered them, we had never gone back. They were from a shop in Ireland, and I had them shipped here.

"Oh my God, my favorites!" She exclaimed.

She immediately pulled out one of the chocolates, popping it into her mouth. I watched as she chewed, watching her lips move. I wanted those lips to be around my cock. I wanted to do so many things to her and for her.

"Would you like one?" She asked.

"Yes," I whispered.

She nodded and picked one out, setting the package to the side and crawling to me.

Her breasts swayed back and forth, hypnotizing me.

Fuck, I was going to cum. I was going to cum, but I couldn't. I couldn't feel her. Penny held the chocolate to my lips, and I parted them for her, taking it into my mouth. The flavor burst on my tongue, the sweetness making me moan. She grinned, leaning forward and kissing the side of my head. Her hand slid down, stroking my cock for just a moment.

I let out a low growl, damn near losing control.

Penny went and grabbed another present, standing up. She came back to me, standing over me and parting her legs slightly. I sucked in a breath, looking up and seeing her pussy right in front of my face.

She grinned down at me and slowly opened the present. The wrapping paper fell to the floor around us, and I sucked in a breath, drawing in her scent.

"Mistress," I gasped. "This is torture."

"I know," she purred. "But you're being such a good boy for me. And you've gotten me so many wonderful things, things that I'll be able to use on you."

"Yes, Mistress," I said.

Penny pulled out the next item, making a little noise. This one was another sentimental item, something that I had painted just for her. It was a picture of her as a goddess, embellished with gold leaf.

"Rum," she whispered. "Maybe we should have kids."

I grinned, the idea making me happy. We had talked about

it many times and wanted them but were waiting a little longer until the time was right. Still....

"Your wish is my command," I grumbled, looking up at her. "I will do whatever you want, Mistress."

"I know you will," she whispered. She held up the painting, her eyes glistening with tears. "This is really beautiful."

"Thank you, Mistress," I gasped.

I let out a little growl, stroking my cock faster. Her praise was edging me, getting me closer and closer to cumming.

The final present was ready to be opened. Penny went to it, picking it up carefully. She opened it as slowly as possible. Taking her time pulling the ribbon apart. Peeling back the wrapping paper and small strips that she placed in the pile next to her. She opened up the final box, her eyes glimmering with mischief.

She pulled out a small slip of paper and read it. "This is perfect," she said. "How did you know?"

How did I know that she had wanted to go on vacation to Ireland again? Because I had seen her search history on her laptop, but also because Kat had told me.

"Oh, you know," I said, winking at her. "A little birdie told me."

She let out a happy breath, looking around her. Tears filled her eyes for a moment, and then she smiled. "Thank you, Rum," she said.

I nodded, fighting off a soft groan. My cock was so fucking hard for her, my heart beating fast. I was ready to explode, more cum dripping from the tip of my cock.

Penny and I stared at each other for a few moments, and then a sensuous smile slowly curved her lips. She lifted her hand, gesturing towards me. Ushering me to crawl to her. I let out a moan and obeyed, crawling across the floor to her. She spread her legs, reaching out and grabbing one of my horns.

"Thank you for all of the wonderful presents," she whispered. "Now you can taste me."

"Thank you, Mistress," I said.

She tugged on my horns, pulling my mouth down to her pussy. I immediately lapped at her, licking her clit. She let out a long moan, her head falling back.

I reached up, gripping her thighs with my hands as I pulled her body closer. The taste of her burst on my tongue, a perfect flavor. She was already wet, and I drove my tongue inside of her. Her grip on my horns tightened, and she cried out, grinding against me.

She yanked me back, turning my horns, and surprising me as she rolled me onto the floor before climbing on top of me and sitting on my chest.

She leaned down, still gripping my horns and pinning me to the floor.

"Are you going to be a good little bull for me?"

"Yes, Mistress," I whispered.

"Are you going to give your cock to me?"

"Yes," I groaned. "Please, Mistress. I'm so hard. I'm so hard for you. My cock aches to be buried inside of you, my goddess."

"Soon," she said. "I promise the wait will be worth it. Stay here. I have something to get first."

CHAPTER 2

Penny

I left Rum on the floor, his monstrous cock waiting desperately to be touched.

All of the presents he had given me were beautiful. I knew he was going to do something, but I hadn't known how touching it would be.

I had plans for us tonight, but that strap-on...

Now, he was going to take the monster cock he gifted me.

I went to the bedroom and grabbed the lube, a blindfold, a towel, a soft leather bridle with reins that I hadn't shown him yet, and the present that was carefully wrapped that I would give him at the end.

I went back into the living room, placing everything on the sofa that was against the wall. Rum lifted his head, his eyes wide.

"Get on your hands and knees," I said.

Rum immediately obeyed, letting out a long grunt as he turned over on his hands and knees. His ass was facing me now, his cock still hard between his legs.

I smiled to myself, picking up the bottle of lube, the bridle, and the reins and going to him. I set the bottle of lube down on the floor and then went around to his head, kneeling down on the floor. He looked up at me, seeing the bridle and reins.

"Oh fuck," he whispered. "Penny..."

I arched a brow. "No?"

He narrowed his eyes, contemplating.

"You have your safeword," I said. "If we need to stop, tell me."

"No," he said. "I'm good. Just surprised."

"Good," I said, smirking.

I leaned forward and fit the bridle around his head, loving how flustered he was.

"Are you going to ride me and pull on the reins?" he huffed out.

"Yes," I said, smirking. I gave the reins a little tug.

That drew a moan from him.

I reached for the strap-on that he had bought and stood, pulling on the harness. Rum watched me with heated eyes, his cock hard and pulsing. I winked at him as I clipped everything, letting out a happy sigh.

There were very few things in the world that were as exciting as a new harness.

I reached for the cock, fitting it in place.

"Ten inches?" I asked, running my hands down the shaft.

"Don't let the power go to your head," he snorted.

I grinned, sticking my tongue out at him. "Disrespectful little pet."

"Never," he said, letting out a little moan again. "Penny, I'm dying here."

"I know," I said. "But I like torturing you."

"If it pleases you, Mistress," he said, letting out a breath.

I went around to stand behind him and grabbed the bottle of

lube, rubbing some along the cock. This thing was big, and I couldn't wait to use it on him.

"Are you certain you can take it?" I asked.

"Yes," he rasped.

"We'll see," I said.

I ran my fingers down his ass, spreading the lube over him. I teased him for a moment, enjoying the way that he gasped. My little bull wanted to be bred, wanted to be fucked by me. I loved him so much. I loved that he wanted this as much as I did.

"Please," he rasped.

I smiled as I guided the tip of the strap-on towards him, slowly pressing it against him. He let out a loud moan, and I let out a little gasp as he slowly began to take it.

I hadn't been sure if he would be able to, and I still wasn't sure if he would be able to take the entire length, but I enjoyed watching him take the first couple of inches.

He let out a loud hiss, a growl rumbling through his burly chest. I leaned down, grabbing the reins that were attached to the bridle around his head, giving them a fierce tug.

"Are you sure you're going to be able to take it, little bull?" I whispered.

"Give me more, Mistress, please," he begged.

I pushed more inside of him, my nipples hardening. I was so turned on by him taking it, by him giving everything to me. I loved being his Mistress, and I loved that over the years, we had found a dynamic that really worked for us. Occasionally, I would ask him to do whatever he wanted to me. For the most part, he liked to submit to his human Mistress.

To think that I didn't even know about monsters when we met, and here I was a few years later, happily with a Minotaur.

I loved everything about him, loved being with him. I loved to be his pretty Penny. He let out a long groan, one that made me even more heated. I desperately wanted to just pound into him, to fuck him like I wanted him to fuck me.

Soon I would be taking his cock, riding my little bull.

"You look so good taking my cock," I said, smacking his ass.

I pushed a little more inside of him, slowly easing in. I went further and further until half of it was inside of him.

He let out a little yelp, his fingers digging into the floor.

"Is that all of it?" he asked, his tone almost hopeful.

"Only half," I chuckled, giving his ass another slap. "I can stop if you want."

"No," he grumbled. "Please, Mistress, give me more."

I fought a smile as I slowly pushed more inside of him. The two of us worked together until, finally, he was taking the entire cock.

He let out a long moan, and I slowly eased back before thrusting in again.

This brought out a little yelp, and I leaned forward, reaching around so that I could stroke his cock.

The sound that came out of him was desperate, his breath hitching.

I grinned, stroking him for just a moment before leaning back, yanking the reins hard, and thrusting into him with as much force as I could give.

Within a few moments, the two of us found a rhythm. One that had him making all sorts of sounds, one that made me moan with excitement.

"I'm going to cum," he gasped. "Mistress, I can't stop myself anymore."

I leaned back over him, reaching down to stroke his cock.

"Cum," I growled, finally giving him permission.

He let out a long groan, his breaths becoming heavy pants. With a loud roar, he finally came— his hard cock shooting ropes of cum onto the floor. I stroked him fast as he came, enjoying every moment of it.

Finally, his muscles weakened some. I leaned back and pulled out of him, standing up and unbuckling the strap-on.

Rum was still panting, and he turned over, collapsing onto the floor.

I went over to him and stepped over his chest, looking down at him. His eyes widened through the haze of his orgasm.

I leaned down and grabbed the reins, tugging his face close. "Are you going to eat me out?"

"Fuck," he whispered. "Yes! Please sit on my face."

I smiled and let go of him. Rum reached up, his hands sliding up my thighs. The roughness of his palms made me shiver, and I slowly lowered myself over his face.

With a grunt, he tugged me down, not caring if he couldn't even breathe. I gasped as his tongue lapped me, burying straight inside of me.

"Fuck," I cried, my head tilting back.

He groaned, his tongue lapping at me. I was so fucking wet from everything we had done. My blood rushed with ecstasy, the pleasure rushing through me.

Hell, I wasn't going to last long, either.

My body shivered, my muscles quaking as he fucked me with his tongue harder and harder— doing exactly what I loved. My pussy pulsed, my gasps coming quicker as he drove me closer and closer to the edge.

He moaned against me, eating me out eagerly.

Fuck. I felt the edge of the orgasm coming, and within moments it became a wave. I screamed out, letting the feeling of absolute pleasure rush through me.

He licked up every drop, his tongue lapping inside of me until it subsided. I groaned, my head spinning as he sat me on his chest.

The two of us looked at each other, both of us cracking grins.

"That was amazing," he said, running the back of his fingers over my thighs.

"It was," I whispered, my head spinning. It was still hard to think. "Absolutely perfect."

Rum chuckled, and I rearranged myself, laying over his body. I wrapped my arms around his torso, laying my head on his shoulder.

"I love you," I whispered. "So much."

He stroked my back, running his fingers through my long hair. "I love you too. More than anything else in this world. My heart's flame."

Tears filled my eyes, and I nuzzled him, the two of us basking in our glow.

After a few minutes, I remembered his Christmas present. I sat up, my eyes wide, startling him.

"Your present!" I said.

I slid off him and then stood, going to the couch. I grabbed the towel and tossed it to him, giggling as he caught it with a grunt.

I grabbed his present while he wiped up his cum, and then went back over to him.

He was still sprawled out on the floor, so I sat back down on his chest.

"Fuck," he mumbled. "I'm going to get hard again."

"That may or may not be the plan," I teased, holding out the box.

He raised a brow and then took it, shaking the box. I snorted, giggling as he held it to his ear.

"Should I guess?"

"No, you dummy," I laughed, drawing a wide grin from him. "Just open it! It's something I know you've been wanting."

Rum smirked and then pulled on the wrapping paper, slowly opening it. I gave him a flat look, one that made him chuckle.

"Two can play at that game, right?"

I rolled my eyes, which only made him laugh more.

He finished unwrapping it, revealing a hand-crafted wooden box. On the top, there was an engraving of our names.

"Oh," he whispered, running his fingers over it. "This is already too much."

He sniffled, which immediately made me tear up. "No, don't do that," I hissed. "Don't cry."

He made a noise and then opened the box, revealing a beautiful set of handmade paintbrushes. He let out a gasp and grabbed me, moving me so that he could sit up and I could still straddle his lap.

"Penny!" he exclaimed.

I smiled, loving his reaction.

I'd been holding on to these for a while, and keeping them a secret had been hard. Especially since he was nosy.

"These are too much!" he said, his voice wavering.

"Never," I said, leaning forward. I grabbed his nose ring, tugging him close. "Never too much for my minotaur."

Rum made a sweet noise and kissed me, the two of us wrapping each other in our arms. He held me tight and then broke away, letting out a happy breath.

"Thank you," he said. "These will be perfect. I will make beautiful art with them."

"You're welcome, baby," I said, pecking his cheek.

I felt something hard rubbing against me and arched a brow, looking down between us. His cock was hard and pulsing again.

"Already?" I asked.

Rum made a noise, clearly flustered. "I can't help it! I have a gorgeous naked goddess in my lap, and she just gave me paint-brushes!"

I laughed and then took the box, setting it on the side. I then shoved him back onto the floor, giving him a wicked look.

"Maybe we have more riding to do after all," I said.

"All night long," he chuckled.

With that, we spent the rest of Christmas Eve in each other's arms, giving and receiving until dawn.

You're a Mean One, Mr. Meduso

NOAH AND MEDUSO

'TWAS THE NIGHT BEFORE CHRISTMAS,
IN THEIR HOME IN BRAZIL,
WHERE MEDUSO AWAITS,
TO BEND HIS MATE TO HIS WILL...

IN THIS HOLIDAY TAIL,
YOU WILL FIND THE FOLLOWING:

INTENTIONAL USE OF DRUGS
BDSM
SUBMISSION
BONDAGE
TENTACLES
ELECTRICITY
IMPACT PLAY/GUT PUNCHING
EXTREME DOMINANCE/POSSESSION
CONSENSUAL NON-CONSENT
AND MORE.

CHAPTER 1

Noah

I stepped onto our wraparound porch, looking out over the lush trees. The sun was setting, and even though it was a humid 85°F, it was Christmas Eve, and my monster and I were in the celebrating spirit.

I could hear the glasses bumping each other as Meduso pulled them down from a shelf in the kitchen. I stole one last glance at the forest around us before going back inside.

We had decided to spend the winter months at one of our favorite getaway homes in Brazil. This was the same one we'd spent our honeymoon in, and we both had many sexy fond memories here. Every time we visited, I was reminded of when we had decided to solidify our bond. And I was reminded of all the things that had come after that...

"Five years," I said, giving him a smirk.

Five years since I had sold my soul to the devil without a shred of regret.

Meduso looked up, giving me a devilish smile. He still was a bastard, still a dick, still very much a monster that wanted to devour me and control me, but he was also sweet. He was mine as much as I was his.

We loved each other, having built a life together over the last few years that we both loved.

"Ah yes," he said, scowling. "Did you think I forgot?"

"No," I said, going to the bar where he stood. "Was just thinking about all the things we've done together... and things we've agreed to."

Prior to our trip, Meduso had sat down with me to talk about yes's and no's again, discussing what we were both comfortable with. It came up about once a year, a general check-in to make sure we were both still getting what we wanted. I loved it, but he had asked more this time— and all with a dark, thirsty glint in his eyes.

Our list of yes's had grown to include darker things— things that I craved more than I realized.

His tentacles set the glasses down as he popped a bottle of whisky, a little growl of excitement working through him.

"One drink. A shot," he said, giving me a pointed look. "That's all we are having tonight. I want you to remember everything I do to you."

A shiver worked up my spine, the anticipation burning through me.

I wanted whatever punishment he was going to give me. He had been very purposeful about not touching me the last two days, which was driving me insane. He'd also made it clear that I wasn't allowed to cum until he allowed me to, which was also making me crazy.

"I want you," I whispered, getting lost in the dark thoughts.

"I know, little prince," Meduso said, arching a pale brow. "Do you still consent to everything we discussed, even if you are unaware?"

"Yes," I said, holding his gaze.

He held it for another beat and then nodded, his expression becoming almost unhinged.

"And you know I love you?" he asked.

"I know that very much," I said.

Well, fuck, now my curiosity was truly peaked.

The last of the sun dipped over the horizon, casting an amber glow through the house. He slid my drink over to me, and I took it, raising it for a toast.

We clinked glasses, and I took the shot. The heat burst down my throat, and I let out a little hiss.

Meduso downed his, letting out a happy sigh. "Come here, little prince."

I went around the bar to him, his tentacles immediately surrounding my body and tugging me close to him. His skin gave off a soft blue glow, and I could almost hear the electricity humming through him.

I wrapped my arms around him, enjoying his touch. He kissed the top of my head, offering me softness.

That made me nervous.

"You're making me nervous," I whispered, breathing in his scent.

He chuckled. "Am I, little prince?"

"Yes," I said, looking up at him. I narrowed my eyes, wondering what he was up to.

One of his tentacles slid up my shirt, and I let out a little breath.

"Fuck," I mumbled, heat moving through me.

"So deprived," Meduso teased, the tip of his tentacle moving around to my nipple.

Fuck. I let out a groan, my eyes fluttering. My cock started to harden, and he tugged me even closer, our cocks now pressing against each other through our clothes.

"Please," I whispered. "I've needed you."

"Only two days," Meduso said. "Such a needy little slut."

"I am," I rasped, moving my hips.

He growled, his tentacles now binding me completely. I felt one slide down to my belt, slowly undoing it.

"Fuck, I'm just going to cum in my pants," I said.

"No, you will not," he said, giving my face a light slap. "Look at me, human."

Oof, it had been so long since he'd called me that. I felt the thrill run through me, the sting of his darkness drawing me in.

I looked up at him, swallowing hard. I felt his tentacle slide into my pants, stroking my cock.

"Please," I moaned. "Fuck."

I felt my head sway, my vision dotting for a moment. Meduso made a noise.

"Hmm. Are you okay?"

"Yeah," I said, blinking. The dots went away, but I frowned. "Weird."

Meduso only smiled.

The tentacle wrapped around my cock, the other playing with my nipple, giving it a twist. I gasped, arching against his body.

I felt my muscles relax more, my cock pulsing. I looked up at him but found that my vision was swimming again.

"Wha the fuc?" I asked, but my words were slurred.

His fanged grin became fiendishly cruel. I squinted at him, his glow swamping my vision.

"Fuck," I said, slumping against him.

"Submit, little prince," he whispered, his lips pressing against my ear. "Just let it take over. Give in to it."

I tried to pull away from him, but it was no use. My thoughts began to dim, and within a few moments, I found myself falling into darkness.

· · ·

I CAME TO, blinking dizzily as I became aware of my surroundings.

I was naked, chains bound around my ankles and wrists. My thoughts began to rush as they became clearer, my heart pounding in my chest.

"Meduso?" I rasped.

Fuck. Pain worked through me as my nerves became more and more awake.

A sudden shock jarred me, and a scream left me, my dry throat ragged. I yanked against the chains, desperate for it to end.

It stopped, but my blood was still rushing, and I was fully awake now. I looked down, seeing that there were electrodes on my body, even one on my cock.

"Fuck," I gasped. "Oh fuck. You fucking monster!"

My voice was already hoarse, my throat feeling like it had been used.

My cock started to harden at the thought, even though I should have been scared. I looked around desperately, trying to see where he was, but there was only darkness aside from the light above my head.

I yanked against the chains again, looking up and down. I was strapped to a St. Andrew's Cross.

Fucking hell, I didn't even know where we were. Was this our house? It couldn't be. We'd fucked in every room there.

Unexpectedly, another shock burst through me. I moaned and then screamed as it became more intense, my cock becoming harder.

"Fuck," I cried. "Fuck. Fuck."

I panted as it slowly died down, my entire body burning with energy now.

"Meduso," I moaned.

I slumped against the chains, shaking my head.

CLIO EVANS

"Is that really all you can handle?"

My head snapped up, and I watched as my mate emerged from the darkness. He was completely naked, his tentacles waving around him.

"Meduso," I growled.

He cocked his head, a cruel smile playing on his lips. "Oh? Are you upset? You don't like being drugged and chained up?"

I made a noise, not sure how to answer that.

He stopped when he was right in front of me, his tentacles sliding over my body. I gasped as he plucked away the electrodes, replacing them with his tentacles.

I barely had the chance to open my mouth before his tentacles lit up, electricity bursting through me. I screamed, my voice breaking as he shocked me.

His hand darted up, gripping my throat. He squeezed the sides of my neck, cutting off my sound even as he continued to shock me.

Tears blurred my vision, and he pulled them away, still gripping my neck.

"You're so pretty when you cry," he whispered.

He leaned forward, his tongue lapping up one of the tears. I tried to jerk away, but he held me still.

His grip on my neck loosened enough for me to suck in a deep breath. I groaned, tears streaming down my cheeks.

"Just remember that if you're good for me, you'll get rewarded," he said.

I opened my mouth again, but his hand came up, hitting me in the stomach. The breath was knocked out of me, my head spinning as pain cracked through me.

Fuck.

I wheezed, my eyes glossing over. Fuck.

I was turned on. My cock was impossibly hard, an erotic buzz burning in my blood.

Meduso growled. "Fucking slut. You like that pain."

I couldn't deny it. I couldn't say I hated it.

His hand curled into a fist before striking me in the abs again, drawing out a grunt from me at the burst of pain. My breath was knocked out of me, my chest heaving as I tried to suck in air.

He struck me again. And then again. My head fell back, a hoarse scream leaving me.

Fuck, I was so turned on.

One of his tentacles wrapped around my cock, starting to stroke it.

"Meduso," I gasped. "Please."

"Please, what?"

"Please fuck me," I rasped. "I'm desperate."

"You haven't earned my cock yet," he growled. "Why would I just give it to you?"

"Please," I whispered.

"No," he said, his tentacles wrapping more around my body. The appendages crossed over my muscles, binding me. "Not yet, little prince. Soon, but not yet."

My body ached from being punched and shocked, but my cock didn't care. All I could focus on was the moments of fleeting pleasure and the way that my entire being needed *him*.

Meduso leaned in, brushing his lips over mine. I groaned against him, his taste a comfort.

He broke the kiss, his tentacle stroking me faster.

"Please," I rasped.

"Do not cum," he growled, pressing his forehead to mine.

"I can't stop myself," I cried. "You're stroking me!"

"If you cum, then you will get punished," he said, nipping my ear.

The little bit of pain made me even harder. Fuck, there was no way I would be able to stop myself.

My legs were already chained wide, and I felt a tentacle slide up my leg and thigh, the tip moving around to my ass.

"Fuck," I rasped. "Please. Please. I can't stop myself!"

"Don't you dare cum," he snarled. "If you cum, then your life is going to be hell!"

My hips thrust desperately as the tentacle began to tease my entrance. Pleasure burned through me, the threat of cumming getting stronger and stronger.

There was no way.

"I can't," I said, my eyes tearing up. "Please don't. Please don't fuck me with that thing."

He laughed, the tone cruel and dark. "You don't make the rules here, little prince."

"Please!" I cried out.

The back of his hand smacked my jaw, the sting making me pant.

"No," he snarled. "You will cum. when I tell you, little prince, or face the consequences."

CHAPTER 2

Medusa

One of my tentacles drove deep inside my mate while the other stroked his cock, his expression one of terror and lust. That was exactly how I liked him, and right where I started to feel my own control slip.

Noah let out a cry, his head falling back.

I knew he wouldn't be able to stop himself from cumming. I grinned, wanting to punish him so badly.

I had never met another soul in the world that could take my darkness as a gift, but he accepted everything I gave. I loved that about him, cherished that.

I struck him in the stomach again, enjoying the way his breath left him. Sweat glistened on his skin, tears streaming down his cheeks.

I began to move my tentacles faster, drilling them into him repeatedly.

"Fuck you," he gasped, letting out a sharp cry.

I looked down right as he started to cum, his hot seed hitting me and dripping down onto the floor. His hips thrust, his lungs heaving painful breaths as his cock gave every drop.

"Pathetic," I sneered.

I reached forward, undoing the chains quickly. I let him fall to the floor, enjoying his little yelp of surprise. His muscles quivered, and I leaned down, running the back of my fingers down his spine. He let out a little breath, his heart pounding in his chest.

"*You're a mean one,*" I hummed, thinking of the only holiday song I'd ever enjoyed. "*Mr. Meduso. You really are a—*"

"Monster," Noah growled.

"*You're as cuddly as a cactus, charming as an eeeeeel—*"

"I hate you," Noah said, but he let out a helpless laugh.

I smirked and pushed his head down to the floor. "Clean it up, little prince, and then you'll worship your king."

He groaned, but he obeyed, licking up his cum from the floor. I watched with satisfaction, waiting until he was finished to grip his hair and bring his little mouth to my hard cock.

I couldn't wait any longer. I wanted to feel my cock down his throat, and then I wanted to be inside of him.

His lips parted with a gasp, taking the tentacled tip of my cock into his mouth. I groaned at the warmth, thrusting my hips forward.

Noah gripped my thighs, taking as much of my shaft as possible. I drilled into him, my hips jerking forward as I started to fuck his throat.

He groaned, making muffled sounds in the back of his throat as I fucked him. I wound my fingers in his hair and my tentacles around his body, enjoying the feeling of taking him.

His nails scraped over my skin, and I shoved my cock in further, feeling him choke. I waited a few moments and then pulled out, watching as he gasped. Tears still fell from his eyes, but they were glazed over with want.

He wanted this as much as I did. To be taken and used by me.

My little prince.

I'd give anything to him and take everything he had. His soul was mine, his body and mind too. I loved him more than anything, and it was moments like this— where his own depravity was burning as bright as mine— that I fell for him all over again.

"You're such a little slut," I growled. "Look at me."

Noah looked up at me, his chest still heaving with breaths. He was kneeling in front of me, his skin marked from where he had been bound and shocked.

His lips drew into the slightest smile.

I arched a brow, making my decision.

"Because it's the holiday, I'm going to do things a little differently," I said, gripping his jaw. I held it firmly for a moment, letting out a soft growl.

I leaned down, and in one swift motion, I picked him up and threw him over my shoulder. Noah let out a little moan, but he didn't fight me. I smiled as I carried him through the room, going through the darkness to a door against the wall.

"Where are we?" Noah asked.

"A basement," I said, carrying him up the stairs.

"Do you have a basement at the house?"

"It's one that I have out by the shed," I explained.

"And we've never played in it?"

"Nope," I said, hitting the top step. "I wanted to keep it for an occasion like this. I like to surprise you, as you know."

Noah made a little noise, but I could feel him smiling. I stepped outside and looked around us, knowing that we were still completely alone. I headed towards the house, glancing up at the sky.

I'd lost track of time with him, the sky now completely dark. The stars burned above us, a galaxy spread out like specks of paint on paper. The air was humid and the exact opposite of the city that we called home around this time of the year.

Within a few minutes, I plopped him down on our massive bed, spreading him out in the center. Neon light poured off my body, casting shadows around us.

Noah stared at me, raising a brow. "Do I finally get to worship you?"

"If by worship you mean taking my cock, then yes."

I climbed onto the bed, leaning down to kiss him. He sucked in a breath, his arms winding around my neck. He pulled me close, my tentacles surrounding him and gripping his muscles.

I spread his legs, my hands sliding over his smooth skin to his cock. I gripped it, stroking him. Within a few moments, he was hard again, his body arching against mine as we kissed.

I was hungry for him, hungry to devour him. My little human was perfect for me and had taken my darkness so well. My soulmate, the man that belonged to me and me alone. Not many souls out there could handle a nightmare like me, but he loved me. He loved me even though I was evil because he knew that I loved him too.

The taste of him was a comfort, and my tongue met him as I pushed him down into the blankets. His legs wrapped around my hips, his cock rubbing against mine. His hips thrust up, his body becoming more and more desperate to be taken by me. I was so hard, and my control was finally unleashed.

I broke the kiss and rolled him onto his stomach beneath me. I pinned his hands down with one of mine and then kissed down his spine. He let out a soft moan, his skin flushed with heat.

"Meduso," he groaned. "Please. Please fuck me."

I growled, spreading his ass with two of my tentacles. He let out a little cry as I pressed the tip of my cock against him, testing to see if he could take me.

"Please," he rasped again.

I shoved my cock inside him, enjoying how he cried out. I

couldn't stop myself anymore, and I gave in to the wave of lust that was coming down on me.

I growled as I thrust into him harder, pulling back out and then going in again. He took my entire cock, his body made for me.

He *belonged* to me.

He was mine to fuck, mine to hurt, mine to love.

I fucking owned him.

He gasped, letting out little moans as I started to fuck him harder. "Please don't stop," he whispered, his fingers digging into the blankets.

I wasn't going to stop. There was no way in hell I'd be able to at this point. I needed to fill him with my cum, to fuck him senseless.

With every thrust, he let out a cry. Over and over again, his voice echoed around me. The sound of our skin slapping together echoed through the room, my tentacles tightening around his muscles.

I loved watching him beneath me, loved fucking him like this. After all the dark things I had done to him, this was my gift. This was my present for him being good, for him letting me do everything.

I slowed down my thrusts, making them hard and powerful. The rhythm changed, made him gasp, and a tentacle of mine reached around and started to stroke his cock again.

I wanted my little prince to cum, and then I wanted him to take my load.

"Meduso," he gasped. "Fuck, I don't know if I can cum again."

"You will," I snarled.

He had no choice. I had decided that he would cum again, so he would. Even if it took all night, I would fuck him and stroke his cock until he cummed.

"I can't," he cried. "Stop!"

"No," I snarled, feeling a flash of excitement run through me.

"Stop! No!" he cried.

For a moment, I wondered if he was being serious, but he hadn't used his safeword.

A snarl came from me, a monstrous one. I grabbed him by his hair, dragging my cock out of him and turning him back over onto his back. He tried to kick at me, but my tentacles gave him a brutal shock.

"You fucking bastard," I snarled. "I'm trying to give you my cock, and this is how you act?"

I pinned him down again, using my tentacles to hold him in place. He let out a pained moan as I slammed my cock back inside of him, giving him every single inch.

I grabbed his cock and started to stroke him, even as he tried to push against my tentacles that kept him still. His cock began to harden, his breaths becoming pants as I slammed into him.

"No," he moaned, but he didn't fucking mean it.

"Liar," I chuckled.

I stopped thrusting for a moment, and his eyes flew open, making me grin.

"What if I stopped right now?" I asked. "After depriving you for so long. After you wanted this so badly. You've been aching for my cock, desperate to be fucked."

His cheeks were flushed, his eyes closing slightly. "Fuck," he mumbled.

"That's right, little prince," I said, easing my cock back inside of him.

His lips parted as he was filled with pleasure, his eyes fluttering.

"Fuck you," he moaned.

I grinned again, dragging my hips back and pumping

forward. We found another rhythm that had him back to whimpering with each movement like he was in heat.

'My little prince," I said, "so eager to take a monster's cock. Do you remember your first time? The first time I gave you this gift?"

"Yes," he rasped. "I remember!"

"The first time I came inside of you," I huffed. "That I marked you as mine. I own you," I growled.

"You own me," he whimpered. "Fuck!"

"Your body belongs to me," I snarled.

"Yes," he gasped. "*Yes*. Only you."

"Good," I said, tipping my head back.

I lost myself in the pleasure of taking him, of fucking my little human. I moaned as I thrust in and out of him, knowing that I was only moments from cumming.

Noah let out a sharp cry, and I looked down at him as he started to cum again.

His cum filled my hand, shooting out over his stomach. I grinned at him, giving three more thrusts before my orgasm finally crashed into me.

I came inside my mate with a roar, letting every drop fill him. Pleasure burned through me, my hips pumping as I gave everything I had.

"Thank you," he rasped. "For your gift."

I moaned, leaning forward. I pressed my forehead against his, breathing in his scent. He let out a little chuckle, kissing my cheek.

"You always know how to push my buttons," I whispered, kissing him back.

"I like to," he said. "I love you."

"I love you too," I said, slowly pulling out of him.

My cum started to flood out, so I moved across the room, grabbed a towel, and returned to him. The two of us spent a couple of moments cleaning up, and then I climbed into bed with him, pulling him close.

He wrapped his arms around me, making a happy little noise.

"I have other gifts for you, too," I said. "This was just the first one," I chuckled.

"Oh? You didn't have to get me gifts," he said.

"Well, gifts for both of us," I said. I thought about everything I had planned and couldn't help but smile.

"I also got you a gift," Noah said. "Maybe I can give it to you once I can walk again."

I let out a laugh, relaxing into the blankets. "Well, we're here for a few days, so you can give it to me whenever."

Noah snorted and leaned up, giving me a kiss.

"This was a good gift," he said, yawning.

"Sleep, and maybe you'll wake up to another."

With that, he nodded and closed his eyes, curling into me. It was Christmas Eve, and while I had never been one to celebrate the holidays, being with Noah had given me an excuse to have a little bit of fun.

I couldn't wait to give him his next gift...

O Horny Night

AL, LUNA, AND QUINN

'Twas the Night before Christmas,
In the snow laden trees
Where a werewolf and werecat,
Hunt for their human with glee...

In this Holiday Tail,
you will find the following:

Breeding with pregnancy
Primal Play
Double Penetration
Triple Penetration
Threesomes
BDSM
Honorifics such as 'daddy'
And more

CHAPTER 1

Quinn

I sat down on the couch between Al and Luna, and all three of us sighed collectively.

Even with the three of us, it had been a struggle to get our children packed up, to the babysitter, and then being okay with us leaving them alone. Luna and I had practically snuck out, followed by Al.

"They'll be okay," Al said with a chuckle. "It'll be morning before they know it, and then they'll be surrounded by presents and family at the cafe. Plus, it'll be good for the kids to feel like it's just them. Well, them and the babysitter."

I snorted. The babysitter was a friend of the Barista— one with six arms and could juggle our pack of spawn easily.

Luna let out a happy sigh. "It's nice to just be us. I love them dearly, and I'm sure I will miss them by morning. Still, it's nice to not worry about them knocking the Christmas tree down again because one of them wanted to mark their territory."

"That was only once," Al grumbled.

I laughed, thinking about our sons. Not one, not two, but three werewolf boys that went between their monster and human forms constantly. One moment they'd be eating dinner, and the next, they were gnawing on the table because their monster teeth took more time to come in properly.

"They'll have fun with the kids," I said. "And be spoiled rotten tomorrow."

Luna giggled and leaned into me. I closed my eyes for a moment, basking in the happiness of being sandwiched between my werewolf and werecat.

"We have plans for you this evening," Al said, his arm moving around me. "Christmas Eve plans."

I felt his claws rake through my hair, and I let out a little breath, a chill working up my spine.

"Fuck," I mumbled. "Yeah?"

I loved the feeling of his claws on me.

He let out a little chuckle, and Luna looked up at me, her eyes shining with mischief.

"How do you feel about a run?" she asked, raising a brow.

Of course, she knew the answer. It didn't matter how fucking tired I was. I'd run from the two of them just so I could get caught.

"Sounds fun," I said, smirking. "A little Christmas Eve hunt."

Al and Luna both growled, and I stood up, turning to look at them. Al pushed up the sleeves of his favorite plaid lumberjack shirt, sitting forward.

Luna looked at him, smirking. "I'll outrun you, wolf. And if I catch her first, you have to do what I say."

"When hell freezes over, kitty," he chuckled. A wicked grin revealed his sharp fangs. "But sure. And if I catch her, you'll have to obey me without sassing back."

"Never," Luna snorted.

"Go on, little pet," Al said, his voice dropping. "Go out into the woods. We'll give you some time to run, and then we'll find you."

"Make sure you're bundled too," Luna said. "More layers to pull off."

Fuck. I swallowed hard, enjoying the bolt of excitement that went through me. The three of us always loved to have fun every moment we got, but a chase.... It had been a little too long since we'd had one.

I went to Al and kissed the top of his head and then to Luna. She pulled me a little closer, stealing a kiss on the lips before patting my ass and turning me loose.

"Go," Al snarled.

Fuck, having a werewolf growl at me shouldn't turn me on, but it did.

I went to the front door and slipped on my boots, pulling on my coat and scarf. I tied my blue hair back and then went out.

The air was cold and still, the moon reflecting off the snow.

Fuck, it was a good night for them to hunt me.

With a little huff, I took off running from our cabin. My feet sank into the snow as soon as I passed the tree line, and I cursed under my breath.

My heart started to pound as I thought about the two of them chasing me.

Who would get to me first? Luna would win from time to time, although Al never actually submitted to her.

My pussy throbbed, and I let out a little moan. I ran as fast as possible, picking up my feet even as the snow grew denser. Eventually, I was able to find a path, one that was easier to trot along.

I paused and grabbed a branch, turning around and dusting the path behind me so that my footprints wouldn't be as easily picked up. I then jumped as far as I could, hitting another area and taking off running.

Over the last five years, I'd gotten a lot better at running from the two of them, even in the snow. I would never forget the first time that Al took me on a hunt, and the thrill of being taken by both of my mates was one that I would never grow immune to.

My heart pumped in my chest, my blood burning with excitement as I ran faster. Every now and then, I would pause again to brush off my footprints and try to change the direction, hoping it would throw them off somewhat. Although there wasn't much I could do, in the end, it would be a matter of who would be faster. And part of me wondered if Luna might play dirty this time.

A little giggle left me as I ran faster, the thought of her tricking Al making me laugh. I ducked through trees, going deeper and deeper until I was fighting a bramble of branches.

I stopped for a moment, dragging in icy breaths. Little puffs parted my lips, like little clouds in the air. I looked up at the sky, seeing the moon peeking through the branches.

A lone howl echoed through the woods, sending another chill up my spine. I wasn't sure how long the two of them had let me run, but now I knew that they were out to get me.

My two monstrous mates out to find me, to hunt me. Whoever got to me first would get to do whatever they wanted to me, and I couldn't wait to see what that would mean.

I sucked in a breath and then turned, looking at the terrain around me. There were some rocks that went up to a ridge. I stole another look behind me and then went towards it.

I was careful as I started to climb, and it wasn't too high up, so I wasn't worried about falling. Within a few moments, I made it to the top, and I was able to take back off into the depths of the forest. I kept my footsteps light, moving slow to try to stay as quiet as possible as I moved.

A low growl echoed to my left, one that was far off enough for me to know that they weren't right on me but that they were close. Closing in.

A little thrill ran through me, and I felt my excitement grow even more.

I wanted them to fuck me. To use me, to breed me.

I swallowed a moan, trying to stay silent, but... there was a part of me that wanted Al to fill me with his pups again. I was on birth control, but....

Fuck. Actually, I had forgotten it the last couple of days with everything going on.

Another growl, this one definitely belonging to Luna. I couldn't tell how far away she was, but I decided it was time to run as fast as I could.

This was the fun part.

I found a path between the trees and started to run down it. Another howl cracked through the cold sky, but I didn't let it slow me down.

My limbs pumped as I ran, my blood hot. My pussy still throbbed, the idea of one of them catching me becoming something that I wanted more and more. I knew that it would happen. It was only a matter of time.

The sound of branches cracking to my right had me going left, and I heard a low snarl.

"*Got you.*"

Al appeared on the path behind me, blocking my way. I turned around, only to find that Luna was right there. "Fuck," Luna laughed. "I think that's a tie."

"No," Al growled.

I yelped as his burly arms suddenly wrapped around me, and he threw me over his shoulder. He took off running, and Luna let out a very fierce growl.

I gasped as I was jostled up and down, Al running faster and faster. I gripped his fur, hoping that he wouldn't drop me.

"You fucker!" I heard Luna yell.

I couldn't help but laugh as Al went to the center of a copse of trees, ones that formed a circle around a small clearing. He pulled me down, plopping me down with a snarl.

I let out a squeal as he lunged at me, his jaws snapping in my face. I laid back in the snow with a gasp.

His claws jerked at my clothing, ripping a hole at the crotch of my leggings.

"I'm going to devour you, little pet," he snarled. "Breed your little cunt for Christmas."

I gasped, feeling a mixture of panic and euphoria. My nipples hardened as he ripped open the front of my shirt, exposing me to the cold air.

I groaned as he lowered his jaw between my legs, his eyes burning as bright as the moon as his tongue lapped out. He dragged the tip over my clit, drawing out a scream of pleasure from me.

"I— I forgot to take my birth control," I gasped, letting out a moan as I melted against him.

I heard rustling from the trees behind us and arched to look. Luna came into the clearing, her body naked.

Fucking hell. I immediately became even wetter, a puff leaving my lips.

"No birth control, hmm?" Luna asked, coming to us.

Al chuckled, his tongue still lapping at me. I groaned as Luna knelt, pulling my head and shoulders into her lap.

"Did you plan this?" I groaned.

"Of course," she said, laughing. "I mean... I planned to win. But Al was determined to catch you first."

"Fuck," I huffed.

I couldn't feel the cold as my pleasure started to build. It felt like my body was on fire. I gasped, arching against Al.

Luna leaned down, running her claws over my skin. "Do you want him to breed you again, kitten?"

"Yes," I cried, my hips bucking.

Al growled and gripped my hips. He plunged his tongue deep inside of me, drawing a scream from me.

Luna gave a warm laugh and leaned down, ripping the rest of my clothes so that my breasts were exposed. I made a noise as her rough tongue swirled over my nipples, pleasure shooting through me.

Fucking hell, they were going to make me implode.

"Daddy," I groaned, the word slipping out of my mouth.

Al paused for a moment, lifting his head in surprise. My cheeks immediately reddened. Where the fuck had that come from?!

"That's new," Luna said, smirking. She looked up at Al, waiting to see what his response would be.

"Say it again," he snarled.

My heart pounded in my chest. All of the momentary embarrassment immediately turned into lust, giving in to what I wanted.

"Daddy," I whispered.

"Again," he growled, pushing my legs back further.

"*Daddy*," I cried.

"Do you want your Daddy to fuck you, kitten? To give you more pups?" Luna asked.

Did we want more? We'd talked about having more before and just hadn't decided on when. But even when the three of us were tired, we loved having our family. And we wanted to keep growing.

"Yes," I gasped. "I do. I want more. I want more of your pups, Daddy. I want you to breed me and fill me with your cocks."

Al let out a low growl and pushed his hips between my legs, both of his cocks hard and ready.

"Are you sure?" he asked, his eyes holding my own.

"Yes," I said.

He looked up at Luna, as did I.

"Yes," she said, grinning. "Of course. We've talked about it before, and we knew we'd want more kids. Hmm... maybe we'll have a little girl this time, and Al can turn even grayer."

"Fucking hell," Al groaned. "I'm going to knot you, kitten. I'm going to breed you and give you everything I have."

"Please," I whispered.

He leaned down, nuzzling my cheek for a moment. The tenderness made me smile, and then he leaned back, his expression turning wicked again.

"Call me Daddy again and beg me to breed you for Christmas, little pet."

M y little kitten moaned as our mate spread her wide, his hand gripping his two cocks together. They throbbed with need, his knots pulsing.

"Daddy," she gasped. "Please. Please breed me. It's all I want for Christmas."

I stroked her bright blue hair, letting out a long purr. I was so wet just from watching the two of them and had many things planned for once we returned to the cabin.

Al and I had noticed she'd forgotten her birth control the last couple of days but hadn't said anything.

Al growled again, one that sent a chill even up my spine. Quinn gasped as he pressed the head of one of his cocks against her, teasing her.

"Fuck," she cried, writhing between us.

I leaned down again and sucked her breast, sucking on her nipple. I could smell her arousal, could feel how much she wanted us.

"Please," she moaned. "Please give me your cock."

Al grunted. "You're going to take both of them, little pet. Both of my cocks, and both of my knots."

"Yes," Quinn said.

Al growled as he slowly began to push both of them inside of her, going slow and gentle. I continued to play with her breasts, enjoying the little noises she made.

"So big," she moaned.

My pussy throbbed as I listened to her. I reached down as Al pushed more inside her, circling her clit with my fingers. She instantly arched up, letting out a sharp gasp.

"I can feel you squeezing me," he growled. "Can feel your tight little cunt gripping my cocks, getting ready for my knots."

Quinn groaned as the two of us worked her together. She took his cocks slowly until, finally, both of them were all the way inside of her. Stretching her wide, making her writhe.

I continued to rub her clit, sending tremors of pleasure through her body. She shivered, her eyes fluttering as he dragged his werewolf cocks back and then thrust back in.

"Fuck!" she cried, her voice echoing through the forest. "Daddy!"

"Take them," he snarled. "Take Daddy's cocks like a good girl."

Fuck, I was so turned on.

"I want to eat you out," Quinn gasped, looking up at me.

I leaned back and then nodded. Fuck, I wanted that too.

I made sure her head and torso were cushioned from the snow and then moved, placing my pussy right above her head. She reached and brought me down as I leaned over her body, watching as Al fucked her harder and harder.

Quinn's tongue circled my clit, drawing a gasp from me. I moaned, only for Al to grab me and kiss me. His hot tongue slipped into my mouth, and I tasted our mate.

I moaned as her little tongue pushed inside of me, tasting how wet I was from watching her and Al. He grunted as he slammed into her hard, and I felt her breath against me as she gasped.

I broke our kiss with a growl. "Daddy," I whispered.

His eyes burned with lust, a moan leaving him. "Fuck, little sub. Hearing it from you too...."

I kissed him again as he panted, moaning as Quinn ate me out. I was getting closer to cumming, my orgasm building.

Al broke our kiss this time and growled, driving his cocks into her over and over. "I'm going to fill this little human pussy," he snarled. "All because that's what she wants for Christmas."

Quinn groaned as she sucked my clit, and I cried out, feeling my orgasm crash into me. Pleasure washed through me right as Al let out a howl, shoving his knots inside our mate.

I moved to the side as Quinn cried out, watching as she came around his knots. Her body arched up, her eyes fluttering. Her cheeks and nose were bright red, her skin covered with faint lines from our claws.

Al groaned, filling her with his cum. I let out pants, my head spinning as I watched. I loved watching him fill her, and I felt excited knowing this could mean our Quinn would be pregnant again.

I leaned down and kissed her, cradling her face. She smiled against my lips, pulling me down for a hug.

"I love you," she murmured. "I love you both."

"I love you too, kitten," I whispered.

"I love you both too," Al groaned. "Fuck."

He let out another groan, his knots sealing in all the cum he was pumping inside of her.

I settled next to her, wrapping my arms around her to keep her warm. Al leaned down, the warmth of his body keeping her from shivering.

She let out a little moan. "Fuck. There's so much from both of them."

Al only let out a grumble, making both of us giggle. I loved it when he was mellow like this, and it only happened occasionally after cumming so hard.

The three of us lay there for a few minutes, my thoughts finally becoming cohesive. I looked up at Quinn, smiling at her.

"So I have a Daddy kink now, I guess," Quinn said.

"I think we all do," Al mumbled.

I laughed even harder now. "It's true. I did get off on calling you Daddy. Although Master is fine too."

"Hmm, we'll save Daddy for when we want him to go feral," Quinn said, reaching down and running her fingers through his fur.

"I'm always feral for the two of you," he said. "Always."

"For your little pussies," I teased.

Al lifted his head, sticking his tongue out at me. "For that too, brat."

Quinn giggled, relaxing between the two of us.

"When you're able to stand again, we should get her back to the cabin," I said, raising a brow.

"Mmm, we can warm her up," Al said, looking up at her. "I can move... maybe. My knots aren't going anywhere."

"You carry her, and I'll grab clothes," I said.

Quinn made a noise as Al pulled her close and lifted her. Her legs wrapped around his hips, and he easily held her to him.

Within a few minutes, we made it back to the cabin. I opened the door, welcoming the warmth of our home.

Al carried her upstairs, heading for our bedroom. I tossed the clothes into a pile on the floor and followed them, stepping over the toys that our boys had left scattered in the foyer.

Al groaned as he laid back on the bed, keeping Quinn seated on top of him. She sat up, slowly moving her hips and drawing a little gasp from him.

"Little pet," he growled.

I chuckled at them as I went to our dresser, pulling out a toy and lube. I smirked as I went back to the bed, climbing onto the mattress and seating myself behind Quinn.

Our bed was huge, large enough to sleep the three of us comfortably. Of course, we'd added on to the house so that we could have more rooms in case one of us needed space. Quinn had a little office space where she wrote when she wasn't at the Cafe with Trixie or Lucy.

Quinn arched back, letting her head fall so that she could look at me. I gripped her hair, brushing away some of the water droplets from the snow that had melted.

"What's that?" she asked.

I planted a kiss on her crimson lips and then pushed her down, happy with the little yelp that I got from both of them. I studied her ass, licking my lips. I ran my hands over her hips, giving her a little slap.

"How about triple penetration?" I asked.

Quinn let out a little gasp, looking back at me. Al growled, watching me from the stack of pillows he was laying on.

"I don't know if her body can take that," he said.

"Yes, her body can," Quinn said, giving him a dirty look. "I popped out three fucking kids. Let's try."

Al laughed. "True. I won't say no. I'm quite enjoying the view I have right now."

I smirked.

I loved her enthusiasm, and I also loved the idea of making her scream all over again. I wanted to make her cum again while she was still knotted to him because I loved the sound he made when she squeezed his knots.

"Are you sure, little kitten?" "Yes," she said. "Was this the plan that you talked about?"

I smirked as I began to circle her ass, pouring some lube on my fingers and teasing her. She let out a little gasp.

"One of them," I said.

With my other hand, I dragged my fingers over his knot inside her pussy, tracing it and drawing out moans from both of them.

When they were stuck like this, I could do whatever I wanted to them. I could do whatever I wanted, and they wouldn't be able to do anything to stop me. A little thrill ran through me, and Al's growl was a reward.

"Fuck," he snarled. "Luna, woman, you're going to kill me."

"Don't stop," Quinn moaned.

I smirked and leaned down, teasing her ass with my fingers as I ran my tongue over the base of his knots.

Al's hips bucked up, his groan mixing with hers.

I could taste both of them, could taste both of their cum. I eased two of my fingers inside of her ass, and Quinn yelped.

"Fuck," she whispered.

She let out a sharp little cry, and I moved my tongue down to her clit. It was engorged and ready to be sucked, and I knew that she was turned on. I took her clit between my lips and started to suck as I eased my fingers inside of her.

"I have to make sure that you fill her with all your cum, Daddy," I said, pulling a growl from him.

"The moment I'm unknotted from her, you're going to be spanked and fucked, little sub."

I giggled and then went back to sucking her clit and playing with her ass. She groaned, her pussy clenching his knots and making him cry out too.

Fuck, this was heaven. Absolute perfection. I couldn't think of a better way to spend Christmas Eve than to be with both of them.

"Please," she whimpered.

"Don't stop," Al growled. "Fucking hell, this feels good."

I started to thrust my fingers in and out of her, moving them in a slow rhythm that matched the way that I sucked her clit. I then grabbed the toy that I had brought with me, one that was smaller than the others but would still do the trick.

I pulled back for a moment, putting lube on the tip of the rubber cock. I then pressed the head of it against her, slowly easing it in.

Quinn cried out, her body tensing for a moment and then relaxing.

I began to pull it out and then drove it back in, listening to her sharp cries and moans.

"I'm so full," she gasped. "Fuck."

"Basically, three cocks inside of you," I said. "Such a good girl," I purred.

She moaned as I kept going, gasping every time I went in.

Her pussy clenched Al's knots, pulsing and making him growl. Within a few moments, her gasps became pants.

I knew that she was close. I kept going, kept working at the same rhythm, until finally, she came with a sharp cry.

I looked up, enjoying watching her orgasm crashing through her. Pleasure spread through her body.

"Fuck!" Al snarled, his hips lifting.

I sat back with a satisfied smirk as he came again, filling her with even more cum. Even though she had two knots inside of her, some of his milk leaked out.

I leaned forward, catching anything with my tongue.

"There's so much," she panted. "Fuck. There's so much."

"Good," I purred. "We have to make sure we fill you with as much of it as possible."

Quinn nodded weakly, collapsing on our mate.

Al held out his hand, and I grabbed it, allowing him to pull me up next to his side. He grabbed my face, pulling me into another kiss.

"Mm," he grunted, relaxing into the bed. "I can taste us."

"Good," I said, licking my lips. "Are you okay, kitten?"

Quinn made a little noise, giving us a thumbs up. "I'm good."

Al and I snorted, and I settled against him, wondering what else he had planned for our Christmas Eve.

CHAPTER 3

Al

A couple hours later, I had finally pulled my knots free of Quinn, and we had cleaned up. And even though I had just chased her in the woods, pushed her down into the snow, and bred her, I still wanted to do more.

I glanced at the clock, seeing that it was close to midnight. It didn't matter though, because it was just the three of us for tonight.

The three of us made a quick snack and then sat in the living room to eat. I leaned against the couch cushion, deciding what I wanted to do next. All of the plans that I had made had almost been derailed simply by one of my mates calling me daddy, but I still had things that I wanted to do... that I would do.

"How are you feeling?" I asked, looking up at both my mates.

Quinn gave me a soft smile. "Full. Good. Warm and fuzzy."

"Good," I said.

"I'm feeling good too," Luna said, smirking. "More than good."

Good. I had figured as much, but it never hurt to check in with them before doing more things.

"Luna," I said, drawing her feline gaze. She arched a brow, listening. "There's a present underneath the tree, one that's just for you. It has your name on it. Go ahead and open it."

Quinn leaned forward in her chair, curious about what was going to happen. I enjoyed both of their expressions, feeling warmth in my chest. I was so lucky to have two amazing mates, both of them loving me as much as possible and me loving them as much as possible too.

"Little pet," I said, looking at Quinn. "There's one under the tree for you too. Open it."

Quinn slid down to the floor on her knees, crawling over to the tree. I sucked in a breath, watching both of their asses happily as they picked up their presents. I hadn't wrapped them the best, and within a few moments, they were opening them up.

"A paddle," Luna said, arching a brow. She smirked as she looked up at me.

"I got two ball gags," Quinn said excitedly.

"Little sub," I said, looking at Luna. "Help our little pet put one on. And then have her help you."

"Yes, Daddy," Luna said, a low purr leaving her throat.

I immediately felt a wave of lust.

Fuck, all this time, I'd had them calling me Master. And I loved that, but there was something about them calling me Daddy...

I felt a tug of lust, a low growl leaving me.

"Can I still call you Daddy?" Luna asked sweetly.

"Yes, little sub," I said. "You may."

"Thank you, Daddy," she said, smirking.

Fuck, I was going to spank the smirk right off her pretty face.

I watched as she went to Quinn, pulling her into a quick kiss before taking the ballgag from her.

Fuck, I couldn't wait to see them both wearing one.

I watched, my cocks already starting to harden again as Luna helped Quinn. She winked at me, and then Quinn helped her too. I leaned forward in my seat, my cocks already starting to harden.

"Good girls," I said, my deep baritone voice becoming more commanding. "Now, Luna. Take your paddle."

Both of them took in breaths, their beautiful lips parted by the balls between them. Quinn let out a little moan, still waiting patiently on her knees.

Luna picked up her paddle, turning to look at me.

"Bring it to me," I said.

She nodded and stood, bringing the paddle to me. I looked up as she stopped in front of me.

I ran the tips of my claws up her thigh, drawing a shudder from her. I took the paddle from her, cocking my head.

The ball between her lips was beginning to glisten.

I leaned back in my seat, patting my lap.

"Lay over my lap, little sub," I commanded.

Luna nodded with a moan, draping her body over my legs. I shifted her slightly so that her ass was right where I wanted it to be.

Fuck. This was perfect. Having one of my mates over my lap like this while the other watched us.

I looked up at Quinn. "Touch yourself for us," I commanded.

Quinn let out a soft groan and obeyed, sliding her fingers down to her pussy. Light from the Christmas tree washed over the three of us, casting shadows around the room.

I ran my hand over Luna's ass, patting both of her cheeks.

She sucked in a breath through her nose as I slid two of my fingers over her slit.

"Aw," I crooned. "My little sub is so wet. So wet for her Master," I said.

She cursed, but her words were muffled. She lifted her head, trying to keep any spit from dripping around the ball gag.

"No," I tsked. "I want you to relax. Get it nice and wet like you would my cock. Nice and wet like your pussy, little sub."

She moaned and nodded, relaxing again.

I slid my fingers inside of her, enjoying the noise that she made. Another noise came from Quinn across the room, and I looked up, watching as she slid her fingers inside of herself.

Fuck. My cocks immediately hardened, and I groaned, thrusting my fingers in and out of my mate. Luna cried, her muscles tensing as pleasure rushed over her.

I pulled my fingers free, slapping her ass. She gasped, and I squeezed her ass cheeks. Warming them up for the paddle.

I played with her, glancing up at our mate with each noise she made. She was losing herself to pleasure as she watched us, the scent of her arousal mixing with Luna's.

Fuck, I loved both of them so much.

I slapped Luna's ass again, enjoying her hiss. I rubbed the spot, reaching for the paddle and popping her with it.

She groaned, her body arching in my lap.

"No, no, little sub," I scolded lightly, grinning to myself. "No tensing up. Relax. Give in to me."

She relaxed again, letting out a long breath. I rubbed the paddle over her ass before lifting it again, slapping her ass with it. The sound echoed through the room, followed by a chorus of moans.

"My good girl," I praised. "Taking it all for your Daddy."

She nodded.

"Good," I whispered, feeling a flash of hunger.

I wanted to devour her.

I growled, bringing the paddle down again. She gasped, but she took it well.

"Little pet," I snarled, looking up at Quinn.

Her eyes opened, burning with lust.

"I want you to count to five," I said. "Count with your fingers."

Quinn nodded and held up her hand.

I brought the paddle down, bringing out a cry from Luna. Quinn held up one finger.

I spanked her again, watching as Quinn held up two fingers.

Again. Three.

Again. Four.

I spanked her once more, drawing a sharp cry from her. I then put the paddle to the side, leaning down and kissing her ass.

She let out a little noise, and I lifted her, seating her on my lap. I spread her thighs, leaning her back against my chest.

"Take your ball gags off," I growled.

Both Luna and Quinn obeyed, both letting out pants.

I gripped Luna's thighs and lifted her, looking at Quinn.

"Help guide my cocks inside of her," I said.

"Yes, Daddy," she said, coming to us.

She knelt in front of us, and I felt her hand grip my cocks. Luna and I both groaned as she helped me push inside of her, the head of my cocks spreading her wide.

Quinn leaned forward, flicking her tongue over Luna's clit. Luna groaned, her head falling back.

I lifted her and then brought her back down, pushing my cocks all the way inside of her. Luna moaned, her pussy gripping me as she took them.

Quinn reached up, rubbing Luna's clit as I began to thrust

in and out of her. I brought her up and down, over and over again.

I let out a primal growl, closing my eyes as pleasure washed over me.

"Fuck," I grunted.

Luna groaned as I took her, her claws reaching back and digging into my forearms.

Fuck, I was getting close to cumming again.

I felt Quinn's hand grip one of my knots, giving it a gentle squeeze. I let out a long growl, and Luna let out a cry as she suddenly came.

I gave another thrust, pushing both of my knots inside of her just as I started to cum. I held her still, sinking my teeth into her shoulder as I filled her. She groaned as my knots began to swell, slumping back against me.

I pulled my teeth away, licking the marks with a moan. The taste of her blood sang on my lips, and I leaned back, fully satisfied.

Quinn stood up, giving Luna a kiss. Luna pulled her down next to me, the three of us relaxing.

"This was a good Christmas," Quinn said, grinning.

"It was," I agreed. "Also, there are other presents too. I just wanted to have some fun first."

"Mmm," Luna purred, still lost in the waves of her orgasm.

I chuckled, closing my eyes for a moment.

I still had the rest of the night to sleep next to the two women I loved most. Over the last few years, we built a life together. One that I cherished. There were times we'd still help with creature world problems. Being close with the Barista meant that would always be the case, but... It was peaceful.

I was happy.

"I love you," I said. "And I'm excited to see our boys in the morning."

"Me too," Quinn said, laying her head on my shoulder.

"I bet they're asleep by now," Luna chuckled.

I snorted. "The moon is almost full."

"Fuck," Luna snorted.

"Well... We'll tip the babysitter," Quinn said.

The three of us nodded, relaxing again.

It was a Christmas Eve I'd never forget.

Jingle Bell Rock

MELODY, ICARUS, AND DALUS

'TWAS THE NIGHT BEFORE CHRISTMAS,
AFTER A CONCERT BACKSTAGE
WHERE THE PHOENIX TWINS
HAVE A GIFT FOR THEIR MATE...

IN THIS HOLIDAY TAIL,
YOU WILL FIND THE FOLLOWING:

FULLY SHIFTED SEX
COLLARING
BDSM DYNAMICS
TABOO ELEMENTS
DEGRADATION
PRAISE
SPITTING
SIZE DIFFERENCE
AND MORE.

133

CHAPTER 1
Melody

I walked through the crowd, ignoring the bodies pressed against mine as I made my way to the front. I could feel my phone going off with messages in my purse, so I slipped my hand down and plucked it out right as I squeezed through two men.

It was freezing outside, but within the venue, it was warm. And not because there was a Phoenix shifter singing on stage.

A familiar hand grabbed my hip, and I yelped as I was yanked back and to the side, lips pressing against my ear.

"You don't listen very well, little songbird," Icarus growled.

"I was trying to find you," I whispered, biting back a moan as he pressed his body against mine.

I could feel the hard cock in his pants through my dress. He fit it against my ass, the heat of him surrounding me like an infernal blanket.

His arms circled around me, and I was pulled from the mass of dancing bodies, dragged towards the front of the stage, where two bodyguards blocked the entrance to the back. They didn't even bat eyelashes at us as we went through, the two of us going around.

Over the last few years, the three of us had done a lot of things we hadn't expected. Dalus' music had slowly started to pick up, and he was regularly playing concerts at large venues now. He had a band— and Icarus played manager/lawyer, while I helped with other things like social media and scheduling.

I loved it. We both loved seeing Dalus live his dream, even if it meant working Christmas Eve. But hell, we were happy. I could listen to my mate sing for the rest of my life and never grow tired. We lived our life between home, Creature Cafe, and the road.

"Told you to meet me by the guards, and then you didn't answer your phone," he snarled, steering me towards a small room.

His hand circled my wrist and tightened, tugging me faster.

"I got lost," I said.

"Bullshit," he said. "You scouted this venue like three times."

It was true, but I wasn't going to tell him that. I smirked to myself. "Maybe I was running from you."

He growled, opening the door to the room.

He shoved me inside, and I turned as he kicked the door shut behind him, damn near launching myself at him.

The sound of Dalus' music thumped around us as our lips met, the heat becoming explosive. I heard the lock on the door click, and Icarus grabbed me, turning and shoving me against the wall.

I groaned as he pushed my dress up, pressing his hard cock against my ass again. I writhed against him with a helpless moan.

"Icarus," I gasped.

"Run from me," he chuckled. "As if you could ever escape."

I groaned, heat flashing over me. I pushed my ass back, grinding against him.

"Feel this, little songbird?" he breathed.

"Yes," I whimpered.

"My monster cock, so hard for your wet cunt. I can smell you," he growled. "I could practically taste how much of a slut you are, even when you were lost in the crowd."

Fuck. His words burned through me, lust not far behind.

His cock throbbed against me, and I moaned.

He spun me around, spreading my legs with his knee. My pussy pulsed with need, desperate for his attention.

Icarus smirked, his eyes burning in the dim lighting of the room. His dark hair was perfect, his smooth skin covered with a very short trimmed beard.

He reached into his pocket, pulling out a small box. I looked down at it, my gaze lighting up.

"What's this?" I whispered.

"A gift," he said. "One I want you to wear before I fuck you like I'm in heat."

He opened the box and pulled out a collar. I let out a happy gasp, reaching out to run my fingers over the buttery crimson leather.

At the center, there was a golden bell.

"That's why you told me to wear this bra," I whispered.

Icarus had specifically told me to wear a crimson and black lingerie piece that had straps that cupped my breasts just right.

The hum of the music began to fade as the song ended. We heard the crowd rumble with claps, the faint sound of Dalus' voice as he announced they had one more song before the set was over.

"Three minutes," I said, looking up at Icarus.

"Five," he growled.

He lifted the collar out, circling it around my neck. Warmth spread through me, a smile playing on my lips.

Icarus let out a happy hum. "Stunning," he said, flicking the bell.

It rang, making us both grin.

He leaned down, stealing a heated kiss. I groaned, tasting him. He kissed down my jawline, his hand circling the back of my neck and squeezing.

"I'm going to fuck you," he whispered. "I'm going to fill you with my cum. And then I want you to wait with your legs spread for me to bring Dalus after his set is over. Understood?"

"Yes, sir," I breathed. "Thank you for the gift."

"Anything for my songbird," he said, kissing down my neck.

I sucked in a breath as he lifted my dress, pulling it over my head and throwing it to the floor. He growled, pulling back to study me. I could feel the flash of heat as his eyes roamed over my body, his lips tugging into a smirk as he fit a finger underneath one of the straps of my bra. He popped it, and I gave out a startled cry.

He leaned down, sucking one of my nipples through the fabric. My head fell back, pleasure curling through me.

I was so wet for him. Fuck.

He sucked and then bit, chuckling as I yelped.

He turned me around again, pushing me against the wall. I groaned as I heard him undo the buckle of his belt, the metal clinking as he let his pants fall to the floor.

"Fuck," I breathed. "Please. Inside me. Now."

Icarus snarled as I spread my legs. He grabbed my hands, pinning them on the wall above me. I kept them there, pushing my ass back as his fingers slid down to my pussy.

"So wet," he said. "So needy. Have you touched yourself today, little songbird?"

"Yes," I rasped. "I wanted you earlier, but you were busy."

"Did you use the toy I bought you? The one that's shaped like my monster cock?"

"Yes," I whimpered.

"Good girl," he praised softly, his fingers thrusting inside of me.

My entire body shivered with a wave of pleasure, my breath catching.

He pulled his fingers free, tsking at how wet I was.

"I can take you," I said, looking back over my shoulder at him.

"Good," he said.

I felt the head of his cock against me, and I gasped.

"Icarus," I moaned. "*Fuck* me."

He cursed under his breath but didn't wait a moment more. In one swift thrust, he drove his hard cock inside of me. I cried out as he filled me, heat rushing through my body. He groaned, leaning forward to kiss my neck. I shivered, letting out little whimpers and moans as he began to pull his cock back out and then thrust forward again. He growled as his hands fell down to my hips, and he gripped them hard as he began to fuck me.

The bell on my collar jingled with every movement, his growls falling into the same rhythm as my gasps.

Fuck, he was huge. But I took every inch, the feeling of being fucked brutally making me even more turned on.

The sound of our skin slapping against each other echoed through the room, coupled with groans and grunts. The end of the song was close, and he let out a curse, his nails digging into my skin.

"I'm going to take you shifted," he huffed. "After my brother fills your cunt, little songbird."

"Please," I breathed. "Please. Please!"

He drilled into me harder before crying out. With one last thrust, he started to cum, driving it deep inside of me.

He heaved out breaths, sliding his hand around. His fingers slid over my clit, making me gasp.

"Fuck," I moaned.

He thrust harder, his cock still hard even though he was still cumming. My pussy spasmed around him, squeezing him tight as he began to rub my clit hard.

"Fuck," I gasped, my head falling back on his chest.

"You really think I'd fill you with my cum and not make you orgasm?" he snarled.

"Never," I whispered, gasping again.

Fuck, I was right on edge.

He rubbed faster, and I screamed, my orgasm crashing into me like a glorious wave. He kept going, still rubbing me as it went through me.

Fuck! I writhed against him, squeezing his cock. I wasn't able to stop my scream as he forced another orgasm out of me, finally pulling his fingers away.

He pulled his cock from me, his cum dripping down my legs. I leaned against the wall, panting.

"Couch," he rasped, picking up his pants. "Legs spread. Don't clean up a fucking drop."

"Yes..." I dragged in a breath. "Fuck. Yes, Sir."

Icarus finished buckling his pants and then leaned forward, stealing a kiss. I groaned, leaning into him. I wanted more, even though I was still burning from the two orgasms he'd just given me.

"Be a good girl," he whispered. "I'll be back with my brother, and then the three of us will be off for the evening to celebrate the holiday and each other."

I nodded, letting out a little hum as he flicked the bell again and then opened the door and slipped out backstage.

Fuck.

I looked down at myself. I was a mess.

And I was still horny too.

I groaned and went to the couch, seating myself in the

middle and spreading my legs. Icarus's cum dripped from me, and I closed my eyes for a moment, thinking about how much I wanted him again.

My pussy pulsed, and I moaned.

Waiting was going to be torture, but it would be worth it once they got back.

Then, the real celebration could start.

CHAPTER 2

Dalus

I set Melody's guitar in its case, running my fingertips over the rosewood. She had made this one for me, a present that she had given me when my music had taken off.

I had played it at every show since.

I smiled, seeing the inscription on the inside of the body, before shutting the case and latching it close.

From your little songbird.

I felt my chest swell with warmth. Warmth and need.

We had plans tonight, and I was ready to get to them.

I felt my brother's gaze on me long before he was at my side, his hand settling on my shoulder. The rest of the band was standing around, talking about the show.

It had been another sold-out venue, and I was riding high on the adrenaline and excitement. This was also the last time we were playing a fucking Christmas song until next year, so that was also exciting.

"Dalus," Icarus said, his voice immediately sending a dark thrill through me.

Fuck. I did my best to mask my surprise as Melody's scent hit me. I could smell her arousal on him like perfume.

"Hey," I said, looking up at him.

The rest of the bandmates were monsters, too, ones that did very well blending in with the world of humans. About four years ago, we had formed a band— naming it, shockingly, Phoenix's Ashes. Icarus and Melody had helped launch us into the world, and since then, we'd been on a roller coaster.

I loved it. I loved that they both supported me and was thankful that I was able to share the music I created with the world. I had lived for a long time, but now that I was able to make my dream come true...It felt like I was reborn.

And in a way, since Melody, I had been reborn.

As exciting as it all was, though, I hungered to be in bed with her, especially after catching her scent.

"Your wife is waiting," Icarus said, giving me an almost brotherly smile. "She said we have to be on the plane soon. Flying out to see Ella and Naomi."

That was partially true.

"Bye, Dalus," my drummer chuckled, giving me a wave.

My bass and electric guitarist both smirked too.

No one asked about Icarus, nor did they care. The four of us were doing what we loved, got along well, and were touring the States before heading to Europe soon.

"I'll see you guys later," I said. "In a week, we'll get ready for the next show. But everyone, enjoy the time off."

"You too," they said.

Icarus gave me a tug, steering me down the steps of the stage to the back rooms. We moved silently for the one I knew Melody was in, but a group of fans rounded the other corner at the same time.

The squeals were almost horrifying, and Icarus sighed as we were surrounded. I could barely understand the words they were saying, my thoughts solely focused on Melody now.

I signed a few shirts, but when someone reached out and grabbed my arm, Icarus shoved me back with a snarl.

"Security," he barked.

They were on us within seconds, escorting the people away.

"That was a little harsh," I said.

Icarus spun, his eyes darkening as they met mine. "No one touches you without my permission. Or have you forgotten that, brother?"

Fuck.

"Right," I whispered, feeling desire stir.

"It's Christmas Eve," Icarus said. "And your present is waiting, being a good girl and everything."

I felt a rush of excitement and smiled. "Thank you."

Icarus turned without another word, going to the door.

We slipped inside, and I damn near fell to my knees as he shut the door behind us, locking it.

"Fuck," I rasped.

Melody was on the sofa, her legs spread with Icarus' cum dripping out of her pussy. Her fingers were on her clit, her skin covered with a sheen of sweat.

She was wearing nothing but a piece of lingerie that hugged her breasts and a red collar with a bell.

"Songbird," I moaned, my cock hardening.

Icarus stepped behind me, his hands intertwined in my hair. He yanked my head back, forcing me to look up at him.

"Merry Christmas," he whispered. "Open your mouth."

I obeyed him, parting my lips.

He spat, still gripping my hair as it slid down my throat. I groaned, my heart pounding in my chest.

"Say thank you," he said.

"Thank you," I whispered.

"Swallow," he said.

I obeyed him, swallowing.

"Now, go make our mate cum."

"Yes," I said.

He let go, giving me a little push. I groaned as I got up, going to her and kneeling between her legs.

"Dalus," Melody whimpered. "Fuck. I need you inside of me."

"I'm going to clean you up and make you cum first, little songbird," I purred.

I pushed her legs wide, digging my fingertips into her thighs. Melody let out a little cry, sinking back into the sofa as I leaned forward and licked her.

The taste of my brother's cum was salty on my lips, and I felt my cock immediately harden as I circled her clit with my tongue.

"Fuck," she gasped. She reached out, gripping my hair and pulling my face into her pussy.

Today had already been an amazing day, but all of it fell away as I buried my tongue deep inside of her. I let my body partially shift, enjoying her squeal as my long tongue unfurled inside of her. I felt the heat shimmer over my body, felt the lust burning up inside of me.

I grunted, drinking in her essence. Tasting both of them, knowing that this was a gift I'd wanted for days. It was hard to find time to just be with the two of them when we were on the road, but now we were on holiday, and I could let go.

"You can shift," Icarus' silky deep voice said. "I already paid for this room's renovations. Made them think you were a true rockstar, you know."

Fuck.

I grunted, letting go. My body began to shift as I kept fucking her with my tongue, listening to her cries as my bones

145

and muscles snapped and grew. I shifted into the form of a monster, of a massive phoenix.

Melody writhed beneath me, her scent driving me wild. I stopped fighting myself, feeling my cock lengthen and harden to its full twelve inches.

I was hungry for her. Hungry to fuck her, to take her.

"Dalus," she whimpered. "Please!"

I didn't stop, plunging my tongue in and out of her. She cried out, her hips bucking as she got closer and closer to cumming. I could feel her squeezing my tongue, her whimpers making me so hard.

"Fuck, I'm going to cum," Melody gasped.

Icarus came to the two of us, sitting on the couch next to her and pulling out his cock. He started to stroke it, watching the two of us with burning eyes.

"Make her cum," he growled, looking at me.

Fuck. I could feel precum dripping from the tip of my cock. I drove my tongue deeper, and Melody screamed, finally cumming hard. She arched against the couch, her breaths becoming ragged.

I pulled my tongue from her, rising up. My wings spread behind me, the air shimmering with heat.

"Put your cock inside of her," Icarus growled, stroking his cock harder. "Fuck her. *Hard.*"

I nodded, eager to obey.

She spread her legs as wide as possible, her pussy glistening as I pressed the head of my cock against her opening. Her gaze locked with mine, her lips parting with a moan as I slowly began to push inside of her.

Melody cried out, her voice a song I forever wanted in my head. I snarled as I pushed my cock inside of her, easing in until I was as deep as I could go.

Her pussy pulsed around me, her eyes fluttering as I pulled

out and then drove back in. The bell around her neck rang, jingling with the rhythm of my hips.

"Dalus!" she cried.

My monstrous body shuddered, my blood simmering as I began to pump into her. I pulled my cock out before slamming back in, looking down to watch as her little human body took me.

"Good boy," Icarus huffed, stroking his cock faster.

The three of us moaned together, a couple of feathers loosening from my body and floating down to her arched body.

Beautiful. She was beautiful. A gift. My little songbird was the love of my life, the reason I sang. The reason I wrote music.

She reached up, her fingers curling into my feathers and gripping. I groaned, fucking her harder. The couch creaked from the pressure, coupled with her and Icarus' sounds of need.

"Fuck," Icarus moaned. "Fill her up, brother," he rasped.

Pleasure burst through me, and I closed my eyes, pumping into her faster until she let out a cry. Her pussy clenched around me as she came, and I felt myself give in.

I started to cum, shooting hot ropes of cum inside of her. Ecstasy burned through me as I lost myself to her body, cumming harder than I had in what felt like forever.

I moaned as I slumped forward, pressing my head against her chest. Melody let out a helpless moan, ruffling my head.

"Fuck," she whispered. "That was fucking hot."

I nodded and leaned back, slowly pulling my cock from her. I began to shift back into my human form, wearing nothing but a smirk.

Melody grinned through her heavy breaths, holding her arms open.

I went to her, planting a kiss on her soft lips.

"Hi, baby," she said, kissing my forehead.

"Hi," I breathed.

We both looked over at Icarus, his hand still on his hard cock.

He raised a brow, his lips twisting. "Oh. You don't think you're both finished, do you?"

"No," I laughed.

"I've already cum three times," Melody said, her brows raising.

Icarus snorted. "I'm sure you can give me more, sweet Melody."

CHAPTER 3

Icarus

I was still hard from watching Dalus' monster cock fill Melody, from seeing the outline of it inside of her as he drove in and out. She had been so small compared to him, his hands alone wider than her hips. She'd taken him, taking every inch.

I leaned forward, looping a finger around her collar and tugging her forward. Her lips met mine, her groan sweet on my lips.

She could and would give me more orgasms before we had to leave for our flight.

She broke our kiss, moving so that she could straddle my lap. Her hand gripped my cock as we kissed, stroking up and down.

I shuddered, breaking the kiss to growl. "Two more," I said. "Two more before we leave for our flight. I want you to scream for me."

"I have to be able to walk to get on the plane," she teased.

"I can carry you," Dalus chuckled.

Melody looked back at him, dragging him into a kiss.

I watched the two of them as she kept stroking my cock, the

bell jingling around her neck. I reached up and circled her nipples, pinching them as they made out.

She yelped, her breath catching. Dalus kept her mouth on his as I leaned forward, biting her breasts. She moaned, her hot pussy grinding against me. She stroked my cock faster, giving into the flames of lust.

I wanted to shift, to fuck her in my monstrous form. I wanted her cries to echo for everyone to hear, knowing that they would wonder how much pleasure she was feeling.

I lifted her in one swift motion, turning her so that her back was against my chest. I seated her on my cock, groaning as I was enveloped in her heat. She squeaked as she took it, and I could feel how turned on she was through our bond.

"Little songbird," I growled. "Taking my cock like such a good girl. My brother warmed you up so well."

"I want your full cock," she gasped.

"You'll get it," I said. "I'm going to shift while inside you, sweetheart. Dalus, make her cum while I fill her up."

"Yes, mate," he breathed.

A shiver of delight worked through me, and I pushed my hips up, ensuring that every inch of my pulsing cock was inside of her. Melody groaned, her muscles spasming with pleasure.

I began to let myself shift, my cock growing bigger as my body began to change.

"Fuck, you feel good," she rasped. "Oh fuck!"

"Good girl," I praised. "You're doing so well."

I groaned as I became more and more monstrous, trying to force my shifting to be slow so that she could adjust to my size. Melody writhed against me, her head falling back on my shoulder with a gasp.

Dalus leaned down, burying his face between her legs. She cried out as he began to lick her, his tongue swirling around her clit. I could feel her grip me, squeezing me more and more as I continued to shift.

Within a few moments, my little human mate was tiny in my lap, my massive cock buried inside of her as Dalus licked her. My massive clawed hand circled her waist, lifting her carefully before bringing her back down on my cock.

She screamed, her voice echoing through the room. I growled, listening to the sound of the bell and her cries, and we began to move together.

"Fuck, I'm going to cum," she gasped.

Dalus groaned, his breath hot on the base of my cock as his tongue circled her clit.

Melody cried out, her orgasm overcoming her. I growled as she squeezed me, feeling how fucking close I was to cumming myself.

I pumped into her, filling her over and over again. I let the primal part of me take over, the one that wished to fill my mate with my cum.

Fuck. I let out a roar as I started to cum, giving one last thrust right as I started to fill her. She gasped as the heat spread through her body, my cum dripping out of her.

"Fuck," she gasped.

Dalus was still playing with her clit, and not two seconds later— another orgasm washed over her. She whimpered, writhing against me as she came.

Finally, the three of us slumped together, a pile of heavy breaths and groans.

I closed my eyes for a few moments, letting the pleasure of being with them float through me.

I started to shift back, chuckling at the audible sigh from Melody.

Dalus stood, going to one of the bags on the floor and grabbing a towel. He came back to us, kneeling down before our mate and cleaning her up.

"You will have to carry me," she said, grinning.

"Happily, little songbird," Dalus chuckled.

I looked up at the clock on the wall and raised a brow. "Fuck. We need to leave."

Melody looked up and cursed. She started to stand, but I pulled her back, stealing one more kiss.

"Merry Christmas, little songbird," I murmured.

Her eyes softened, and she smiled. "I love you. Merry Christmas."

I smiled happily as she leaned down and grabbed Dalus' face, giving him a kiss too.

"Merry Christmas," he said, grinning. "Naomi is going to be pissed."

Melody snorted. "Not the first time she's smelled your cum on me. They'll be happy to see us for the holiday, and we'll be an escape route from the royal family if needed."

True. Naomi and Ella were hosting the Naga family at their home, and we were going there to be together but also to rescue them if needed. Naomi's parents were great, but some of the others were annoying as hell. Then, tomorrow morning, all of us would be crawling to the Cafe to see everyone else.

The three of us got dressed quickly, trying to be somewhat presentable.

Never mind that there was definitely cum on my pants.

"I have clothes we can change into on the plane," Melody giggled, studying Dalus and me.

Dalus smirked. "Always prepared."

"You have to be when you're mated to two Phoenix shifters. You never know when you'll be on fire."

I laughed, grabbing a couple of our bags and hoisting them over my shoulder.

The three of us turned to look at the room, and Melody winced.

"Fucking hell. Well. They will certainly think you're something."

"It's fine," I said nonchalantly, going to the door. "Already paid for. Now, let's go, *mates*. There are still more presents to be opened."

Melody and Dalus both looked at each other, grinning with excitement. The three of us left the room, heading off into the snowy evening to celebrate the holiday together.

Princess, It's Cold Outside

NAOMI AND ELLA

'TWAS THE NIGHT BEFORE CHRISTMAS,
IN THEIR BEAUTIFUL HOME
WHERE THE QUEEN AND HER PRINCESS
WERE READY FOR SOME FUN...

IN THIS HOLIDAY TAIL,
YOU WILL FIND THE FOLLOWING:

SQUIRTING
WAX PLAY
BONDAGE
PRAISE
TAIL SEX
SEX TOYS
AND MORE.

CHAPTER 1

Ella

"We have two hours," Naomi said, giving me a knowing smile. "I think we should celebrate early."

The two of us sat in the living room, the Christmas tree in the corner casting a sparkling glow over everything. It smelled like chestnuts and fresh bread. We had everything for dinner ready to go, and I'd already snuck in a few bites of different things.

The windows in front of us showed a world of white, but I couldn't feel the chill inside.

Especially not in the arms of my beautiful Naga mate.

"What do you think, princess?" Naomi hummed, lifting a brow.

She was gorgeous. Stunning. Even after being together for a few years, she could steal my breath with her looks. She was wearing a sheer crystal top, one that suited her perfectly.

"Yes," I breathed, leaning in.

She met me halfway, her tail curling around my body as our lips met. I groaned at the softness, the taste of her perfection.

Her hand slid up my chest, over the dress I was wearing.

Her family, along with Melody, Icarus, and Dalus, would be here later. But for now, it was just the two of us.

For now, we could celebrate the holiday together.

Over the last few years, I had fallen even more in love with her— if that were possible. Our lives were very different now, especially with her getting ready to assume the throne within the next few years. Never had a Naga ruled with a human at their side, but no one batted an eyelash. Her family loved me, even though there were moments I felt like I was about to get devoured.

Her father was ready to retire and spend time with his wife and husband, and said that he didn't want to pass the crown down because of death. That was also different, but it worked better for everyone.

Five years ago, I didn't even know if I could be worthy of love. I certainly didn't know that I would gain someone that cherished me, along with an entire family that supported me. Holidays used to be my least favorite time of the year, because even when I had been surrounded by friends, I had felt alone. I had felt the pain of not having anyone that was mine, and it haunted me like a dark cloud from September to January.

But it was different now. I had been able to pull myself out of that. I was able to relax and enjoy things.

And even in moments that I felt it creep up again, Naomi was there for me. Soothing me, loving me, giving me space if I needed it and pulling me close if I wanted. She was my Queen, my love, and everything that I could ever want.

Heat worked up my spine, my nipples hardening as her hand slid around the back of my neck. She raked her nails through my silver hair, eliciting a helpless groan from me as she gripped it.

"So cold," Naomi whispered, leaning forward to kiss down my neck. "Do you want me to warm you up?"

A shiver worked through me, and I felt her tail moving. Wrapping around me, binding me to her.

"Please," I gasped as she scraped her teeth at the base of my throat.

She smiled against my skin. Fuck, she was always able to turn me on in a matter of seconds.

"I want you," I moaned. "Fuck. I always want you, though."

"And I always want you," she murmured, smiling.

I leaned into her, running my hands up her hips and tugging on the dress she wore. I pulled it off, tossing it to the floor.

"Now you," she said, pulling my clothes off.

I was wearing a beautiful blue satin dress that she had picked out for me. It fit me perfectly, and came off easy.

I whimpered as she stripped me. The moment I was completely naked, her lips went to my nipples.

"Fuck," I groaned, my head tipping back.

She sucked them, her hands gliding down to my thighs. She pushed them apart, her fingers gently brushing over my clit.

It felt like lightning struck me, pleasure curling my toes as I gasped.

"Naomi," I rasped.

I felt the tip of her fangs teasing my skin, the sharp tips threatening to pierce me.

I loved it when she bit me.

I was so wet already, my blood humming as she circled my clit and sucked on my breasts. I closed my eyes, giving in to her completely. I was hers; body, mind, and soul.

I arched against her, wanting to give her more. Desperate to give her whatever she wanted.

She moaned against me, her fingers working their magic. I gasped, my eyes flying open as I felt another wave of pleasure burn through me.

Fuck, she could make me cum so easily. So freaking easily.

I looked up, remembering that our living room had windows.

Massive windows.

"Naomi," I moaned. "Windows."

With a little hiss, she drew back, looking at them. If looks could shatter glass, they would have.

"I'm sure the forest would love to see us fuck," she said, but she was already sweeping me up.

I wrapped my arms around her neck and legs around her hips as she carried me out of the living room and down the hall towards our bedroom.

"What are you going to do to me?" I asked with a giggle.

"Devour your pussy and make you scream," Naomi answered. "Fuck you so that you're stupid at the family dinner."

"Hey!" I laughed as she tossed me onto our bed.

She smirked as she stood at the end of the bed. My gaze roamed over her body, appreciating everything.

"Gods, I love women," I sighed happily.

"Me too," she snickered. "Especially when they're blushing like a virgin."

Fuck. My pussy clenched at her words.

"Lay back, little princess. I said I wanted to warm you up, and I know exactly how."

My eyes widened, but I obeyed. I relaxed into the soft blankets as she went to her closet— the closet of all things pleasure and orgasm. My muscles tingled with excitement as I watched her go in.

She'd told me I wasn't allowed to go in there the last couple days, and now I would find out why.

I swallowed hard, the anticipation killing me.

Would she spank me? Would she whip me? Hypnotize me? Bind me?

I wanted her to do all of the things. Anything and everything.

I looked up at the mirror over our bed, smirking.

She was right, I was flushed pink. I spread my legs, my pussy glistening.

Naomi came back into the room with a small bag, bringing it to the bed. She leaned down, stealing a kiss from me.

"Do you know your safeword, sweetheart?"

"Yes," I breathed.

"Good girl. You'll use it if you need it?"

"Yes."

"Good," she hummed.

"Do whatever you want to me," I said. "Gods know I'm already wet for you."

"Of course you are," she teased, pinching one of my nipples.

I let out a pleased gasp and she reached into the bag, pulling out a blindfold. She slid it over my head, condemning me to sweet darkness.

I swallowed hard as I listened to her reach into the bag again. I felt her fingers wrap around my wrist, sliding a cuff over them. Within a few moments, I was bound to our bed.

"Good girl," Naomi murmured. "You look so good spread out like this."

Her fingertips traced down my body and I sucked in a breath as they dipped between my legs.

"Goddess," I gasped.

Naomi chuckled, her fingers pulling away. She left me wanting more, my pussy aching for her touch. For her tongue, her tail, anything she offered me.

My ears strained as I listened to her movements. She disappeared for a moment and then came back to my side.

I heard the sound of a lighter and felt a shiver work through me. I trusted her entirely, but it still made me nervous.

"Do you want this?" she whispered.

"Yes." I nodded, my breath hitching.

What did I want? I wanted her. I wanted whatever she wanted to do.

I could feel her smile.

My little princess, her voice crooned in my mind.

I smiled right as I felt something hot drip onto my stomach. I gasped at the momentary sting, amazed at the warmth that followed it.

It was hot wax, I realized.

I moaned as more dripped onto me. She created a line up my stomach, up to my breasts. I hissed as a drop landed on my nipple, a combination of pain and pleasure following.

Good girl, she praised.

I gasped as I felt the tip of her tail slide up the bed between my legs. I was already spread wide for her, my ankles cuffed like my wrists were.

"Fuck," I groaned.

I felt her scales glide over my skin, the bulbous tip of her tail teasing my clit.

Another drop hit my other breast, making me groan. Pleasure worked through me as the stinging kisses of the wax filled me with infernal lust.

My beautiful girl, Naomi whispered. *Such a good little princess.*

The tip of her tail moved down, teasing my entrance. I gasped as she began to ease it in.

So wet for me. So eager to be fucked.

"Yes," I gasped. *"Please."*

My voice was a ragged beg, my body straining as she began to ease her tail inside of me. I gasped as more wax hit my skin, the little bites of pain contrasting with the pleasure of taking her tail in a way that sent me straight to the edge.

Do you want your cunt to be fucked, little princess? Would that warm you up?

"Please," I cried. "I want you."

"I know you do," she chuckled.

Her tail thrust into me right as more wax dripped, my cry echoing through our room. It pulled back out, before thrusting again, finding a rhythm that had me pulling on the cuffs that bound me.

I groaned, shivering as she fucked me. I fell into the darkness, allowing erotic ecstasy to grip me.

I hissed through clenched teeth as more wax hit my skin. Her fingers pinched one of my nipples as I whimpered, my head arching back as her tail drove in and out of me.

"Fuck," I cried. "I'm so close."

Her hand slid down my body, her fingertips circling my clit. The pleasure was immediate, the rush making me scream.

Cum for me, princess.

As if I could stop myself. I gasped, caving into her command.

My orgasm gripped me. I cried out, yanking against my restraints as I cummed.

Naomi slowly pulled her tail free and then lifted my blindfold. I groaned, my head spinning.

She leaned down, kissing me.

I panted, staring up into her brilliant eyes. "Your turn."

Naomi

E lla lifted her head, looking down at her body. She was covered in crimson and evergreen wax, my little Christmas present.

"How did you feel about the wax?" I asked.

"Good," she said, her eyes lighting up.

I leaned down and kissed her again, unable to get enough. I glanced up at the clock, noting that we still had plenty of time to do more and still be presentable before everyone came over.

"It stung but it felt good," she said.

"Good," I said, stealing one more kiss.

Ella groaned as I started to kiss down her body. I paused, trailing the tip of my tongue over her skin. I avoided the wax, creating a little trail until I made my way to her pussy.

Ella yanked against her restraints, her wrists and ankles pulling on the cuffs bound to the bed. Her chest heaved with a little breath, another noise of pleasure as I dipped my tongue inside of her.

She tasted like heaven, especially after just cumming. I drove my tongue inside of her, fighting off a laugh at her little squeak. I could hear her heart hammering in her chest, her body arching with pleasure as I continued to play with her.

I ran my fingers up her thigh, and then rested it right above her pussy. With my thumb, I began to rub her clit in circles.

"I thought you were done with me," she gasped. I only chuckled, because I was never done with her.

There had been times over the last five years that I had stolen her for a few days just so that I could make her cum as much as humanly possible. I reveled in the fact that I was able to make her feel so much pleasure.

Ella gasped, the sound of the chains rattling through the room.

I lifted my head for just a moment, giving her a stern look.

"Do you want me to stop, Little Princess?" I asked.

Ella's eyes widened, her head immediately shaking. "No," she gasped. "Please don't stop. Please."

I smirked, and then went back down to her pussy. I sucked on the folds of her cunt, and then buried my tongue deep inside of her again. She let out a little squeal, and I began to lap at all of her essence. I rubbed her clit, and then slid two of my fingers inside of her. I found a rhythm with my tongue and fingers, doing everything I could to drive her straight back to the edge. I wanted her to cum again, I wanted to hear her cry. I wanted to hear her scream

Ella let out a broken cry. "Fuck! I'm so close! Please don't stop!"

I wasn't going to. I smiled against her pussy, closing my eyes with a moan as I devoured her.

Eating her out was still one of my favorite things to do.

Her walls clenched around me, her breaths becoming more ragged as her hips lifted.

I pulled my tongue free, thrusting my fingers harder inside

of her. There was a little spot that always made her cum, and I knew the moment I hit it, she would be crying out.

"So desperate," I whispered. "Such a needy little pussy. Stop fighting yourself and give in to me."

"Yes!" she cried. "Please! I'm so close—"

Her words were interrupted by a scream right as I hit that spot. Liquid gushed out between her thighs, and I smirked as it drenched the blankets under her.

We always had extra blankets and bedding for moments like this.

She let out ragged gasps, her body convulsing. I slowly pulled my fingers free, bringing them to my lips and licking them clean.

Ella lifted her head, giving me a dazed look.

I chuckled and then kissed back up her body, planting one on her forehead. I then slowly undid the cuffs around her wrists and ankles.

Ella melted into the bed with a sigh. "Fuck. My head is spinning from cumming so hard."

I smiled. That's what I liked to hear.

"Good," I purred. "Hmm. When you're ready for more, let me know."

"More?" she gasped, looking up at me.

"Yes," I said, raising a brow.

I leaned back, reaching into the bag on the bed and pulling out a black strap-on for her to wear.

She beamed, reaching for it. I watched happily as she gripped the cock, running her hands over it.

"Yes," she purred. "Okay, I can do more."

I laughed, her excitement endearing.

"Please. I love it when you let me use this on you," she said, giving me a pleading look.

"Me too," I chuckled.

We saved it for special times like this.

I loved the life that we had built together. Over the last few years, we'd continued to find happiness. And even with the responsibility of the Naga throne growing closer, I couldn't stress when I had her around.

The Barista had done his job well. Not to mention, I had gained new friends out of it too. Icarus and Dalus had become two people I'd never believed I would care about, but I did. And Melody— she was wonderful.

Inside our world, we had created second families and third families even. There were times throughout the year where we popped in to see Trixie, the Barista, and Lucy.

I certainly never believed I'd call the devil my friend too.

It made me happy. I'd also come around on pets and even ended up getting a cat of my own, one that loved our Morticia. Not that I had never not loved Ella's pets, but this was the first time in my life that I had my own.

I was thankful to have my Little Princess with me. To be able to share moments like this, solace and comfort interspersed with pure pleasure and need, overtaking the banality of everyday life.

I gave her the strap on and watched as she slid on the harness. I wanted her to fuck me, and I wanted to make her cum as she filled me.

"Good girl," I praised. I loved watching how she lit up when I murmured such words, her expression giving me a little thrill.

She buckled the harness and then looked at me, waiting to see what I wanted next.

I reached for her and in one swift motion, laid out on the bed with her seated on top of my hips.

She let out a little thrilled laugh, her heart pounding in her chest. I could hear the rush of the blood, and could smell her arousal. She was turned on and a little uneasy when I put her on top of me like this.

"You're on top princess, but I'm still in control."

She nodded, her gaze melting into mine. I gripped her hip, winding my tail up and around her torso.

"There's lube in the bag," I said. "Do what you want to me."

"Wha— what?" She gasped, her eyes widening.

I raised a brow. "You heard me, Little Princess."

"Fuck," she mumbled. "Whatever I want?"

"Yes," I said with a smirk.

Oh, I liked this. I liked the uneasiness, the surprise. I liked the way her lower lip quivered, her breath hitching.

"What do you want to do to me, Little Princess?" I asked.

She let out a curse and then leaned down, kissing me. I opened my mouth, our tongues meeting. She groaned, the tip of her tongue brushing my fangs.

I growled against her, the urge to sink my fangs into her burning through me.

I would wait, though. I wanted to see what she would choose to do.

Ella broke our kiss, trailing her lips down my jaw and then neck. I closed my eyes with a little moan as she kissed her way down to my breasts, sucking one of my nipples tenderly.

I loved the way she felt, the softness of her thighs against my hips. I was already turned on from playing with her, and could feel my slit slowly starting to open.

Ella's hands moved down my body as she kissed my breasts, her fingers pressing into my folds. I gasped, pleasure working through me.

She was gentle, searching for all of the little ways she could please me. She kissed down my stomach where my scales began, her lips sending shivers through me as she made her way to my slit.

She spread my slit, her tongue flicking over my clit. I groaned, gripping the blankets beneath me.

Fuck, her tongue felt amazing.

It took every ounce of control to not take over, fighting myself to give in to the pleasure. Part of me wanted to flip her over and make her cum again, but I liked the way her tongue felt. I liked the little breaths of surprise.

She slipped two fingers inside of me and I groaned, heat rushing through me. Pleasure echoed through our bond, working through me in waves.

She began to move her fingers as she played with my clit, drawing a groan from me.

Fuck.

I couldn't stop myself.

My tail curled around her body, and in one swift motion, I moved the two of us. Ella let out a surprised squeal and then a laugh.

"Shush," I hissed.

Ella grinned, her cheeks flushed and eyes sparkling. "And here I was thinking you'd really let me be in control."

I hissed at her again, but she only laughed, wrapping her arms around me to kiss me. I moved the two of us off the bed, bringing the lube with me, my tail wrapping around us, cocooning us completely. I let out a little growl, tipping her chin up.

"Sorry," I said. "I tried."

She laughed again and then stole another kiss. "It's okay, I like it when you take over," she giggled.

I smirked, running my hands down her body to the strap-on that was around her hips. I gave the rubber cock a hard tug, arching my brow.

"Don't stop, princess," I whispered, my voice husky.

Ella's hands fell back down to where my skin turned to

scales, her fingers slipping inside of me. I let out a gasp as pleasure worked through me, my head tipping back as she began to make the same motions again.

I sucked in a breath, focusing on the feeling of her against my body. I could feel her warmth, so very different from my own. Ella continued to tease me, her lips trailing down my chest. She kissed her way down to my breasts, her tongue swirling around my nipples as she continued to play with my slit.

"Ella," I rasped. "My Little Princess."

I groaned as she continued to finger me, my tail curling tighter until it was against her body. I took the lube and poured some in my hands, rubbing it over the cock strapped to her as she continued to steal moans from me.

Once the cock was lubed up, I tossed the bottle to the side and stole a deep kiss from her. Ella groaned against me, her breath pitching. I kissed up her jawline, whispering in her ear. "I still want you to fuck me."

She moaned helplessly, giving me a nod. "Yes, my Queen," she whispered.

That sent a little thrill through me, one that made me growl. Ella looked down between us, pulling her fingers free and wrapping them around her strap-on.

She eased the tip inside of me and I moaned, a chill rushing over my skin at the pleasure of being filled by her.

It had taken time for me to be able to learn how to give in to her too, and I loved that I was able to. I felt safe with her, and while I preferred to be in control— I still loved moments like this.

"Fuck," I cursed, moving my hips forward.

I took several more inches. I cupped Ella's face, kissing her again. Our tongues met, the taste of her making me hunger even more.

With my tail wrapped around the two of us, she began to move her hips, thrusting in and out of me. Our touches were heated, needy. We only had so much time before we had to get ready, and I was desperate to cum for her.

I was desperate to make her cum again.

"Good girl," I gasped. "Fucking your Queen like a good little princess."

"Yes," she gasped. "Whatever you want," she moaned, her hips moving a little faster.

Her fingers slid against my clit again, rubbing in quick circles as she set a carnal rhythm.

I watched her face through half closed eyes. Her lips quivered, her brows drawing together with a moan. She leaned down, taking one of my nipples between her teeth and giving me a gentle bite.

That sent a bolt of ecstasy through me and I let my head fall back. I looked up at our mirrored ceiling, and grinned.

Fuck, that had been a good investment.

I could still see the red and green wax that covered my mate's body, a faint redness from the heat still lingering. I watched as she drove into me, her body shivering just like mine.

"I love you," she rasped.

"I love you too," I said, my eyes closing.

I was getting closer and closer to cumming. My muscles coiled as I went towards the edge, her fingers working my clit as she pumped inside of me.

I let out a cry as I suddenly cummed, my body tensing as it took over me. Ella let out a little gasp of delight, watching me cum with a heated gaze.

I relaxed with a groan, my heart beating wildly in my chest.

Ella slowly pulled out and then leaned forward, resting her head against my chest. I held her close, my mind spinning from cumming so hard.

"Did I do good?" she whispered.

"Yes," I said, smiling. "Amazing, Little Princess."

"Good," she whispered, her arms wrapping around me.

I held her close for a few minutes and then let out a sigh. I looked up at the clock, and cursed under my breath.

"Fuck. We need to get cleaned up. Get the wax off you, the bed changed, bathed."

Ella looked up too and her eyes widened. "Oh shit. Well. At least Melody and the guys wont give a shit if we smell like sex."

"No, but my parents will smirk the entire time at dinner, and I don't want that," I hissed.

Ella laughed. "Fair. Ok, let's get to it then."

It took about 45 minutes, but we were able to make it right as the doorbell rang through the house.

I cursed under my breath, looking at Ella.

We both looked like nothing had happened. The bed was changed, we were cleaned up, and looking gorgeous as ever.

She made a face and the two of us went to the living room.

"Oh fuck," I cursed.

Some of our clothing from earlier was on the floor.

I leaned over the couch and snapped it up, opening up a closet door in the hall and tossing it in.

Ella snorted. "Sometimes I wonder if we really have it together."

"We don't," I said, shaking my head. "Worth it, though."

Ella went to the door, opening it.

Melody, Icarus, and Dalus were on the other side, about as disheveled looking as we had been not long ago.

We all stared at each other for a moment and then burst out laughing.

It was going to be a holiday night we all would remember.

A Holly Jolly Orc

ALEX AND JASPER

'TWAS THE NIGHT BEFORE CHRISTMAS,
AND JASPER COULD FEEL IN HIS GUT
THAT THE TIME HAS CUM
TO TURN HIS HUMAN INTO HIS SLUT...

IN THIS HOLIDAY TAIL,
YOU WILL FIND THE FOLLOWING:

SPANKING
DADDY KINK
BREEDING W/O PREGNANCY
FORCED ORGASMS
CNC
HONORIFICS (DADDY/BOY)
RIMMING
DEGRADATION
PRAISE
AND MORE.

Jasper

The moment I stepped into our cabin, I shut the door behind us and lifted Alex in the air.

My mate let out a breath, one that was almost a squeal, as I turned him around, shoving him against the wall.

"Jasper," he gasped.

"Alex," I said, raising a brow.

The two of us stared at each other for a moment and then broke out into stupid grins.

It was Christmas Eve, and the two of us had just dropped off our children for the evening. Loved all four of them to death, but I wanted my hubby alone, hard, and screaming my name.

Alex wrapped his legs around my waist, letting out a breath. His fingers slid down my chest, tugging at the scarf tassels. "Daddy," he whispered.

"Boy," I growled, feeling my cock harden.

How I ached to be inside of him right now. Fuck.

"We're not worrying about our orc brood tonight," I growled. "Not one worry. Just you and me tonight."

"Yes," he said, his expression softening.

Fuck, I loved that look. I leaned forward, brushing my lips

against his. He groaned against me, and I could feel his cock hardening in his pants.

I grunted and turned, carrying him through the foyer and up the staircase to the house's second floor. Our bedroom faced where the sun rose each morning, designed by Alex himself.

We'd built a cabin, one that was perfect for both of us and our family. It was cozy, sturdy, and exactly what we both had wanted.

I loved knowing that every piece of wood in this house had been chopped and shaped by me. I loved that the designs were his.

We made a good team.

"You want your Daddy to fill you up for Christmas, boy?" I asked.

"Please," he groaned. "Fuck. I've missed you this week."

"I've missed you too," I said.

I'd flown back this morning after having to visit a couple of the lodges. Alex had stayed with our kids this time since we were so close to the holiday. It had been a little stressful flying back in, catching up with our family, and then taking them to the babysitter— but we had done it. Plus, tomorrow would be a day for us to remember between presents, family, games, and more.

The Barista and his family, along with all the friends we'd grown close with over the years, would meet at Creature Cafe for a day of festivities.

Orcs loved any excuse to party, and I was no exception.

"I got all the shopping done," he said softly, holding on to me as I took him to our bedroom.

"I got some things, too," I chuckled. "I know we already got them a lot of presents, but Lea told me she wanted to learn how to shoot a bow...and well."

"Oh gods," Alex snorted. "Hell. We already have axes flying through the house sometimes."

"Don't worry, little mate," I chuckled. "Us orcs won't hurt you."

He laughed as I laid him out on our bed, hovering over him. I stole another kiss, my cock hardening.

"I need you," I breathed.

"I need you too, Daddy," he moaned.

I growled as I pinned him down beneath me. My body was massive compared to his and I chuckled as I looked down between us, seeing the shape of my cock.

"I want you to breed me," he whispered.

His words were both dirty and loving. I sucked in a breath and moved to the side.

"Strip for me," I said, giving his thigh a pat.

He sat up and slid off the bed, moving to stand in front of me. His face was shaved smooth, his blonde hair short. He was wearing a flannel shirt with jeans and boots.

My city boy had roughed up some over the last few years, and it always made me smirk.

His belt jingled as he undid it and pulled it free. His bright blue eyes held mine as he began to undo the buttons of his shirt. He pulled it off, followed by the one underneath.

My hand went to my cock, and I could feel a heat creeping through me. I wanted to rut into him, to fill him with my monstrous seed over and over.

"You have that look," Alex chuckled as he pulled off his pants.

"What look?" I asked as I undid my kilt.

My cock sprang free, and Alex whimpered, his eyes falling on it.

"Fuck. You're already dripping."

"I wasn't kidding when I said I needed you," I snarled.

Alex raised a brow, pulling the last of his clothing free, and kicking the pile away. His cock was hard and aching, just like mine.

"Come rub it against mine," I commanded, leaning back on the bed.

I kept myself propped up on my elbows, watching as Alex stepped forward between my thighs. I could have trapped him there if I wanted, and the thought made me smirk as he pressed the tip of his cock against mine.

Fuck. Even the slightest touch from him was enough to make more cum drip from the tip of my cock. It glistened in our bedroom lighting, rolling down the head. The piercings along the bottom glinted too, and I was ready for him to tease them.

Alex grunted, shivering. With a little curse under his breath, he moved one leg and then the other, taking a seat on me. His thighs were balanced against mine, his knees on the bed around my hips.

He thrust his hips forward, pressing his shaft against mine. He shook his head with a snort.

"Your cock is so big, Daddy. Big and green and all mine."

"Yes, it is, boy," I whispered, watching as he tried to fit his hands around the two of us.

"Spit on them, boy," I commanded.

Alex nodded and leaned down, letting his saliva drip from his lips. He used it as lube, rubbing it over our cocks as he started to thrust his hips.

"Good boy," I growled, my breath hitching as his cock rubbed against mine.

Fuck, it felt good. It felt good to be with my mate, to have him seated on me. Our cocks together, hard and needy.

I watched as he moved, watching as he fell further and further into his lust. I loved watching him completely let go, submitting, and succumbing to subspace.

All for me. Because he trusted and loved me.

"Will you let me cum, Daddy?" he asked. "Please?"

"Yes," I said, fighting off a smirk.

It had been too long since I'd forced a few orgasms out of him, so I'd let him have this one exactly how he wanted.

Then, I'd see how long we could go tonight before the two of us fell asleep in our bed.

"Keep humping me," I growled. "I like watching you struggle to hold our cocks together. Mine is so big compared to yours. Does it feel good, boy?"

"Yes," he moaned. "*Fuck.*"

Alex kept moving, his head tipping back as his lips parted on whines and gasps. Within a few moments, his cum shot from the head of his cock, landing on my own. He let out a soft cry, his hips still moving until he was completely done.

Fucking hell, my balls ached. My cock throbbed, the feeling of his warm cum on me nearly sending me over the edge.

But I had control. And I wasn't ready to spill my seed yet. Not until I had my mate beneath me, begging his Daddy to fill him up.

"Clean up your mess, boy," I growled.

Alex nodded, letting out a little breath as he slid off my lap and to the floor. I sat up more as he gripped my cock, swiping his tongue over his cum. He licked me eagerly, the sounds drawing a groan from me.

"After you're done, there's something for you in our dresser. Clean me up well, then go to it and get your new present," I huffed.

Alex's gaze lit up as he kissed up my cock, taking the head between his lips for a moment and sucking.

"You little slut," I gasped, curling my fingers for a moment as pleasure shot through me.

Alex chuckled and cleaned up the last of his cum before

standing. I watched through narrowed eyes as he went to our dresser and opened the drawer, reaching inside.

He pulled out the new paddle, his gasp of surprise making me smirk.

"Oh, Daddy," he whispered.

He ran his hand over the wood grain, turning it over.

On the back side were the raised letters saying 'Daddy's cum slut'.

I fought off a chuckle, knowing it would sound diabolical. But, I'd had it made just so I could spank him hard enough to leave those words on his ass for a couple of days.

"Fuck," he grunted.

I could smell how turned on he was, even though he'd just cum. He turned, holding the paddle in his hands. He walked back to me and then slowly knelt in front of me.

His submission never failed to floor me. For a moment, I felt a sense of wonder. This human, this man, my mate and center of my world— I loved him so much. I loved him more than I ever believed possible.

"Good boy," I whispered.

"Daddy, will you please use this on me? It's all I want for Christmas," he said, his gaze locking with mine.

"Of course," I said softly. "Of course Daddy will. I've been wanting to ever since I got it."

I leaned forward and took the paddle from him, tipping his chin up with one of my fingers.

"How hard do you want me to go, boy?"

"As hard as you want," he said. "I want you to use me, Daddy. I want to please you."

"You always please me," I chuckled.

He gave me a smile. "I want you to get what you want for Christmas too. I'd like to be able to walk tomorrow but... it wouldn't be the first time we said that I strained my leg."

I snorted. It was true. There had been a time where we'd gone harder than we ever had the night before a school event, and I'd told everyone that Alex had strained his leg in the night when stepping on a rogue shoe. The only person that had narrowed their eyes was the Barista, but it was with a smirk and snort.

"Hmmm. Okay, boy. I'll let you walk tomorrow, but we'll push it some. Use your safeword if I go too far," I said, my voice becoming stern.

"Yes, Daddy," he said.

"Good. Come on," I said, standing.

Alex stood up, and I reached down, throwing him over my shoulder. He grunted but didn't fight me.

I smirked as I carried him to the closet door. I opened it up, went to the back of the closet, and hit the panel that opened up another door.

Had to be fucking sneaky with nosy orc kids around. I loved our little green quartet, but when they were home, the house was their fort. Which meant they occupied every nook and cranny, aside from this space.

I stepped inside, the lights coming on for us. It was a small room, but large enough for Alex and I to play in. The walls and floor were padded, so no screams could escape. There were all types of things in here, from whips and paddles to spanking benches and a cross to chain him up on.

Five years and we'd only gotten kinkier.

Hell, there had even been a couple times I'd let him top me.

I set Alex down, giving him a little push to the spanking bench. "Go get yourself situated, boy."

"Yes, Daddy," he breathed, his voice thick.

His cock was already half hard again, his heart thumping in his chest. I watched him as he went to the bench and draped his body over it, putting himself in a kneeling position that pushed his ass out but still supported his body.

I stared at his ass for a moment, my cock giving another hard throb.

Fucking hell, I was hanging on by a thread. But it would be worth it.

I loved him. I loved him, which meant I wanted to give him whatever he wanted.

What he wanted tonight was for me to turn him into Daddy's cum slut.

And my boy would always get what he wanted.

CHAPTER 2
Alex

My cock was already hard again as I listened to Jasper go to one of the drawers in the room, rummaging through it. Our new paddle was amazing, and while it made me a little nervous, I wanted that stamp on my ass as he fucked me.

Fuck. I let out a little groan, closing my eyes for a moment.

Holidays had never been my favorite time of the year, until Jasper and I got together.

Now, I always looked forward to them. Jasper was a celebratory Orc, which meant he liked to do especially fun things together.

Like turning me into his cum slut.

Not that I wasn't already.

"I can hear your thoughts turning," Jasper chuckled.

His voice was always deep and soothing, even when he was edging me.

"Are you sure you want me, boy?"

I gasped, almost offended. "Of course, I want you, Daddy. More than anything. I want you to use me and breed me however you want."

"Good," he said.

He moved back across the room to me, and I felt the warmth of his body behind me. A chill worked up my spine, and I swallowed hard.

"So eager," he whispered.

The edge of the paddle ran over my skin, the wood deceptively soft. It was almost comforting, except I knew how it would feel.

Jasper leaned down, kissing my lower back. He set the paddle down on my upper back and then spread my ass, spitting.

Fuck. My cock throbbed against the bench I was on. I'd just cum so much, but he could always turn me on again. Even if I didn't want to.

"I want to get you nice and ready for my monster cock," he said. "Nice and ready to take your Daddy."

"Yes," I gasped.

He chuckled again and gave my ass cheek a slap before standing. He went past me, disappearing for a moment before returning with lube and a plug.

I lifted my head, my eyes widening.

"Fuck," I mumbled.

His tusks gleamed, his smile beaming as he held it up. This was the toy that wrapped around my cock while another part of it was in my ass, vibrating the entire time.

Fuck. *Fuck.*

"You know what else I want for Christmas, boy? I want you to cum until you beg me to let you rest."

"Yes, Daddy," I whispered, my cheeks burning with heat.

Jasper opened up the bottle of lube and poured some of it on my ass, his fingers rubbing it against my hole and then pushing inside.

I let out a little moan, the pleasure of being filled making my cock throb. I was going to cum again, and I knew that even after that, he would make me cum *again*. He would make me cum until he was satisfied, until I was begging him to stop.

"Daddy," I gasped.

Jasper let out a low growl, slipping another finger inside of me. He then reached down, fitting the ring around my cock while slowly pushing the plug inside of me. I gasped as it stretched me, letting my head fall for a moment as pleasure worked through me.

"Oh, my good boy," he said.

The deep timbre of his voice echoed around me, a blanket of comfort while also the very thing that turned me on.

I loved it when he praised me and I loved it when he degraded me– a double-edged sword, driving me closer and closer to cumming again just for him.

I whimpered as a toy filled me, knowing that soon I would be taking something much bigger.

Jasper slapped my ass, the sound cracking around me as I gasped.

He chuckled, and then came around to face me. He tipped my chin up, forcing me to look up at him.

"Open your mouth," he growled.

I obeyed him instantly, parting my lips for him. He leaned down, his tongue slipping into my mouth. I groaned as he grunted, his fingers curling into my hair as he stole a heady kiss.

"That's my good boy," he breathed, pulling back. He gripped my head a little harder, moving his hips so that his hard cock slapped my face. "See what you do to me, boy? It's a problem. One that only you can solve."

"I'm sorry, Daddy," I rasped. "I'll take care of it."

"Yes, you will," he said. "But not yet."

His cock slapped my face again, drawing a whine from me. I

wanted his cock inside of me, whether it be my mouth or ass. I didn't care, I wanted him to fill me.

"Not yet," he whispered again.

He let go of my head and then reached for the paddle, taking it from my back. He then moved around to my ass.

He reached down and hit the button on the toy that was buried inside me.

The vibration immediately started, drawing a low cry for me. It was intense, set on a setting that would immediately make my cock leak pre-cum. I gasped, my muscles tensing as the feeling of pleasure burned through me.

"Gonna milk your cock for Daddy," Jasper whispered.

He ran his hand over my ass cheeks, squeezing one and then the other. I moaned as he squeezed one of them a little bit harder, smacking me with a growl.

I cried out, another bolt of pleasure shooting through me. The ring around my cock moved in a way that had me harder than I thought possible, little electric shocks of need zapping through me.

Jasper smacked my ass again, warming up my body so that he could hit me harder without breaking skin. I gasped as he spanked me with his hand, light pats that brought the blood to the surface.

He kept going until I could feel the heat of his palm before he touched me, my skin growing more and more sensitive until my ass was tender. He took a step back, letting out a satisfied growl.

"Look at you," he growled. "Your ass is bright red, your cock hard. Your ass is filled with this little thing, and you're already moaning like a bitch in heat."

"Yes, Daddy," I whimpered, my hips jerking as the toy continued to vibrate.

"Tell me you want to be Daddy's cum slut."

"I want to be your cum slut," I gasped. "Please. Please. I need you to fill me. I need you to let me taste you. I'm desperate."

I gave in completely now, letting all thoughts and worries drift away as I sank into submission.

"Please," I begged. "I want to be your cum slut."

"Why? You don't deserve it. You're already whining just from this tiny toy," he chuckled.

He smacked my ass, drawing a cry from me.

"Please, Daddy. Please. I'm begging you," I rasped. "I'm not worthy but if....if you want me to be your cum slut, I will be."

He was silent for a moment. My heart pounded in my chest, panic almost creeping up.

Finally, he spoke. "Good," he praised.

I let out a breath of relief, but it was a moment too soon.

He brought the paddle down, and I cried out as pain flashed through me. The sound of the wood on my skin echoed through the room, my blood rushing through me as my back arched.

"No," he growled, one of his hands pushing on my back to keep me still. "Arch up like that again boy, and we won't do this for pleasure. Understood?"

"Yes, Daddy," I whispered, tears filling my eyes.

"You asked for this," he growled. "You're gonna take it. Understood?"

"Yes," I moaned.

"Yes, *what*?"

"Yes, Daddy," I whimpered.

His hand spread over my back, and the paddle came down again. I cried out as the pain snapped back, the heat stinging relentlessly. But then, it was followed by unreasonable waves of pleasure.

The toy was still milking my cock, still buried inside of me and humming with a continuous outpour of pleasure.

He spanked me again and I yelled. *Again.*

My vision blurred with more tears, but holy hell. They felt *good.* The pain was harsh, the pleasure was brutal, but I wanted it more than anything else.

He spanked me again, pain searing me. Over and over until I let out a sob, and my body gave in.

I started to cum, my cock shooting ropes of hot cum.

Jasper laughed, his voice almost jolly. If I didn't know any better, I would have believed he had just seen the funniest thing.

"You came from me spanking you," he laughed.

I panted, tears running down my face and now cum dripping from my spent cock. But the vibrations didn't stop.

Jasper didn't stop.

The paddle came down again and I screamed. Every spanking was becoming more and more brutal. My ass was fucking sore, my skin aching between every blow.

"Daddy's little slut," Jasper chuckled, spanking me again.

I cried out, another choked sob leaving me. My body trembled, the pain almost becoming too much.

Jasper paused for a moment, rubbing his hand over my ass cheeks gently. He rubbed them and it felt good.

"I can read it now," he whispered. "Daddy's cum slut. Such a perfect boy for me."

His praise was a relief, giving me a sense of fulfillment.

I sniffled, letting my muscles relax for a moment. Jasper tossed the paddle to the side and then pulled the plug free, pulling the ring from around my cock.

Fuck. I let out a sigh, my chest heaving. I slowly turned my head to look back at him.

Jasper held my gaze as he ran his hands down my back, pressing his hard cock against my ass. I groaned, feeling my cheeks flush with heat. I squeezed my eyes shut for a moment, another tear slipping free.

"Aww," Jasper whispered, his voice gruff. "Don't cry, boy. Don't cry. Daddy's got you now. Daddy's going to give you your reward."

I nodded, and my cock started to harden.

Again.

Fuck.

Jasper lifted me, making me yelp in surprise. He carried me to a table with a cushioned top, placing me on my back on it. He pulled my ass to the edge, pushing my knees back.

My cock throbbed now as he loomed over me. The table was at the perfect height for him to bury his cock inside of me, but instead, he grabbed my hands and had me hold onto my knees.

"Don't let go," he commanded. "Keep your legs back like this no matter what I do. Understood?"

"Yes, Daddy," I huffed.

I looked down between my legs, gasping as Jasper took my cock between his lips and began to suck me.

I was so close to cumming that it hurt. I couldn't give any more, I had already cum so much. But Jasper took my cock as deep as possible and I whimpered in pleasure. His hands reached up, his fingers pinching my nipples.

I cried out from the sting and ecstasy.

"Daddy!" I moaned.

He kept sucking my cock, moving his head up and down.

I grunted, knowing I couldn't stop myself.

"I'm going to cum," I gasped. "Fuck. I can't stop."

He rubbed my nipples in gentle circles now as he sucked. I let out a cry, feeling another orgasm take me. I started to cum again, my eyes squeezing shut as more cum shot out of me.

Jasper swallowed, slowly pulling his lips free as I gave the last drop.

I panted, my muscles relaxing.

But, he was still teasing my nipples.

"It's too much," I gasped. "I'm so sensitive."

"I know," Jasper whispered, licking his lips. "My sensitive boy."

His gaze burned with lust as he watched me, the rough pads of his fingers still circling my nipples.

Part of me wanted to push his hands away, but I couldn't. I had to keep my knees up like he had commanded.

"Daddy," I gasped.

I was spent. There was no way I could cum again. I'd given everything I had.

He kept rubbing them in circles. The tenderness became an ache, but he was patient.

He was so fucking patient.

I gasped, writhing slightly beneath him.

"Don't worry, boy," he whispered. "We have all night. Your little cock will get hard for me again."

"No," I moaned. "I can't. Stop!"

He shook his head, his eyes glinting. "No. Daddy knows what's best."

"Please," I begged.

"No," he said.

"It's too much," I rasped. "Please don't."

"Boy," he growled. "Your cock is mine. Do you understand me?"

I let out a cry as he pinched both of my nipples.

I couldn't help it. My cock was already starting to lift again.

"Please," I rasped. "Please."

He pinched them harder.

My cock hardened completely now.

"Fuck," I whimpered.

My ass still burned from being paddled, my legs feeling like jello. I took in a shivering breath as he smirked, knowing that he owned me.

"Disrespectful," he said, shaking his head. "Here I am trying to give you a reward. Your Christmas present. And you tell me you can't take it?"

"I'm sorry," I whimpered.

My cock was standing straight up as Jasper lowered himself to his knees. His fingertips dug into my hips as his tongue ran down my ass, burying inside of me.

I cried out from the invasion, but it was a welcome one. Pleasure burst through me, my cock bobbing as my Daddy started to eat me out.

"Fuck," I gasped. "Fuck! Daddy!" I moaned.

His tusks rubbed against me as he drove his tongue in and out, holding me still on the table. I closed my eyes, my head spinning as he fucked me with his tongue.

I cried out as pleasure shot through me. It was intense and made my cock hurt.

"I can't cum again," I cried, but he didn't listen.

He knew he'd be able to force me to.

I wanted him to force me.

Fuck.

Daddy continued to fuck me with his tongue as his hand slid around to my cock, gripping it. I cried out as he began to stroke it fast, jerking me over and over until I was sent straight back to the edge of cumming against my will.

My cries became louder as I felt another orgasm start to build.

"No," I cried, but it fell on deaf ears.

Jasper continued until finally, I let out a helpless scream and started to cum again. Fluid burst from the head of my cock, dripping down his hand as he pulled his tongue free and stood.

"Good boy," he whispered, bringing his cum covered hand

down to my ass. I groaned as he used it to lube me up, pressing the head of his cock against my opening.

"Daddy," I whispered, my eyes widening.

"Do you want your final present?"

"Yes," I rasped.

It was true. I wanted it more than anything else.

"Good boy," he whispered.

He thrust forward, and I yelled as he filled me with his entire cock. The piercings along the bottom rubbed against me, his cock spearing me.

"Ohhh fuck," he groaned, shuddering. "Fuck, you feel so good, boy."

"Thank you, Daddy."

He growled as he began to thrust in and out of me, pulling his cock out and shoving it back in. I groaned as he took me, happy to know that I was pleasing him. I loved it when he used my body, when he turned me into his little slut.

"Are you Daddy's cum slut?"

"Yes," I rasped.

Jasper groaned, fucking me harder. The table groaned beneath me as he pumped into me, driving his cock in.

I watched him in awe, tears streaming down my cheeks. My chest felt warm, my heart bursting with joy as he took me.

I was his and his alone. Mated to an Orc that loved me. That cherished me.

Jasper grunted, shaking his head. "I can't stop myself from filling you," he moaned. "You feel too good."

"I'm yours," I whispered.

"Grab my nipples," he growled.

I let go of my legs and obeyed him, reaching up and pinching his nipples. He immediately growled, his eyes rolling as pleasure washed over him.

The noises coming from him were primal as he rutted into

me over and over. I pinched harder, groaning as his tempo became a constant pounding.

"Daddy," I whispered. "Please fill me. Please."

"Yes," he groaned. "Fuck!"

He let out a roar and with one last thrust, buried his cock deep inside of me. His cock shot liquid, his seed filling me with searing heat.

He let out a low groan, his cock twitching as he kept cumming, until finally, he gave me the last drops.

The two of us stilled, panting. I moaned, my muscles relaxing.

"Fuck," he mumbled. He gave me a gentle squeeze.

I could already feel my head spinning from his cum, the ecstasy of getting high from him already overtaking me.

"How do you feel?" he asked.

"Good," I whispered.

He chuckled, his cock still buried inside of me. "I love you, Alex. Merry Christmas."

"I love you too," I said, smiling at him. "Thank you for the presents."

He snorted, kissing my chest. "Always more where that came from. But I think a hot bath together, a massage, and some food sounds good?"

"Yes," I said, grinning.

It would be perfect— spending the rest of the night together, basking in the warmth of our love. Then tomorrow morning, we would wake up early and have an amazing day with our family.

Hark! The Herald Angels Cum

GABE, CAM, AND SETH

'Twas the Night before Christmas,
Where two fallen angels await
To do many naughty things
To their human mate

In this Holiday Tail,
you will find the following:

Cockpockets
CNC
Degradation
Praise
Chasing
Blood Drinking
Sounding
and more.

Cam

"It's too big, Gabe. It's not going to fit."

"It's going to fit."

"It's *not* going to fit."

I raised a brow and turned, looking through the kitchen doorway towards our living room. I glanced at my hands, which were both covered in bread flour, and then wiped them on my apron.

I crossed the kitchen and peeked around the corner.

Now, both of my brows shot up.

An evergreen tree was being shoved through the front door by Gabe while Seth watched, his arms crossed and head shaking.

"We already have a Christmas tree," Seth said.

"I fucking want another one," Gabe growled.

Seth looked up at me helplessly, and I snorted, raising my hands. "Don't look at me, little kismet. He wants another tree."

Seth made a face, but his lips tugged into a grin of defeat as Gabe managed to shove the tree into the foyer.

Gabe stepped in, covered in green needles and snow. His black wings shook behind him, sending it all to the floor.

He slammed the door shut, staring at Seth.

"It fits," Gabe said, still staring directly at our mate.

Seth let out a small laugh, breaking the tension. I shook my head with a sigh.

"Drama kings," I said.

"Seth is," Gabe retorted. "It's okay. I'll remember his arguing later when my cock is inside of him."

Seth's ears turned pink and he shuffled. "Listen. I just don't know why we need two trees."

"I like *one* holiday," Gabe said. "One. And this is the one."

It was true. Gabe only ever became festive around this time of the year. He decorated our house, covering the outside with Christmas lights and building an abominable snowman out front in the yard.

You'd think it was for his tiny half siblings, but it was for him.

"You know how I am," Gabe snorted.

Seth sighed, but he was still smiling. "Okay fair. Truce?"

"Not a fucking chance," Gabe chuckled, his fanged jaw splitting with an evil smile.

Seth groaned. "Fuck."

"I'm going back to my bread," I snorted. "The two of you can fuck out your frustrations."

The two of them looked at each other again and I rolled my eyes, going back to the kitchen. I finished dusting the bread dough with flour and then cut a nice pattern on the top, putting the pan in the oven.

I heard a groan, one that wasn't quite as annoyed as before.

Mm. Fuck. I set the timer on the bread and then washed my hands, pulling off my apron and hanging it.

We had dinner mostly ready for the three of us, and Gabe had already said that he had plans for us tonight as well too. It made me excited, wondering what he had in store.

I came back into the living room, not surprised to see that the tree had been pushed into the corner next to the other one and Seth was straddling Gabe's lap.

"Can't leave the two of you alone," I chuckled, going to the sofa.

Gabe smirked, patting the seat next to him.

I sat down and Seth leaned over, giving me a warm kiss. I took a deep breath, relaxing.

"Bread will be ready in 40 minutes," I said.

"Hmm...." Gabe hummed. "Enough time to have a little bite to eat first, right?"

"I think so," I said.

Seth grunted, giving us both knowing looks. "Fuck," he mumbled. "Please?"

Gabe chuckled. "What was that, little kismet?"

"Ugh," he sighed. "You're so mean to me."

"Yes. So so mean," Gabe teased.

"Go on," I said, giving Seth a smirk. "Tell him what he wants to hear so I can touch you."

Seth let out a breath. "Will you please devour me, oh mighty angel of Christmas?"

Gabe barked out a laugh, one that was almost frightening. He took Seth off his lap, making him stand up.

"Little kismet," he said, his laugh dying. "I'm going to give you a head start. On the count of five, I'm coming after you. Go."

"Fuck," Seth grunted, taking off down the hall.

"One," Gabe growled.

I listened to our human mate run, giving Gabe a knowing look.

He looked back at me, smirking. "What? You like it."

"I do," I said.

"Two," Gabe called. "I want you to hunt him with me."

"Oh?" I asked.

"Three!"

We both heard the back door open, and Gabe grinned hungrily.

"Sly dog. Alright, we're having a little excursion." Gabe leaned forward, his muscles tensing like a lion about to spring for prey. "Yeah. We'll hunt him together. Will your bread be okay?"

"We'll be back in time," I said, feeling the excitement.

It wasn't fair, of course. Seth couldn't hide from us. And he could only run so fast as a human.

But I'd be lying if I said I didn't like to terrorize him just a little sometimes. Perhaps it was Gabe rubbing off on me after all of these years.

"Four," Gabe whispered, leaning in to steal a kiss from me.

I groaned, parting my lips so that he could kiss me deeply. His wings curled around us for a moment, his hand sliding to my cock.

"Fuck," I gasped.

"Five," he growled, stealing one last kiss before standing up.

"Rude," I grunted.

"Don't worry. Once we drag our naughty mate back, I'm going to show him what it means to have the holiday spirit."

I raised a brow as Gabe went out the front door, lifting off into the sky.

This would be fun.

I went to the door and pulled on my snow boots quickly, and then stepped outside. The sun was starting to set, turning the clouds above us a blushing pink. It was cold, but it didn't chill me the way it would our human.

I chuckled and took off running, breathing in the crisp air. I could smell him as I broke the tree line, taking off into the forest that surrounded us.

He hadn't covered his tracks very well. I ran faster, glancing up above to see Gabe in the sky, a monster.

I missed flying at times like this, but it wasn't in the painful way that it used to be. I'd learned how to move damn near just as fast on the ground.

I could hear Seth's heart pounding. I paused, looking around.

"Little kismet," I chuckled. "Why did you run so far? You know he's going to destroy you now."

I heard shuffling but stayed still, waiting.

There was movement to my right, a blur of shadow. I held my breath for a moment, listening intently. I then smiled to myself, glancing up at the sky again.

Found him.

Good. Give him a couple of more moments and then we'll ambush him.

A shiver worked up my spine. Gabe was hungry today.

Our little kismet was in for a treat.

CHAPTER 2

Gabe

I circled the treetops, giving Seth a few more moments of peace. I could hear his heart pounding in his chest, and I knew that Cam was near him.

I loved him. I loved him so much. Therefore I was going to rip into him tonight. I had so many things planned, things I wanted to do to him to celebrate the holiday. It came around once a year, and it was always my favorite time.

Over the last few years, I'd been able to grow close with my father and actually have a somewhat healthy relationship with him. Especially with how much he tried with Luca and Layla.

Tomorrow would be a day spent with monsters and humans alike, with friends and family.

But tonight? Tonight was for my mates and me. Tonight was for pleasure and for pain.

I grinned to myself and then dove straight into the forest. Within seconds, I was descending on my human mate.

Seth let out a startled yell, ducking right as I reached for him. He rolled out of the way with a laugh, only to tumble straight into Cam.

"Et tu, brute?" he groaned as Cam grabbed him.

I landed in the snow, tackling him. Cam chuckled, letting me grab him.

"Sorry, little kismet," Cam said, smirking. "I, too, want to have some fun."

Seth grunted, trying to shove at me. It was no use, though. With a growl, I wrapped my arms around his waist and lifted him into the air.

"Fuck," he grunted, grabbing onto me.

My little human was invincible, but he was still nervous as hell when I carried him in the sky.

"Meet us back!" I called out to Cam.

I took off, my wings pushing us through the frigid air. Snow was starting to fall again as the sun dipped below the horizon, the pinks and purples slowly morphing to midnight blue.

I landed in front of our cabin right as Cam ran up, Seth over my shoulders. I ducked through our front door, taking him down the hall to our nest.

He was so hard. I could feel his cock straining against his jeans, rubbing against my chest.

"Remind me your safeword," I growled. "Before I get a taste of your blood."

"Red," he gasped, squirming against me now that we were home.

I chuckled, baring my teeth as I threw him down into the blankets. He landed with a groan.

"Are you going to behave now, you fucking brat?"

"No," he said.

Cam laughed as he came into our room, slamming the door shut behind him. "Gods, Seth, you're pushing it tonight, my love."

It was stupid but effective.

I lunged for him, straddling him and pinning him down. He tried to fight against me, even though it was futile. Even though we were mated, he was still a human and I was still a fucking monster.

Cam knelt down next to us, grabbing Seth's face and turning it to look at him.

Seth's lips tugged into a rebellious smile.

Oh.

Oh, he wanted me to actually fucking murder him.

"Open your fucking mouth," I snarled.

His smile faltered and he looked up at me, parting his lips.

I spat, watching it drip onto his tongue.

"Swallow," I growled.

His cock was now throbbing. He swallowed with a soft moan.

I sat back and dragged my claws down his chest, tearing the fabric in small places as I moved them down to his cock.

"So hard for your monsters," I said.

"Yes," he breathed.

"Even though you're being a fucking brat."

"I am."

"Fuck his throat, Cam. I'm going to play with the rest of him."

Cam nodded, undoing the top of his pants. He slid them down, freeing his cock. I watched for a moment, letting out a chuckle as one of the eyes on his chest opened, looking down at our mate too.

The teeth that kept my own cock away had already parted, allowing mine to throb against my clothes. Cam grunted as he leaned over Seth.

Seth parted his lips with a groan, taking the head of Cam's cock into his mouth.

I stood up, taking off my clothes and tossing them to the side. I crossed the room, grabbing one of the presents I had wrapped for Seth off the dresser.

Cam grunted, his muscles rippling as Seth sucked his cock. His gray wing spread behind him, his tattoo gleaming in the soft lighting. We always kept a cozy ambiance in here, but it was moments like this that I appreciated it all the more.

Cam reached for a bottle of lube, pouring some on his hand and moving down to Seth's ass. Seth groaned as he began to tease him, to get him ready to take one of our cocks.

They were glorious, and holy hell, had I softened up the last few years. I let out a little growl, ripping open the present.

"This was for later," I growled. "But we'll use it now and see how much of a brat you still want to be."

Seth groaned as he kept sucking Cam's cock, his hands wrapping around the ridged shaft. I pulled out the items in the box and then knelt back down, pulling off his pants and boxers.

His cock sprang free, and he moaned as I stroked it for a moment, his hips jerking up.

I smirked.

I was curious to see if he would hate or love what I was about to do.

I looked back down at the contents of the box. I had bought a set of candy cane sounding needles, along with a sterilizing lube. The teeth that held my cock inside its pocket parted, allowing my shaft to fully harden as I leaned down and started to prep him.

He made a curious noise, but Cam was still keeping him distracted. I glanced up at my mates again, letting out a little hiss.

Too sexy for their own good.

I picked up the smallest needle, one that was shaped like a candy cane. It had a rounded hook on the end, and the straight part had smooth bulges down the shaft. It was striped red and white, my evil instrument of pleasure and pain.

I coated it in the lube and then Seth's cock, rubbing his shaft up and down. I ran the pad of my thumb over the head of his cock in small circles.

Seth made a noise, his muscles clenching. Cam pulled his cock free, both of them looking down at me.

"What?" Seth croaked, his eyes falling on the candy cane hook in my hand. "What the fuck is that?"

"Relax," I said.

"FUCKING HELL," he hissed, recognizing what was happening.

His eyes widened, his muscles tensing as he sat up partially.

"We're going to try it," I said. "Your early Christmas gift."

Seth cursed under his breath, and Cam raised a brow.

"Will that actually go into his cock?"

"Yes," I said.

Cam made a noise, his cock still hard. "Fuck. I want to watch. I want to be inside of him while you do that too."

I nodded, pulling the rod back.

Cam reached for our mate and lifted him, spreading his thighs wide. Seth groaned, leaning back so that his back was on Cam's chest, his head on his shoulder.

Fuck. My cock throbbed as I watched Cam slowly start to fill Seth, pushing his ridged cock inside of him slowly until our mate was fully seated.

"Fuck," Seth cried. "Fuck. You're so big."

"I know, little kismet," Cam breathed, letting out a moan. "Fuck. You feel good."

I leaned forward again, grabbing Seth's cock and stroking him.

"Fuck," he mumbled, his eyes widening as I held the rod to the head of his cock again.

"Are you scared?" I asked.

Seth let out a hiss but didn't answer. I held his gaze for a moment, and then he gave me a small nod.

Fuck. The little hint of fear turned me on even more.

That and the fact that he still trusted me to do this.

"Ask," I said, holding the end of the sounding rod to the head of his cock. "Beg for it."

Seth made a noise, but then his lips parted, his voice soft. "Please," he whispered.

"Please, what?" I asked.

"Please put that inside of me." He let out a helpless groan as Cam lifted him, slowly thrusting back inside him.

I held his cock firm, leaning in to steal a kiss from Cam and then from him. They both let out heated breaths.

"Please," Seth moaned.

"As you wish. Merry Christmas, little kismet," I said.

CHAPTER 3

Seth

I let out a cry as Cam gave a small thrust right as Gabe inserted more of the metal rod inside of my cock.

It didn't hurt necessarily, although it did sting. It also made my cock feel full in a way I had never experienced.

I let out a groan as Cam thrust again, slow and measured.

Fuck, this was torture, but it was the best kind of torture.

I had been a brat earlier today, but it was because I liked driving Gabe crazy sometimes. I loved him too much for his own good, which meant there were moments I also liked to push his buttons.

Cam wrapped his arms around my chest, kissing my neck as he moved again. I groaned, my head falling back on his shoulder as Gabe continued to fill my cock with the candy cane rod.

He had the evil look on his face, the one that I loved even though it made me nervous. His fangs stretched up the side of his face, his black eyes gleaming. His wings were relaxed behind him, draping over the blankets of our nest.

His hand held my hard cock and I hissed as more of the rod went in.

It felt like it should be impossible.

214

He pulled it out partially and then worked it down gently. Back and forth, careful while still pushing me.

My voice melted into cries as the two of them took me together, Cam fucking me while Gabe used my cock how he pleased. I gasped as the ridges of Cam's cock rubbed against my prostate, pleasure bursting through me followed by the stinging pain of the instrument Gabe used on me.

I cried out, gasping as the two of them found a brutal rhythm. More waves of pleasure worked through me as the two of them took me together.

Cam growled, his breath hitching as he got closer to the edge.

"Please," I groaned. "Please fill me. Please," I rasped.

"I will," he grunted, fucking me faster.

Fuck. My cock was so hard and full. Gabe pulled the rod free, stroking my cock faster. I screamed out just as Cam groaned, his hot cum filling me as I cummed too.

Cam moaned, filling me with as much cum as possible. I shivered against him, looking down to see my cum all over me.

Gabe leaned down, licking it up with his tongue. I sucked in a breath, my body humming with pleasure. My cock felt sore and used, but in a good way.

Cam made a noise, relaxing. "Fuck. That was amazing."

"I want to fill him while he still has your cum," Gabe said.

Cam nodded, kissing my neck lovingly for a moment before letting go.

Gabe growled, reaching for me and lifting me off of Cam's cock. I gasped, only for him to roll me onto the floor beneath him. I stared down at his body, my head spinning. His wings spread above him as he pushed my legs back, positioning the head of his cock against my ass.

"Please, Sir," I gasped. "Please fill me."

He growled again, his teeth baring in a monstrous way. I

groaned as he pressed the head of his cock inside of me before slamming forward. I gasped as I took all of him, my moan becoming a yelp of pleasure.

Cam stretched out beside us, running his hands over my muscles as Gabe began to pump into me. He played with my nipples, sending shivers of pleasure through me. I cried out as my mate fucked me, using my body like a little toy that was made just for him.

"Are you my little fuck toy?" he growled.

"Yes," I cried. "Yes. Fuck."

Gabe thrust into me harder and harder, his eyes closing. He groaned in pleasure, his teeth bumping into me as he fucked me deeper.

Cam leaned over me, sinking his teeth into my neck. I cried out, the pleasure increasing to an almost unbearable degree. My cock immediately hardened all over again, our mating bonds becoming deep and more transparent. I could feel how much they both loved me, could feel how turned on the three of us were.

Fuck, I loved them. I loved being their little kismet, loved the life that we had built together.

Cam pulled his teeth free, leaning up to kiss Gabe. I watched as blood dripped from his lips, their monstrous hunger making my cock throb.

Gabe groaned again, his head falling back. His tongue swiped up the remnants of blood, his muscles tensing.

"Please," I gasped. "Please fill me with your cum."

He nodded, the sound of his skin against mine growing louder as he pumped into me.

Within moments, he let out a loud roar, spilling his hot cum inside me. He pinned his hands into the blankets on either side of my head, panting as he kept cumming.

The three of us moaned together, Cam relaxing next to me.

His fingers wound into mine, holding my hand as Gabe laid his forehead on my chest.

"I love you," he huffed, chuckling. "Brat."

"I love you too," I said, grinning. "Even though you crammed a second tree in our house on Christmas Eve."

Cam suddenly sat up, letting out a curse. "My bread."

"Oh fuck," I said.

Gabe and I both watched as he jumped up, leaving the room for the kitchen.

We heard the incessant beeping of the kitchen timer ringing through the house, the smell of fresh sourdough making my stomach growl.

Gabe leaned down and kissed me before leaning back and slowly pulling out. "Let's get cleaned up and check on our little baker."

"Okay," I said, smiling.

Even if the bread had burned, this would be one of the best Christmas' yet.

Barista Baby

THE BARISTA, TRIXIE, AND LUCY

'TWAS THE NIGHT BEFORE CHRISTMAS,
WHEN THE GRIM REAPER WAITS
TO HAVE MILK AND COOKIES
WITH HIS DEVIL AND HUMAN MATE

IN THIS HOLIDAY TAIL,
YOU WILL FIND THE FOLLOWING:

DADDY KINK
CUM DRINKING
SHADOW SEX
COLLARING
LEASHING
DEGRADATION
PRAISE
AND MORE.

CHAPTER 1

Trixie

I yelped as I was plopped on our bed, Lucy already pulling my pants off. I sucked in a breath, heat flashing through me as he yanked them off, his devil's tongue lapping over my clit.

"You naughty little angel," he breathed. "No underwear, Daddy."

The Barista stood in the doorway, watching the two of us with a twisted smile. The car ride home had been excruciating, Lucy having me in his lap while he kissed my neck and played with my breasts. We'd discussed boundaries and limits for tonight too, checking on safe words and how we felt.

I was ready to see what the two monsters had in store for me.

"Of course not," the Barista said, the deep timbre of his voice sending a chill up my spine. "Our angel likes to tease us, little devil."

I would have said something smart back, but all thoughts went out of my head as Lucy plunged his tongue inside of me. I cried out, arching against the blankets as he began to please me just the way I liked it.

My mate was hungry to make me scream, to make me cum over and over. I was hungry for that too.

My voice echoed through our room, followed by the Barista's chuckle. Lucy continued to fuck me with his tongue, getting me ready to take one or both of their cocks.

The Barista left his post, coming to the edge of the bed. I cried out, arching in Lucy's grip as I turned to look at him.

His eyes burned with lust, embers glinting in his beard. We'd had a long week, the Cafe insanely busy from all of the holiday traffic, and this was the first night we'd had alone in a while.

Lucy and I groaned together as the Barista unbuttoned his shirt. I sucked in a breath as he tossed it to the floor.

Lucy's tongue hit a sensitive spot, pulling a scream from me. I reached down, gripping his horns as I ground my hips against him, my eyes fluttering.

"Naughty girl," the Barista whispered. "I want you to cum for him, little angel. Be a good girl for Daddy."

"Yes, Daddy," I gasped.

The sound of his belt unbuckling sent another tremor through me. Lucy pulled his tongue free for a moment and then lifted me, rolling me so that I was seated directly on his face. I gasped, planting my hands on his chest as his tongue thrust back inside of me, his satisfied hum melting into my squeal.

"Oh yes, suffocate him. I'll bring his soul back," the Barista snorted.

Lucy held up a middle finger, causing me to laugh which turned into a gasp as the tip of his tongue started doing things that only monsters could do.

"Fuck," I moaned, digging my fingers into his skin.

The Barista pulled off his pants and boxers, his cock springing free. He stroked it, running his hands down the ridges. His knot pulsed, a little growl leaving him.

He went to the foot of the bed, reaching down and undoing Lucy's pants. Lucy growled, his cock aching to be free. Within a few moments, his clothes were on the floor and the Barista was stroking him.

He groaned, his hips bucking as I moaned and gasped. My pussy pulsed and I closed my eyes, another wave of pleasure rolling through me. I was getting close, so close.

Lucy groaned again, his tongue thrusting in and out of me. His hand slipped over my thigh, his fingers rubbing my clit.

My cry was loud, my ragged gasp that followed it turning into a moan.

The Barista leaned forward, straddling Lucy's chest. His hand gripped my throat, tipping my face up. I gasped as our lips met, the heat exploding through our mated bonds.

I came, my orgasm gripping me hard. I broke the kiss, my head falling back with a cry. My muscles tensed, my mind bursting with ecstasy.

"Good girl," the Barista growled.

I groaned and leaned back, moving off Lucy's face. He licked his lips with a wicked smile.

"Naughty girl," Lucy said, smirking.

The Barista raised a brow. "Open your mouth, little devil."

His eyes flashed with lust, his lips parting. The Barista smirked and looked up at me.

"Go get your present, baby girl, and bring it here."

"Yes, Daddy," I breathed, my muscles still trembling.

I had hints of what was in the box, but the anticipation made my stomach burst into butterflies. I went to our closet and went inside, reaching up for the box.

Hands brushed down my sides and I gasped as the Barista's shadow form encompassed me, surrounding me almost like smoke....except smoke didn't have a hard and throbbing cock.

I sucked in a breath as it reached up, pulling the box down

for me. I turned to look up at it, a groan leaving me as part of the shadow wrapped up my thigh, flicking over my clit.

"Fuck," I breathed.

The present opened and inside there were two collars and a leash. My pussy pulsed as the shadow form lifted one of them out, placing it around my neck.

My heart pounded in my chest and I swallowed hard.

The Barista's shadow didn't have a face, but I could feel it smirking at me. Feel *him* smirking at me.

I ran my fingers over the collar, letting out a breath.

Fuck.

The shadow gave me the box, disappearing and leaving me wet and aching all over again.

Bastard.

I went back to the bedroom to see Lucy on his knees on the floor deep throating the Barista. He groaned as the Barista gripped his horns, thrusting in and out of his eager mouth.

"Come," the Barista said, knowing I was back.

I went to them, my eyes on his cock thrusting in and out of our mate. I loved to watch them when they did things, especially inhuman things. *Monstrous* things.

The Barista pulled out, saliva dripping from his cock. Lucy groaned, his chest rising quickly with pants.

"Fuck," Lucy mumbled, his eyes glazed over with lust.

The Barista smirked, looking over at me. "Put on his collar," he said, taking a step back.

I nodded and pulled the collar out of the box, setting it down on the bed. His collar was black with metal details, while mine was bright pink. Both of them had loops that allowed a leash to be attached.

I knelt down next to him, and he pulled me into a kiss, the taste of the Barista shared between us. I groaned against him, feeling another shudder of pleasure run through me.

Lucy groaned and leaned back, giving me a little smile. "Pretty girl," he whispered.

I winked at him and leaned up, putting the collar around his neck. His eyes glazed over further, the act of wearing a collar always placing him in a more submissive space.

It was one of my favorite places to be, especially when the three of us were sharing time together. Lucy's expression softened, his black wings relaxing behind him.

The Barista reached over us, grabbing the leashes from the box. He then leaned over us, clipping one leash to Lucy and the other to me.

He gave each of us a tug. My breath hitched, my eyes widening.

The Barista hummed to himself, his cock still hard. "I like this," he whispered. "Both of my mates kneeling on the floor, collared and leashed. Do you like being Daddy's little pets?"

"Yes," we both said.

"Good," he said.

He turned, his grip on the leashes firm.

"Crawl with me," he commanded.

I swallowed hard as I obeyed, Lucy obeying too. We crawled behind him as he crossed our bedroom, taking a seat in a chair. His cock pulsed, precum dripping from the tip as he relaxed.

He let out a growl, his burning gaze falling to us. I was on his left side, Lucy on his right.

He gave my leash a tug. "Come sit on Daddy's lap, baby girl."

I nodded and stood, taking a seat in his lap. I gasped as his shadow emerged behind Lucy.

Lucy looked back, his lips spreading into a wide grin. "Oh, I do like it when you're rough with me."

"Of course you do," the Barista chuckled.

227

He ran his hands over my body, cupping my breasts. He leaned forward, his beard tickling my neck as he kissed me.

"Barista," I gasped.

"Yes, baby?" he murmured, his lips leaving a trail of fiery heat behind.

I sucked in a breath, watching as the shadow did the same to Lucy. He groaned, his cock hard again.

"Do you want me to knot you?" the Barista asked.

"Yes," I gasped. "Please."

"Do you want Lucy to play with your clit while I do?"

"Yes," I groaned.

He tugged on Lucy's leash, pulling him between his thighs. I gasped as I was lifted, and then felt the head of his cock against me.

"Do you want the shadow to fuck you while you please our mate?" the Barista asked him.

"Yes. For fuck's sake," Lucy growled, his voice faltering. "Please. I need you inside me."

The Barista chuckled and I watched as the shadow knelt behind Lucy, running its hands over him. He groaned, leaning forward. I felt his breath against my pussy, my clit aching to be touched by him.

"Please," I whimpered. "Please fill me, Daddy."

"Again," he growled.

"Please," I cried. "I need you inside of me. I need you to knot me and breed me."

He growled and slowly lowered me onto his cock as the shadow started to push into Lucy. We both cried out together, our mutual pleasure amplified as it resonated through our mate bonds.

"I'm going to fuck you together, and then Lucy can clean up our milk with some cookies."

CHAPTER 2
Lucy

I growled as B's shadow shoved inside of me, my lips sucking on Trixie's clit as it began to fuck me.

I could feel her pleasure, could feel her being fucked just like I was. I groaned with her, all because our mate was being generous.

Precum dripped from my hard cock, my body shivering with delight. The Barista began to bounce her up and down on his cock, his grunts turning me on even more.

What the fuck had he just said about milk and cookies? My mind had barely registered that, but... Well, I'd find out.

The shadow thrust inside of me and I groaned, losing myself completely. Every movement, every touch, all of it felt sinfully good.

I gripped the Barista's thighs, burying my face against Trixie as he pumped in and out of her. His knot pulsed, her cries music to my ears.

I felt the leash tug, the shadow gripping my hips and fucking me harder. I groaned, my tail wrapping up the Barista's leg.

He groaned. "Fuck," he cursed. "Both of you feel amazing," he gasped.

Knowing that he could feel me through his shadow while fucking Trixie too was enough to send me over the edge. I gasped as my cock shot hot seed again, cumming without even being touched.

I panted, digging my talons into his thighs. He groaned and I looked up right as he and Trixie cummed together.

Trixie cried out, her head falling back as the Barista growled, his knot pushing inside of her before his cum could leak out. I watched in awe as her pussy spread for him, her back arching.

Silence fell over the three of us, only interrupted by our panting. I groaned and leaned forward, swiping my tongue over his knot.

The Barista jerked, letting out a groan. He tugged on the leash, pulling me up so that I could kiss him. My lips parted, our tongues meeting before he leaned back, giving Trixie and I a smile.

"Did you say something about milk and cookies?" I asked.

That earned a laugh from both of them.

"Yes," he said.

"Like....your milk...and cookies?"

"Yes," he chuckled.

I licked my lips, thinking about it. It was a little crazy, but that was nothing new, and I liked the taste of them enough to fucking drink it all day long.

Trixie wrapped her arms around me, holding me to her. I sighed happily, burying my face between her breasts.

"This is heaven," I murmured.

Trixie hummed in agreement and the Barista nodded, closing his eyes and laying his head back on the chair.

Five years I'd been with these two. Five years that had gone by in the blink of an eye. I was still a bastard most of the time and still did things that were questionable, but that was my nature. Still, the three of us had found happiness. We'd built a life together.

I loved our kids. I loved that I was able to be a good father to them, and that I'd even been able to work on my relationship with Gabe. I'd reached out to others too and while I hadn't been able to save all the relationships I had hurt, it was still rewarding to know that I was able to save some.

Tomorrow, I would be surrounded by our family and friends. We'd have gifts for Layla and Luca, and even Bean. I'd gotten him a hunk of demon meat straight from the gates of hell, which would make him happy.

The Barista's hand curled into my hair, stroking me. I sighed again, relaxing.

It shouldn't have been possible for someone like me to find love and happiness, but I had. I was thankful for it, thankful that I had met Trixie and that the Barista had given me a second chance.

I looked up at the Barista, and found that he was looking down at me too. I held his gaze, enjoying the way that his lips twisted into a soft smile. He loved me, even if there were times that he wanted to kick me off of a cliff. But, our relationship was good, and we had done a lot of good things together. And now we had Trixie too, and gods knew that we loved her.

"Should I go get the cookies then?" I asked, sitting back.

"That would be good," the Barista said. "And a cup."

"Fuck. You're really going to have me do that?"

"Yeah, and then I'm going to fuck you."

Trixie giggled. "Sounds fair."

"Shush, you naughty girl," I teased, standing up. "You're not the one getting milk and cookies."

She giggled again as I left our bedroom, going down the hall to the kitchen. Ever since we'd had the twins and then got a dog, too, we'd ended up expanding the house so that there were more bedrooms.

The kitchen was the same as always, the bar had a nice espresso machine, along with different bags of coffee. There was a jar of cookies and a cup already waiting.

That bastard. He'd already had this set up earlier, and I hadn't even noticed.

I snorted and grabbed the cookies and cup, shaking my head as I went back to the bedroom.

Trixie was still knotted to the Barista, her little moans echoing through the room every now and then.

"The things I do for love," I teased, popping open the jar.

"You're a slut and you like it," the Barista quipped.

True. That was very true.

His eyes narrowed on me, his beard flickering with embers. He tilted his head, raising a red brow.

"Little devil," he said, taking on that tone. The tone that I couldn't resist, the one that made me want to kneel at his feet.

"I want you to get yourself hard again. And I want you to grab a flogger, and then I want you to kneel down and flog yourself while you stroke your cock. And if you do well and cum for me again, then you'll be rewarded with milk and cookies."

Fuck. I had already cum twice, and while it wasn't impossible for me to cum again, it would still be a task. Still, I was going to obey him. I set the jar of cookies and empty cup down, and then crossed our bedroom to the wall where our toys hung.

I picked one of the floggers, one that had little spikes at the end. It would sting like a bitch, but it would also feel good.

Plus, I would have the satisfaction of knowing that the Barista enjoyed watching me.

I took a deep breath, a shiver working up my spine. I'd already been fucked by his shadow, and I'd already cum twice.

He had fucked my throat, but I still wanted more. I wanted to taste them, to have the taste of my mates lingering on my tongue for the rest of the night.

I turned around and went back to them, kneeling in front of my mates. Trixie groaned, her eyes opening so that she could watch me. Her cheeks were flushed, her nipples still pink from where one of us had bitten them.

The Barista gave his hips a little thrust, drawing a cry from her. I smirked, loving the sound.

I looked down at my cock, seeing that I was already starting to get hard again. It didn't take much when I was with these two, especially on a night like tonight.

"Go on," he growled. "I want you to punish yourself like the little slut you are, little devil."

I sucked in a breath, running my fingertips over the soft leather of the flogger. I gripped the handle, and then slid my other hand down to my cock. I ran my palm over the rigid shaft, a shiver working up my spine yet again. I was sensitive, aching to be inside of Trixie or even the Barista.

I lifted the flogger, swinging it back so that the tassels smacked my back. The sound of it echoed through our bedroom, followed by a soft cry from me. I then swung it forward, using the motion to send it back to the other side. It splayed across my shoulder and spine, the pain rocking through my body.

"Stroke your cock," he commanded. His voice was gruff, his tone unyielding.

"Yes, Daddy," I gasped.

"*Harder*," he growled.

"Yes, Daddy."

I put more force into the flogger, the constant thud of it hitting me putting me into a trance; my existence narrowed down on the sharp pain heightening my pleasure.

I grunted as I stroked myself harder, faster. A long moan left my parted lips, and I thrust my hips to meet my hand.

"Are you a little slut?" he growled.

"Yes," I cried.

"Do you like being such a needy little devil?"

"Yes," I gasped.

"You're doing so good for me," he said. "And I'm warming up your reward. I can feel our mate's cunt pulsing around my cock. She's turned on by watching you punish yourself, by seeing you helpless and needy."

I gasped, opening my eyes to watch them as I continued. Trixie let out a sharp cry and I watched in awe as she again cummed around the Barista's cock, drawing a primal growl from him.

"Fuck," he breathed.

I stroked my cock faster, groaning. I was getting close to cumming again too.

"Cum for us," Trixie whimpered.

Fuck. Her words broke me.

I growled, striking myself one last time as I started to cum. Hot seed shot from the tip of my cock and I hunched over, gasping as I came hard.

"Lick it up," the Barista growled.

I panted, catching my breath. I groaned, leaning down to do as he asked. I swiped my tongue over my cum, lapping it up.

"Good boy," the Barista rasped. "Come get your reward, little devil."

I groaned, crawling to the cup and cookies. I grabbed the cup and then went to them, kneeling at the foot of his chair.

This sure as hell was going to be a Christmas I wouldn't forget.

CHAPTER 3

Barista

I slowly lifted Trixie up, my knot easing free. She gasped as my cum began to drop from her and straight into the cup that Lucy held ready. She groaned, her head still resting on my shoulder.

"Good girl," I praised, kissing her cheek.

She groaned. "Fuck," she mumbled. "That felt good."

I wrapped my arms around her as the last of my cum went into the cup and then I stood, carrying her over to the bed. She squeaked as I plopped her down on the mattress. I leaned over her, planting a kiss on her lips.

She wrapped her arms around me for a moment, her fingers intertwining in my hair before she let go with a satisfied grin.

I turned, looking at Lucy. "Come here, little devil," I said.

Lucy made a noise as he moved across the floor to me, the cup still in his hands.

I gripped one of his horns and forced him to look up at me with a growl. He groaned, his black eyes fluttering.

"Are you going to fuck me?" he asked, his fangs glistening.

"If you drink your milk, then yes," I said.

He gave me a smug smirk, one that made me grip his horns a little harder.

"Don't smirk at me, you little slut," I snarled.

He liked pissing me off. I glared at him for a moment, my shadow emerging next to me.

His eyes widened as my shadow grabbed the cup from him and then the cookies. I kept his head tilted back as he was on his knees in front of me. I felt his tail curl around my calf, sneaking up my leg and gripping me. I didn't want it to go away. I had found that in moments like this, I liked that bit of contact with him.

"Open your mouth," I growled.

He obeyed, parting his lips for me. His fangs glistened, his eyes dark and glazed over with lust.

I grabbed one of the cookies and dipped it into the cup of cum, offering it to him. He took it into his mouth, chewing and swallowing.

I felt a rush of power run through me, my cock hardening.

I had thought of this idea yesterday when I had been in the middle of a rush at the cafe. I'd been pouring a latte for a dragon and a kraken, and my thoughts had wandered off. What would happen if I made Lucy drink my milk? It was Christmas, after all, and having a little holiday fun was irresistible.

Plus, I had wondered if he would obey me. Would he actually do this? Of course he would, he was my little devil. And he liked doing devilish things.

I grabbed another cookie as he groaned, dipping it into my cum and shoving it into his mouth. He glared at me for a moment, but he didn't dare argue.

"That's right," I said. "You're a slut. My slut. And you do what I tell you, don't you?"

He nodded, swallowing hard. "Fuck," he mumbled.

I held his horns, watching as my shadow held the rim of the

cup to his lips. The shadow tipped it forward, and I watched as my cum began to pour into my mate's mouth. Lucy groaned, but swallowed every drop, his tail tightening around me.

"Good boy," I whispered. "Drink your Daddy's milk."

A drop of it rolled down his cheek, and I leaned down, licking it up. Our lips met in a passionate kiss, and he groaned against me.

My cock was hard again, ready to be buried inside of him.

I heard Trixie's breath hitch, and I looked back. She was on the bed, her legs spread, her finger stroking her clit. I groaned, and stepped back so that Lucy could see her too.

The sound that he made was monstrous.

I chuckled, and then lowered myself to the floor. I was going to fuck him while we watched her. The love of our life, the woman that held our world together.

We both worshipped her, cherished her, loved her.

Lucy bent over onto all fours, and I ran my fingers down his ass. He was still primed from when my shadow had fucked him, ready to take my cock.

"Watch her," I commanded. "Watch her make herself come for us while I fuck you little devil."

"Thank you, daddy," he gasped.

I growled, positioning the head of my cock against his ass. His tail moved, wrapping around my torso as I began to ease inside of him. He cried out, his back arching as he took me.

Pleasure worked through me, my body still humming from the ecstasy of taking Trixie. I looked up at her, groaning as she thrust her fingers inside her cunt, her body arching.

"Fuck," Lucy cursed. "Fuck, you feel good."

"Good," I grunted, gripping his hips.

I thrust all the way inside of him, giving him every inch. My knot bumped against him before I dragged my cock back out and pumped into him again.

His muscles rippled, his eyes feasting on our mate as I took him. The two of us growled together as my fingers dug into his skin, my head falling back as I gave in to my desires.

I could feel their pleasure, their lust, their wants. Trixie groaned as she fingered her clit, while Lucy reached down and started to stroke his cock again.

I cursed, closing my eyes and breathing in the scents of their arousal. I could taste Trixie and Lucy, could feel our bonds tightening as the three of us got closer and closer to cumming again.

Fuck. I couldn't stop myself.

I let out a low growl, giving one last thrust as I started to cum. My knot pushed inside Lucy as I started to fill him and he cried out, his muscles shivering as he started to cum again too.

"Fuck," he growled. *"Fuck."*

We both looked up right as Trixie came, her voice a melody I loved to hear. She was beautiful and wild, her skin flushed and her pussy glistening from my cum.

She collapsed back on the bed with a groan and Lucy and I chuckled, panting as more of my cum filled him.

"So cookies and cum, huh?" Lucy said, turning to look at me.

I kissed up his spine, smiling against his skin. "Thought of it yesterday while working the counter."

"Of course you did," he mumbled. "Is that what you think about when you make customers coffee?"

"Sometimes, little devil," I chuckled.

"Trixie, are you alive?" Lucy asked.

Trixie held up a thumbs up, letting out a tired moan.

We both laughed, and I closed my eyes for a moment, letting the happiness sink in.

"I love you," I whispered, kissing him again.

He shivered. "I love you too. And you, little angel."

Trixie made another incoherent noise which definitely translated to her loving us too.

"Mmm, I think this calls for a group shower, food, and then sleep," I said. "And then tomorrow, we'll get to see everyone."

"It'll be fun," Lucy said. "No one will know that we had such a naughty Christmas."

"Oh, I think everyone will know," Trixie laughed, raising her head.

"We won't be the only ones," I chuckled, thinking about all of our friends.

No. We definitely would not be the only ones who had stayed up doing crazy things to each other tonight. I looked forward to seeing who could walk straight tomorrow.

Monsters had such hungry appetites, ones that only our human mates could fill. I thought about all of the love we had created over the last few years and smiled to myself.

I used to be so bitter, but all of that had changed. I had two mates I loved, and a family. And yes, I secretly liked the dog. Not that I would admit that to anyone...except to the dog when I snuck him treats.

I slowly pulled free from Lucy. The three of us spent the rest of the night in the shower and jacuzzi, and then in the arms of each other.

I was already thinking about the things we would do for fun this time next year...

The Next Morning - Barista

"Here you go," Lucy chuckled, handing me a cup of coffee.

I inhaled it almost immediately, staring blearily around at our family. The three of us had stayed up all night, and even though I technically didn't need sleep, I was still exhausted compared to Trixie. Lucy and I watched as she bounced around the Cafe, chasing after Luca and one of Jasper and Alex's boys.

I was standing next to the counter, away from the Christmas tree and all of the presents. The ornaments that I hung last night gleamed in the morning light, the scent of evergreen and roasted coffee scenting the air.

A massive hand clapped me on the back, and I damn near choked. "Morning," Jasper said. "You look like you had a fun night."

I snorted but didn't hide my smirk. Lucy chuckled next to me, giving my hand a squeeze before intercepting Layla trying to climb on Bean and ride him like a horse through the mounds of wrapping paper.

I chuckled, taking another sip of my coffee. Lucy was adept at making coffee at this point, almost as well as I did, and it always made me happy when he brought me one.

"How's it going?" I asked, giving my orc friend a side look.

"Good," he chuckled, his gaze pinned on Alex as he flipped pancakes in the kitchen.

We'd expanded the cafe, adding a kitchen in the back that could be easily seen from the seating area. We had more food options now, which was nice for both monsters and humans. That was thanks to Trixie and Quinn, both of them coming up with a menu. We'd even added some of Dracon's soups, part of the seasonal menu, for the colder months.

Almost everyone was here, and there was more going on than in a circus. Meduso and Noah wouldn't make it, but they'd sent all of us a picture of their view in Brazil and would be coming home for New Year's.

Quinn, Alex, and Dracon were in the kitchen cooking. Dante and Peter were standing with Al and Luna, watching as more gifts were unwrapped.

The front door to the cafe burst open, and Rum stepped in, dressed like Santa Clause– if Santa were a minotaur.

Jasper and I laughed as there was an immediate uproar from the children, all of them stampeding for him.

"Ah hell," Rum said, his eyes widening.

Penny slid past him before she could be caught in the cross-fire, winking at me before joining Kat and Dell across the room.

"I'm glad I didn't volunteer for that," Jasper chuckled.

Trixie waltzed up, giving me a kiss before I pulled her next to me, watching as Layla and Luca tackled Rum too.

Laughter erupted through the cafe and I felt myself relax even more. It was hard not to. There was so much joy here, so much excitement and love. I had been matching monsters and humans for years, but it hadn't been until the last few that I had been able to see how much good could really come from it.

Rum managed to stand up with a victorious roar, at least four children hanging off him. He moved out of the way right as the door opened again; Seth, Cam, and Gabe standing there with—

"No, they fucking did not," I wheezed.

A hell hound puppy was in Gabe's arm, his smug fanged grin the only thing I could see as he was wrapped head to toe in fabric so he didn't accidentally kill someone.

"Did you approve this?" I hissed, looking down at Trixie.

She patted my arm, looking up at me and batting her eyelashes. "Drink your coffee, Daddy," she said, giving me a bright smile.

My insides melted, which was an unfair advantage. She pecked me on the cheek and then went over to meet them, everyone fawning over the puppy.

Jasper was a goner too, already heading over to them.

Lucy came back to me, giving me a wicked smile.

"Can you control your son?" I hissed.

He chuckled. "Nope, not at all. Plus, this is the last time. I swear."

"Oh, so this was your idea?" I asked, raising a brow.

Lucy made a face. "Oh would you look at that, someone is calling me."

"No one is—"

Lucy snickered as he left me standing there alone.

I'd been betrayed, but it was fine. I found myself smiling as I watched.

"Hey."

I turned to see Naomi with Ella, Melody, Dalus, and Icarus following behind her. They must have come in the back door.

"Morning," I grumbled, taking another sip of coffee.

She grinned, stopping once she was next to me. "My goodness. This is a lot. Aw, you got another puppy."

I sighed but nodded. Gabe looked too damn happy for me to actually be angry, and we had room for another dog.

Bean was a pain in my ass, but he had grown on me.

"I need coffee," Melody moaned.

I looked back at them, raising a brow. "Long night?"

Icarus snorted, turning and heading to the coffee pot.

"Do you want a latte instead?" I asked.

"No, this will do," he said, grabbing five cups for all of them.

Ella grinned, immediately immersing herself into the gaggle of children and presents.

"This is lovely," Naomi said. "Chaotic. But lovely."

"It is," I said.

"I have a favor to ask," Naomi said.

Intriguing. I gave her my full attention now, raising my brow.

"I have a friend," she said.

"For fuck's sake," I sighed.

"Listen," she hissed, rolling her eyes. "Don't be so dramatic. Plus, you like favors."

It was true.

"He needs to find a mate."

"Of course. What kind of monster?"

"He's a Basilisk."

"Fuck no," I said.

She hit my arm, gesturing to Inferna who had swiveled her head at my curse.

"Bad word," she said.

"Yes, bad word," I said, grimacing. "Go back to opening presents."

"Fuck no," she repeated.

Naomi let out a loud laugh.

243

"Fuck no," Inferna said again.

Dante made his way over, snorting. "Inferna, leave him alone and don't say that, please."

His tone was so gentle that I couldn't help but laugh too.

"Okay," I said. "Fine. Basilisk's are dangerous though."

"Come on, you've dealt with worse creatures," she quipped. "He's also a Prince."

I groaned, looking up at the ceiling for a moment. "Fine. Fine. I will do it. Have him meet me here soon. And he better be good, Naomi."

"Thanks," she said, baring her fangs in a grin.

I merely grunted, going back to sipping my coffee.

Layla ran over to me, holding her arms up.

Well, never mind the coffee. I immediately set the cup down and swooped her up, her giggle making me laugh.

"Papa!" she squealed, immediately hugging me.

Fucking ten hells, there was nothing else like this. I held her to me, looking at Lucy and then Trixie.

"We got a puppy!" she said, leaning back with a wide grin. One of her teeth had come out recently, which was both amazing and a reminder that in a blink, she would be all grown up.

Luca wandered over to us, and I knelt down, scooping him up too.

"How are you, my loves?" I asked, not caring that when I was being a dad to them, I was no longer the gruff coffee drinking grim reaper.

They both grinned and started to tell me everything. About last night, about this morning, about their new puppy— who we had already named Roast, apparently.

I sighed happily, listening to them intently.

Soon, I would make another match. And dangerous monster

or not, maybe they would be able to find the happiness I had found.

It was Christmas morning, and I could think of nowhere else I'd rather be than at Creature Cafe with my family.

HAPPY HOLIDAYS FROM CREATURE CAFE!

Little Drink of Venom

A NEW YEARS EVE CREATURE CAFE NOVELLA

To Sam
Thank you!

Note from the Barista

HELLO, MY LITTLE MONSTER LOVING **CREATURE**.
THIS IS JUST A FRIENDLY REMINDER TO MAKE SURE YOU
CHECK YOUR TRIGGERS BEFORE READING.
THIS STORY HAS BDSM, CONSENSUAL NON-CONSENSUAL
SEX, DOM/SUB DYNAMICS, OVIPOSITION, BREEDING **WITH**
PREGNANCY, DOUBLE COCKS, CUM DRINKING, TAIL SEX,
MATING BITES, FATED MATES, ATTEMPTED MURDER,
KIDNAPPING, AND MORE.
IF ANY OF THOSE THINGS ARE NOT FOR YOU— DO NOT READ
THIS STORY.
IF THOSE SOUND RIGHT, THEN MAYBE YOU NEED HELP.
BUT THEN AGAIN, MAYBE I DO TOO...
SINCERELY,
THE BARISTA

The Barista

The Basilisk Prince sitting across from me was an asshole.

"I want them to have red hair and—"

"I don't know what the fuck you think I am," I snarled. "If you want someone to match you with someone based on looks, you're asking the wrong guy. I can't believe Naomi recommended you to me."

Lucas scoffed, baring his fangs at me.

"Do you know who I am?" he asked, his vibrant yellow eyes pinned on me. His pupils were shaped like diamonds, and every few seconds, the tip of his tail would rattle.

In his half-shifted form, he was like a Naga. But in his fully shifted form, he was a massive beast. A giant serpent that would barely fit in my cafe.

I had one friend that was a basilisk, and I steered clear of him if he was in that form. Even as the Grim Reaper, there were some creatures I didn't like to tangle with unless necessary.

"I know that you've already broken some of my coffee cups with your tail and that Trixie is gonna be pissed," I said. "So, you want love?"

"Yes," Lucas whispered. "Is Trixie your servant girl?"

I immediately stood up, fire erupting across my skin.

How much trouble would I get in if I reaped this prince's soul?

He held up his hands, hissing. "My apologies! I didn't know that was offensive."

Silence settled between the two of us. I arched a brow, crossing my arms. Smoke twisted up from my nostrils as I glared.

Creature royalty was just as snobby as human royalty.

"Don't speak her name again, *prince*. And your family is fine with you seeking out a human?" I gritted out.

The only reason I was doing this was that Naomi had asked as a favor and now she would owe me.

I did like collecting favors when the time was needed.

Lucas pressed his lips together, scowling. "What I do is not their concern. I am my own person."

"You're also next in line for your throne," I growled.

"Yes. Well, the world is changing. I want a human by my side. I don't care what gender or sex they are. But I do love red hair. It's pretty."

A basilisk prince with a thing for red hair.

"Alright. Just so you are aware, none of this is guaranteed. If they don't like you, they don't like you."

"Just because you don't like me doesn't mean they won't."

"Just because you're a prince and friend with Naomi doesn't mean I can't kill you," I quipped back.

He smirked, shrugging. "You could try, Barista."

It wasn't a matter of trying.

How was I going to find a human that could deal with this level of alpha asinine ego?

"Also," I said. "You owe me for this."

"I know," he answered, rising from his seat. "I'll hear from you?"

"You will," I said. "Give me some time."

He nodded and left the cooler. The door opened and shut.

With a deep sigh, I pulled out my phone.

I had a human to call.

CHAPTER 1

Drink Me

S ^{am}

I TUGGED the scarf around my face, squinting through the snow as I trekked up the sidewalk to Creature Cafe.

It had already been a day. The worst day. Work had been chaotic, my boss had won the biggest-asshole-of-the-year award, and then I had driven through this snowstorm to get here for a date.

A date with a monster.

Not to mention that there had been a lot of traffic as well. New Year's Eve was this Sunday, and everyone was getting ready to celebrate— even if the weather was being feisty.

At least all of us at the office were off Monday and Tuesday too.

I bit my bottom lip as I pushed open the front door, immediately greeted by warmth and the smell of coffee.

The world of creatures and humans overlapped in many

ways, and this unassuming coffee shop was one of them. I had known about monsters for a few years after walking in on a vampire drinking from a woman in the bathroom at a club.

At least in their case, they were mates. The vampire was also an actual sweetheart, she just had a craving for type B. Type B as in her mate, Bianca.

The two of them were still my friends and had ultimately drawn me into the world of monsters. Which was how the Barista had gotten my info.

I'd been out of the dating scene for a while, hunkering down to focus on work. I worked in software and was currently learning a new language in order to get a certificate to move up. It wasn't hard necessarily, but it took up more time than I realized.

Sometime in the last couple of months, I'd started to get restless.

I'd started to try and go out of my way to meet monsters, which had nearly gotten me in trouble if it weren't for Vicky, my vampire friend. She'd steered me away from the bad ones, saying she had a friend that had a friend that had a *friend*.

Still, I didn't know what to expect.

A girl behind the counter waved at me, her smile bright. I smiled too, walking across the cafe to her. It was dead and I realized that we were the only ones here.

"Hey! Are you here for a date? My name is Trixie, I help run Creature Cafe," she chimed.

I nodded, pausing a moment to take in my surroundings. My eyes wandered, catching odd details here and there.

My eyes widened at the painting in the back corner. "Oh god," I said, grinning. "Didn't expect that in a cafe."

Trixie snorted. "Most people that can see it don't. I think your date should be here soon. The snowstorm is pretty bad so he might be late. What would you like to drink?"

"Hot chocolate and maybe this chocolate croissant," I said, eyeing the pastry through the glass.

"Good choices. You got it," Trixie said, beaming.

I wondered if she was human or a creature as I watched her make my drink. She was like a little pink-haired pixie.

I felt butterflies in my stomach again, nerves working through me.

What would my date be like? What kind of monster? I had no idea and had been torturing myself over it ever since it had been set up.

Hell, maybe I was crazy. Maybe going on a date with an actual monster was an insane idea and—

The bell on the cafe door chimed and I felt a chill work up my spine. I froze in place, my stomach tugging.

I turned around, meeting the bright yellow eyes of an unbelievably gorgeous man. His skin was deep brown with patches of iridescent crimson scales, his long black hair drawn back into a bun.

There was an aura surrounding him, one that reeked of power. His gaze never left mine as he walked toward me, only stopping once he was right in front of me.

I swallowed hard, all of the nagging thoughts about today instantly vanishing.

"Are you my date?" he asked, his lips drawing into a smile. I could see the tips of two very long fangs, way longer than my vampire friend's.

His eyes finally left mine, immediately going to my hair. I found myself reaching up to try and fix it but he caught my hand, letting out a soft hiss.

"*Mine,*" he hissed.

What?

I blinked, feeling a shock run up my arm from his touch.

"Here's your drink and croissant, love," Trixie said.

259

He slipped past me, snatching my coffee and pastry from the counter.

"Hey!" I said, finally coming to. "I can get it. And also, was there something in my hair or—"

"No, your hair is beautiful. You're stunning," he said.

I paused for a moment, feeling a twinge of disbelief.

I'd done a lot of work over the years on being able to take compliments and actually believing them. It was hard sometimes. It was hard to hear what he'd just said and not think that he was lying.

He leaned down, his lips close to my ear. Goosebumps worked over my skin and I found myself wondering if it were possible to melt.

"I've got it, princess," he whispered. "I don't want you carrying anything. I will pamper you. Go pick out a table."

The last part of his words was a bit more authoritative. Heat bloomed in my cheeks and I felt like ripping off all of my clothes, my pussy throbbing.

Fuck. What the fuck was this? He was magnetic, alluring, and sexy.

Instead of getting naked in the middle of the cafe, I clutched my scarf and scurried away— heading towards the little table in the back beneath the minotaur painting.

I was on a date with a creature, one who had just refused to let me carry my own food. I was stuck between wanting to argue that I could care for myself and allowing him to do something for me, but I still sat down— my heart pounding.

He came over to the table, setting my croissant and hot chocolate down. "My name is Lucas," he said. "And I'm excited to meet you. You're exactly what I imagined."

I cocked my head now, arching a brow. "Thanks," I said. "My name is Samantha, but you can call me Sam."

He took the seat opposite of me, looking up at the painting

with a little scoff. I fought off a little smile, amused by his immediate disdain.

"I don't know how they get away with hanging this in here," Lucas said, shaking his head.

"Oh, I think it's wonderful," I chuckled, pulling my croissant and mug closer. I was trying *not* to stare at him, but I definitely was. "The artist is great."

"I think I just prefer to do such things…in private."

"You prefer to suck minotaur dicks in private?"

He scoffed even more now, but it ended on a brusque laugh, his head tipping back.

He was too fucking pretty to be a monster. He looked back down at me, his lips turned in a soft smile.

"Hmm… I think my opinion on this comes from how I was raised. Almost everything I do is kept private and out of the eyes of others," he said, giving me a brilliant smile. "It's not that I don't enjoy sex. It's that I am judged if I show I enjoy it."

"Oh," I said. "Why is that?"

"I'm a Prince," Lucas said casually.

"What?" I asked, blinking rapidly a few times.

Had I heard him right?

He arched a dark brow. "A Prince. Basilisk royalty. I'm next in line for our throne, although the world is different now. But yes, in the underworld of monsters— I will be a King."

His bright eyes fell on me now and I felt my stomach twist again. My gaze dropped to his mouth, his tongue teasing the tip of one of his fangs.

What would it be like for those fangs to sink into me?

Fuck.

His nostrils flared, his eyes flickering. "We're the only ones here aside from the waitress…"

"We are," I whispered, my voice cracking. I cleared my throat, my cheeks heating.

"I can smell your arousal."

Fucking hell. I tore my gaze away from him and covered my mouth, mortified. "Sorry," I whispered.

His hand darted out, pulling mine away from my face. His grip was firm, his hiss making me look at him in shock. "Don't ever look away from me like that again," he snarled. "Your scent pleases me. I want to bend you over this table and fucking claim you. But I'm trying my very best to behave so the Barista doesn't murder me. If it weren't for that, I'd have already claimed you, princess."

His grip softened. I started to pull away, but he let out a little growl.

"Sorry," he said, wincing, letting go of me.

I arched a brow, collecting myself.

"I just...I don't want to scare you."

I fought off a little laugh and took a moment to sip my hot chocolate. "I don't think I'm scared of you, just a little startled."

"Sorry," he apologized again. He cleared his throat and then changed the subject. "How long have you known about monsters?"

"Not too long. Ever since I met my vampire friend. I came across her feeding off her mate. She's good." I cleared my throat as I grabbed my hot chocolate, clinging to the warmth of it.

Lucas nodded, humming. "Good. What are you doing after this?"

"Driving home."

"Absolutely not," he said.

"What do you mean *absolutely not?*" I asked, squirming in my chair.

"You should come home with me where I can keep you safe," Lucas said, arching a brow. "There's a nasty snow storm that's coming in."

"I've driven in the snow," I said. I was terrible at it and it always made me feel like I was about to have a heart attack, but i had still managed.

"Stay with me," Lucas said. "For New Years."

I stared at him for a heartbeat. He was serious despite the fact that I wanted to believe he was joking. This was our first date, and he was already wanting to sweep me off for a holiday.

"I can't go home with a stranger, Lucas. Prince or not. I don't even know—"

"You *know*," he said, his gaze locking with mine.

I felt that dark pull, a carnal need.

He was hard to say no to. In fact, was he even used to people telling him no?

Did the people in his life ever deny him things?

"Come on, princess," he said. "I want to show you what it's like to be with a monster."

I bit my lower lip, the temptation strong.

What did I have to lose, aside from getting axe murdered or eaten alive by this pretty Basilisk Prince? Thirty years on this planet and, at this point, that would at least add some excitement to my life.

If I was murdered, I also knew I would be avenged. Perks of having friends that were creatures.

"Give me two seconds," I said, slipping my hand into my coat.

"Take your time," Lucas said, relaxing in his seat.

The bastard knew he had won.

I plucked my phone out, opening the screen to text Vicky.

> Hey, I think I'm going to go home with this guy. He's pretty convincing. But if he murders me will you avenge me?

Reply bubbles immediately popped up.

Vicky: Of course. What's his name? Also, if the Barista matched you with him, he is safe. But also, if he hurts you then my horde will hack him up and turn him into snake skin boots.

I fought off a snort, sending her his name. I got a thumbs up, which was good enough for me.

Fuck, I was really doing this. I was really going to go home with a monster I'd just met. I was really going to spend New Year's weekend with a Basilisk Prince.

But also, fuck it. There was part of me, a very shameless part, that wanted to know what he would be like in bed. Were monsters any good? Also what the hell did his...

I shouldn't be thinking about that. I shouldn't wonder about the package below.

And yet...

"Alright," I said, looking up at him. "I guess I'll go home with you. My vampire friend said she'll turn you into snake boots if you murder me though."

Lucas barked out a laugh, his fangs glistening. "Alright, princess. Let's get you home."

CHAPTER 2

Snowed In

L ucas

CONVINCING my human to come with me to my vacation home had been easier than I had thought, which was good considering I was ready to have one of my servants disable her car battery.

Was that crazy? Yes.

But her scent was driving *me* crazy.

I'd watched her walk into Creature Cafe, oblivious to me. Oblivious to everything around her. She'd needed the warmth and I could hear her heartbeat quicken once she realized she'd finally arrived to her date.

Fuck, she was beautiful. And now she was all mine.

I fought to keep my eyes on the road and not her instead. The two of us were in my car heading towards my house.

I was fighting off the already overwhelming possessive feeling, the need to constrict her sweet body and claim her. My skin burned, this form itching to give way to my true one.

There was a massive snowstorm rolling in, one that would leave her stranded with me for the entire holiday weekend. I'd planned this out meticulously because this also meant that my family wouldn't be able to catch wind of what was happening–that I was going to claim a human.

I'd told them I would be away for the New Year and would return after my solo-cation. I'd been met with some resistance, but I had also stayed through most of December to appease my parents.

They would riot at first about Sam but eventually would come around. All of them would. Especially since she would already be mine.

Besides, it wasn't their choice. It was mine, and I always got what I wanted.

Even if I had to manipulate my way there.

"How much further until we're at your place?" Sam asked, her voice alone making my cocks harden.

She was smart, gorgeous, and not scared of me.

She had no idea the effect she had on me. Fucking hell. Her scent, her appearance, the little sly smiles I'd see here and there when I wasn't surprising her.

Of course, her shocked expression also made me feel...hungry.

I wanted to know what her expression would be once she took one of my cocks. And when she took both.

My hands tightened around the steering wheel.

"About ten minutes," I said, stealing a glance at her.

Sam was looking out the window as we passed the snow-laden trees. We were one of the only souls on the road, everyone else safely tucked in and ready to hunker down.

"This is crazy," she muttered, pulling her evergreen scarf tighter around her neck and face.

Crazy for her. Not for me. What was crazy was the fact that

I was ready to burn the world down for the little red-haired human and she had no fucking idea.

Her scent spiked again and I fought off a moan.

What was she thinking about? Was she imagining how it would be to be with me? To be with a monster?

Should I take her fully shifted or half-shifted?

Half-shifted would be safer. And I wanted to be safe, despite the way I burned to release myself fully.

"Princess," I said, fighting off my biting tone. "Are you sure you know what you're getting into? Did they tell you that monster's mate for life? Or anything about my kind?"

"No," she whispered. "I have no idea, but...I'm not turning around now."

I nodded, feeling my incisors lengthen. It was getting more and more difficult to control myself, but we were close to home.

"Many creatures have soulmates," I said. "Many of them never get to meet theirs, but in our case— we had the Barista match us. I wasn't convinced he would be able to do it but then I saw you. And I want you, princess. Even now, I can feel my cocks hardening."

"*Cocks*? As in *two*?" she whispered, turning her sweet, but slightly alarmed, eyes on me.

Oh, she would be so fun to tease.

"Yes," I said. "*Two.*"

"Fuck," she whispered.

"I'm going to breed you," I growled, unable to stop myself.

"Oh fuck," she mumbled again.

"Use you. Breed you. Worship you."

"Fucking hell," she cursed again, breathless.

"And if at any point you want me to stop, you need to tell me, princess. Understand?"

"Yes," she said. "Okay. I've never done anything this crazy before. I've never been with a monster."

"You keep saying that word. *Crazy.* Do you want to know something crazy?" I asked, gripping the steering wheel.

"What?" she whispered.

"The way your scent makes me feel. My monster wants to fuck you, constrict you, shove the tip of my tail in your pretty pussy. And I want to lay my eggs inside of you."

"*Eggs?*" Sam gasped.

Yes. Eggs. When she was ready.

I turned down another road, meeting the gate that enclosed my property. It immediately opened for me, everything ready for the two of us.

I had planned this holiday weekend perfectly. The storm just worked in my favor too.

"Almost there, princess," I said, fighting off a smile.

She was nervous and aroused, a little scared but still curious.

"Eggs," she whispered again, this time shaking her head. "Insane. Wild."

Silence fell between us for a moment, and I could hear how hard her heart pounded.

"I want you," she said, her voice barely audible.

Fuck. *Fuck.* Desperation poured into my veins, need nearly making me swerve.

"You will have me," I said. "All of me. Any and every way you want me, princess."

"This is insane."

I chuckled as I pulled up to my home. Well, *one* of my homes. This one was quaint compared to the others, trading the classic opulence I had grown up around for modern architecture.

"I've never been this far out of the city," Sam said, her eyes wide and on the house. "I didn't grow up around here."

"Where are you from?" I asked, curious.

"I'm from Texas," she said. "Which means the snow is strange to me. We don't have snow like this there."

"We don't either where I'm from," I said. "Bundle up, princess. I'll come around to get you."

Before she could protest, I got out of the car and went around— opening her door. I leaned in, pausing to breathe her in. She let out a little breath and then held it, her teeth sinking into her crimson bottom lip.

I unbuckled her, lingering a little longer than necessary before allowing her to get out. The moment she stood, I pulled her close, wrapping my arms around her.

She gave a nervous laugh. "You're so..."

"Crazy," I teased. "And you, princess, need to stay warm for me," I said, shutting the door behind her. "I'm going to carry you inside."

"What? No—"

She squealed as I swooped her up, writhing against me until I let out a little growl.

"I didn't think you'd be able to just pick me up. I'm not exactly light."

"Neither am I," I chuckled. "I'll have to be careful not to crush you while I'm rutting into you."

She shook her head and mumbled a string of curses, but ultimately wrapped her arms around me.

I wanted to worship her. I wanted her to know that she was going to be a princess now, my little goddess, and deserved to be treated as such.

I opened the door and stepped inside, slowly setting Sam down. Her fingers curled into my coat for a moment and I steadied her, fighting my urges.

"Sam," I said, tipping her chin up.

She met my gaze, a strand of coppery hair falling in front of her freckled face. I swept it back and then cupped her jaw, my body aching to shift.

"Let me prove that you belong with me," I growled.

I could see the uncertainty swimming there, but there was need too. The tug that she felt, the pull to *me*.

She was mine. She was meant to be my mate. I would have her, one way or another.

She surprised me by leaning up onto her tiptoes and brushing her lips over mine. I let out a heady growl, immediately kissing her back.

She tasted like heaven.

I broke the kiss before I lost control and devoured her, releasing a frustrated groan. "Consent," I rasped. "Give me your consent to touch you. To ravish you. To show you what it means to be mine."

"You have it," she said, letting out a little moan. "You have it, Lucas."

With that, I finally let part of my monster free.

CHAPTER 3
Forked Tongue

S ^{am}

WITHIN MOMENTS, I was no longer standing in front of a man, but a monster.

I took a step back, not because I was afraid, but because even in this form he was still breathtaking.

His clothes were discarded, left scattered on the floor. I was faced with a towering half-Lucas, half-serpent. His lower body was a tail that was long, ending with a rattle at the tip. Scarlet scales now extended over his torso, neck, and face. His bright yellow eyes burned with a ravenous glow in the dark of the foyer.

I was hot. He was hot. I wanted him to devour me.

The car ride had been torture. If he asked me to rip off my clothes for him, I would.

And now, I'd given him my consent to devour me.

"Sam," he hissed, his forked tongue flicking out

Oh fuck, I wanted that tongue inside of me.

His nostrils flared and he moved forward, his hand darting out and gripping my chin.

I was shivering, I realized, and it was because I was...

Not scared.

In need.

I wanted him so badly that I was quivering for him.

"Princess," he growled. "My little princess. I'm going to make you cum harder than you ever have."

I was struggling to find words, but it didn't matter. Lucas swept me up again, despite my yelp, and carried me to his living room. I sat down on a couch. He leaned down, his lips brushing over mine, and I felt all of my worries melt.

He had chosen to bring me home. He had chosen for the two of us to do this, and so had I.

There was a part of me screaming— what the hell was I doing?! But it was drowned out by the throb in my pussy and the way his touch made my blood heat.

The tip of his tail wrapped around my ankle and tugged, spreading my legs. I parted my lips as he deepened the kiss, giving in to him.

Giving in to the Basilisk Prince.

Lucas drew back, his fingers curling into my scarf and slowly pulling it away. He then took my coat off, tossing it to the floor.

"I'm taking you to my nest, but first, I need you naked," he rasped.

My cheeks felt like irons had touched them, but I still nodded.

It was usually weird to get naked in front of someone for the first time but with him, it felt natural. I wanted him to turn those molten eyes on my body, bare and needy for him.

"You're so..." I drifted off, my eyes falling down his beautiful body.

Now that I was sitting, his waist was at eye level and so was the slit that was slowly parting.

"Oh," I gasped, reaching out.

He grabbed my hand with a little hiss, keeping me from touching him. "Not yet. Soon, princess. I want to see you naked. I want to please you before you touch me."

I wanted to lick every scale that covered him.

"You're so hot," I whispered.

He grinned, his sharp fangs gleaming. "Strip for me, princess. I want to see you."

"Yes, Your Majesty," I said, sticking my tongue out at him.

He made a low growl, but then it turned into a hum. "Most people would get their ass whipped for saying that."

"Why wouldn't I, then?" I asked, grabbing the hem of my sweater and pulling it off.

His eyes lit up, his lips twisting. "Oh. I see. My little human wants to be handled, does she? Do you want me to do evil things to you?"

"If spanking is all you got—"

He shoved me back onto the couch, my wrists immediately pinned above my head. I gasped, now fully trapped beneath him.

"You're a brat," he growled. "A little brat. I will spank you until you beg me to stop. On second thought, maybe I should strip you," he said, leaning down to brush his lips over my jawline.

I shivered, my words dying again.

"Can't have my princess lifting a finger, now can we?"

I tried to yank against him, but it was no use. Instead, that earned me a nip of his fangs on my neck, just enough to make me gasp.

273

"Oh, I like that noise," he chuckled.

His tongue flicked out now, running over my skin. Down my neck, down my chest, and then dipping between my breasts.

My pussy gave a hard throb. I was getting wetter and wetter with every moment that passed.

His free hand lifted the edge of my tank top and then he paused, dragging his claws up.

"What's your safeword?" he asked, pausing for a moment.

"Ice," I answered, groaning as his claws dug in just a little.

"What if you can't speak?"

I held up a hand, making a symbol with my fingers.

He nodded, memorizing both. "You will use them if you need them?"

"Yes," I said. "I will."

"Do you have any limits that I need to know about? Anything that you do like?"

"I like being spanked," I groaned. There were so many things that I wanted him to do to me. "I want you to take me even if I beg you to stop. I want you to use me and make me cum over and over again. I like a little pain with my pleasure."

He chuckled, his expression reminding me of a demon who had just found a little soul to devour. "I think you will like some of the things I will do to you. Use your safeword if you need me to stop and everything will end," he growled his final warning.

Then, in one swift motion, he tore through the fabric.

I gasped, shocked that his talons were so sharp. He held me in place, not allowing me to squirm away.

"Oh, princess," he breathed, tearing the front of my bra next.

I let out a moan as my nipples hardened, begging for his tongue.

"Your body knows it belongs to me," he sneered. "So helpless."

I writhed under him, bucking my hips up. This only made his grip tighten on my wrist above and then I felt...

I lifted my head with a gasp, looking down between us. He did have two cocks, both of them starting to emerge from his slit. Each one of them had hefty knots at the base of their ten-inch shafts, both of them also crimson red.

"Oh, fuck," I groaned.

"Just wait," he whispered, his tongue flicking over my skin again. "Gonna fuck that ass and pussy, princess."

"No," I gasped, writhing against him harder.

He was so strong. So fucking strong, and he had me pinned.

" I like it when you struggle, little princess."

His words were like a searing heat straight through me. I was dripping and desperate to dispose of the rest of my clothing. To bare myself to him completely.

"Are you going to behave?" he asked.

"No, Your Majesty," I said.

"Fine," he growled, raking his claws over my pants.

I squealed as they scratched over me, the fabric tearing and the sharp tips grazing my skin.

"Hey!" I cried. "I need those!"

"Not around me, you don't," he sneered, yanking them down.

He let go of my wrists briefly and before I could sit up, he pulled the rest of my clothing off and then flipped me over.

I squealed, kicking back at him. My heel dug into where his thigh would be if he were human, and he grunted.

But then, he laughed, arresting my hands again and shoving my face against the cushion. I shoved back against him, only to feel one of his cocks now resting against my ass.

He leaned down, his tongue flicking out to touch my ear.

"Lucas," I gasped.

"Who do you belong to now, princess?" he snarled. "Who do you obey?"

"Not you," I gasped.

I'd never been this bratty before. I'd never gone to this type of extreme, but fuck it.

"I won't submit to you," I said.

His whole chest vibrated with a snarl, his claws digging into my hair and yanking hard. "I'm going to make you regret saying that, princess."

"All bite, no venom," I said, shoving my ass back against his hard cocks.

The movement alone made him suck in a breath, and I knew I had truly pushed him now.

It was a dangerous game, exhilarating.

He pinned me down now, his weight pressing into me as he ran his hand up my side, giving me gentle squeezes before raking his claws over my skin.

"One day, I'm going to fill you up with all of my cum. And then your sweet cunt will take my eggs and we will have children. But, until then I'm going to use you exactly how I know you want me to."

I cried out as I was lifted, thrown over his shoulder like he was a caveman.

The rest of the lights in the house were turned off and I was carried into the dark. I could only hear my heart thrashing and his scales over the floor, his grip on me tightening as we went down a hall.

"How big is your house, Your Majesty?" I asked, letting out a squeal as he smacked my ass.

"Who knew the sweet woman at the coffee shop would be so bratty?" he said.

I fought off a little smirk as a door creaked open and I was taken into a massive room with large windows. The snow storm was settling in outside, blotting out the moon.

Snow still boggled my mind and oftentimes I still forgot to check the weather since living here, which had led to me almost getting in trouble before.

Maybe I was in trouble now...

I was tossed onto a pile of cushions. I started to sit up, but that earned me a growl.

Lucas hovered over me, his diamond eyes honed in on me like a lion stalking its prey.

He bared his fangs, giving me a hiss. "You think you can take my cocks, princess?"

There was a hungry need that overruled every sane thought controlling me now. I held his gaze for a second more before looking down his glorious body to where both of his cocks were hard and throbbing.

He slid his hand down to the top one and arched a brow. "Do you want this inside of you, princess?"

"Yes," I whispered, spreading my legs.

His breath hitched and he leaned down, shoving my legs apart further. His tongue flicked over my clit, the two ends both stroking me.

"Oh god," I groaned, tipping my head back. "Please."

He chuckled. "Now you're being a good girl. Say please again. Beg me to give you my monster cocks. Beg me to knot you, to fill you with my cum."

Part of me wanted to tell him to go to hell, but then the bastard turned his head and started to kiss my inner thighs. His lips ran over my stretch marks, his tongue flicking in and out as he tasted me.

"*Please.*"

Constricted

L ucas

HEARING Sam beg me to fill her was enough to make both of my cocks drip with precum.

I was enjoying the taste of her, taking in every part of her luscious body. She was beautiful and I wanted to memorize every curve, every line, every dimple.

But I also wanted to spank her ass for being such a little brat.

Your Majesty. I smiled as I kissed back down her body, flicking my tongue over her clit again.

Her little gasp told me that as much of a brat as she was, she was going to submit to me.

And when she did— when she fully did— it would be the most glorious submission I would ever experience.

"Please," she rasped again, her eyes fluttering as I started to play with her clit more. "Oh fuck. *Fuck.* That feels really good."

278

Every noise she made was one I would dream about for eternity.

I pushed her legs back and dragged her closer, ready to feast on her. She cried out as I tasted her, pushing my tongue inside.

She tasted divine.

A deep growl left me and I closed my eyes, pressing my tongue in further and further until I was stroking her deep. Her cries were music to me, her fingers gripping the blankets and pillows beneath us.

The need to mate her surged, nearly taking me over. I wanted to fuck her, to claim her completely. Over and over again. She was all I could think of, all I would think of from now on.

Mate.

I couldn't mate her yet. I couldn't seal our bond, not on the first date. Not when she was so new to monsters.

And yet...

I drove my tongue in and out of her, holding her body in place as I rubbed her clit with the pad of my thumb. She screamed out, her muscles tensing.

Princess was so close... so close.

I needed to feel her come undone around my tongue.

I picked up speed, lapping relentlessly at her inner walls. My claws dug into her skin as I tightened my grip. Her moans grew louder, more erratic until finally a scream ripped from her lips and filled the room.

"Lucas!" she cried.

The rest of her words were unintelligible as her muscles clenched around me, her cum flooding my mouth. I continued to lap at her, moaning as I feasted on her dripping pussy.

I finally slipped my tongue out, kissing up her inner thighs as I slowly let go of her.

"Princess," I chuckled. "Did that feel good?"

Her head raised and she looked at me like I was insane. "Yes, that felt good you crazy snake man."

I fought off a laugh, smirking against her soft skin. I licked my lips, chuckling. "You scream so well for me, princess."

She moaned, her head falling back onto the cushions.

She was perfect like this. I could see the heat rising from her, could see her red hair splayed out around her. The cold of the storm wouldn't reach us here, not when one of my cocks was about to be buried inside of her.

But first...

"Turn over," I said, easing back.

She looked like she wanted to argue, but ultimately obeyed me. She huffed and then rolled onto her stomach, presenting her gorgeous ass to me.

I wanted to take her ass too. I had to make sure it was ready for me, just like her pussy was now.

"Are you going to obey me, princess?" I asked, looking down at her.

I gripped her ass cheek, sucking in a breath. I gave her a squeeze and then gripped the other, parting them.

"No," she whispered, but we both knew it was a lie.

"No?" I chuckled, squeezing her ass a little harder. "Princess likes punishment, doesn't she? You want me to devour you. To take your ass and breed your pussy."

I watched her pussy throb even though she let out a little growl. "Never," she said, a little more bite this time.

And yet, she lifted her hips enough for me to lean over and push a pillow beneath them.

"I see," I chuckled. "So stubborn. Already a princess through and through. I'm going to fuck your ass, *your majesty*, and hear your pretty screams again."

She started to buck up but I shoved her down with a snarl, only pausing to catch the curve of her lips.

She was such a brat. She was my little brat.

My cocks both pulsed in unison. She was fucking perfect for me in every way.

My control was slipping further and further. I liked the way she struggled against me, how her little screams sounded as she fought against me. She knew what she was doing, and it turned me on.

I loved a woman who knew what she wanted.

"Not my ass," Sam gasped, trying to roll away.

I slapped her right cheek hard. She cried out as my palm smacked, her skin immediately blushing red with my handprint.

"Princess, I swear to the gods," I sneered, my tail now swiping around.

I wrapped it around her body, binding her arms to her sides. She was starting to really fight me now, her heel kicking back.

I slapped her other ass cheek even harder than the other, growling as she screamed.

"You monster!" she wailed. "Let me go!"

"Not until I devour you," I snarled. "A little helpless human. You won't escape me, little one."

Fuck. I was so fucking hard.

I had known I liked this type of play, but doing it with someone who was into it as much was...exhilarating.

Even though she screamed *no*, her scent was dripping with arousal. Her skin was flushed with heat, her muscles quivering as my tail wrapped around her hips and torso. She was losing more and more mobility, her cry of frustration making me chuckle.

"You thought you were in control, didn't you?" I hissed, leaning over her.

My body hovered over hers now, both of my cocks pulsing and dripping. I wanted to bury them into her tight holes, to fill her up with every drop of me. I tightened my tail again, constricting her until her breath caught, and she began panting.

"Lucas," she groaned. "Oh gods."

I gripped my lower cock, rubbing the head against her pussy for a moment. She squealed, her body trying to fight me again.

It was no use, she was bound by me. Bound to me.

"Don't worry, princess. You're not getting your monster's cock yet. Not until your ass is ready for the other one too."

"No," she moaned.

I shifted, using my free hand to trace my fingers down her back. The very tip of my tail rattled as I ran two of my fingers across her hole. I paused, moaning.

Her ass needed to be lubed up, and the only thing that would truly help her take something as large as one of my cocks and knots was some of my cum.

Swallowing a groan, I began stroking my top cock, quickly, finding a rhythm that would send me spiraling soon.

"What are you doing?" Sam gasped, trying to turn her head to look back at me.

"We need to lube up your ass, and my cum will help your body," I huffed, tilting my head back.

I jerked myself harder, groaning as I got closer and closer. I looked back down at her, at how fucking perfect she looked wrapped up in my tail.

"Have to get your ass ready for fucking," I gasped.

With a snarl, I started to cum— spraying my seed straight onto her waiting asshole.

I grunted as I coated her with my essence. I fell forward, planting one hand to her side while I dipped two fingers into my cum and then eased the tip into her ass.

"Oh god," she gasped, bucking against me.

"Nice try, princess," I panted. "Don't worry. I'm going to make your ass feel just like your sweet cunt."

She cried out as I shoved more cum inside of her, making sure to get as much in as possible. I then worked a second finger in, thrusting them in and out.

"Say thank you," I growled.

"No," she groaned. "You fucking monster. Horrible!" she yelled.

I paused and smacked her ass, her squeal making me hard again.

"I told you to thank me, you ungrateful little princess. *Now*."

"No," she gasped.

This time I shoved four fingers inside of her. She screamed, but it turned into a surprised gasp and moan as I began to fuck her.

"Little slut," I muttered. "Such a dirty little princess. Likes to get fucked by monsters. Does anyone else know how much of a slut you are for monsters?"

"No!" she cried. "No, no. Oh god. FUCK!"

Her body started to quake all over again and I watched as she started to cum again, this time just from her ass. This one was short and sharp and within a few moments, she was completely limp in my tail.

I pulled my fingers free and leaned over her, pushing the wild strands of red from her lovely face.

She made a noise, her eyes fluttering. "*Monster*," she whispered, breathless.

"You like it," I chuckled.

She fought off a smile and I leaned in closer, brushing my lips against hers. She moaned, parting them for me so I could taste her.

Both of my cocks needed to be buried inside of her. *Now*.

I drew back, pinning my hands to either side of her shoulders. My torso stretched above her, my cocks now pressed against her ass. The rest of my tail was long enough to wrap around her body and pin her down while giving me room to still move.

She was *mine*.

"Sam," I snarled. "Tell me to fuck you."

"No," she whispered.

"*Tell me!*" I thundered.

Her breath hitched and she groaned, turning her head to the side so that she could look up at me from the corner of her eye.

"Fuck me," she rasped. "Mate me. Take me. I want you more than anything else."

Her words defeated me.

I had no control left. I couldn't wait any longer.

I groaned and reached down between us, easing both of my cocks inside her. One into her pussy, the other into her ass.

She gasped in surprise, her muscles clenching around me.

"You're so big," Sam whimpered, her fingers gripping the blankets under her.

"All yours," I gasped, pleasure burning through me as I eased the first few inches in.

Her body was ready for me, my cum helping her take both of them.

"Fuck," I snarled. "Fuck, I want to bite you so badly. I want to know what you're feeling right now, for our bond to share pleasure."

"Do it," she moaned.

I froze for a moment.

The most primal part of me— the monster that fought against the humanity, the creature that devoured any sense of patience— I felt it overcome me.

Why not take her now? Not another man or creature would lay a finger on her pretty body.

She would never belong to another.

She didn't know what she was asking for but I didn't care.

She had to belong to me.

Now and forever.

Venom

S ^{am}

I REALIZED a little too late that I'd just asked a Basilisk to mate me.

Lucas's fangs sank clean through my flesh and muscles, deep into my shoulder. My scream was drowned out, pain immediately blooming where he held onto me.

Heat injected into my veins and every ounce of excruciating pain was replaced with an almost unbearable pleasure.

My scream turned into another orgasm.

He slammed both of his cocks all the way into me now and I felt his venom start to overtake me. I cried out as a wave of ecstasy crashed into me, my thoughts completely obliterated.

I'd always wanted to be fucked so hard I couldn't remember who I was and fucking hell— I didn't know left from right. I didn't know my name or how the fuck I got here.

All I knew was that I had just been mated to a Basilisk Prince.

His voice filled my mind, along with the weird merge of our emotions. Of the heat between us and the edge of passion sharper than a blade.

Mine. Always mine.

I was crying I realized, tears streaming down my cheeks. Everything felt so good that it hurt.

He groaned and sucked, drawing some of my blood into his mouth. He began to move his hips, thrusting in and out as he fed.

I didn't know he would feed on me, but fuck.

FUCK. Now I knew why humans loved to be with monsters. This was exhilarating, being constricted and fed on by him.

Mate, he hissed into my mind.

"Yes," I whispered. "Oh god, you feel so good," I groaned.

He began to pump into me harder, and I didn't have to ask him how to make it feel good. It was as if our thoughts were in sync, his body immediately responding to my every little wish. His tail tightened more around me and my breath was knocked out of me.

He slowly pulled his fangs free and I felt drops of venom fall on my back.

He growled and I cried out as I felt something thick press against my openings.

"I'm going to knot you," he snarled. "Fuck, you feel so good, little red."

He leaned down and kissed the mark he'd just made, and his gentle touch was enough to send me over the edge again. Pleasure crashed into me again, and this time I squealed as he gave one final thrust— forcing both of his knots inside of me.

Cum started to fill me, both of his cocks filling me up. The two of us moaned together, our bodies one. Lucas gave a soft hiss, his tail slowly unraveling from around me. He replaced it with his arms, pulling me close to him.

I was in a daze, my brain on cloud nine. I could barely think, but fucking hell— I felt amazing.

His knots pulsed inside of me, keeping the cum in.

Lucas nuzzled me, our breaths softening. "You did so well," he whispered.

I nodded, still not processing everything that had just happened. He gave me a gentle kiss, his touch becoming soothing and sweet.

"I need to hear you speak, little red. I need to know that you're okay," he whispered.

"I'm more than okay," I rasped, holding up a haphazard thumbs up.

He chuckled, his tongue swiping over the bite again. I moaned a little, the area sensitive.

Fuck. I'd just mated with him.

I'd just bound my soul to a Basilisk on the first fucking date.

"Oh my god," I whispered. "What the fuck did we just do?"

Lucas lifted his head, letting out a little snort. "Mated."

"Yeah," I whispered, my eyes widening.

My brain was starting to work again finally. I started to turn, only to realize that his knots were keeping me in place.

Lucas let out a little growl, his arms tightening around me. "You're scared," he whispered.

"I didn't think this through! What if we hate each other. What if you hate me and don't want to be with me or what if I don't want to be with you. I don't know how royalty works and —"

"Little red," he purred, "I promise that it will be okay. I know that...this is unconventional by human standards, but I knew the moment I saw you that you were mine. As for royalty, we have no worries about that right now. We will figure that out. Etiquette can be learned."

I started to ramble again but ended up closing my mouth, feeling a sense of comfort wash over me. I realized that it was coming from him and that he was able to help me.

"I shouldn't have mated you so soon," he whispered. "But I couldn't stop myself when you asked me to. I'm sorry, but I have no regrets."

I swallowed hard as he nuzzled me, my breathing finally evening out.

"Once my knots can be pulled from you, we will go relax in my hot tub and I will feed you whatever you would like. I'm fairly good at cooking, despite the fact that most of our servants did it for so long."

"Servants?" I whispered.

That was a foreign concept to me and one I didn't like. I liked doing things myself. I had a tiny apartment that I kept spotless and when I wasn't going out, I liked to cook too. There was something relaxing about day-to-day tasks.

I wasn't cut out to be royalty and already the doubts were tearing into me.

Lucas slid his hand down my side, giving my love handle a squeeze. "Sam, I promise... I promise that I'll win you over."

"You've already won me over," I whispered. "It's just that sometimes lives don't fit together. I've never had anyone do anything for me."

"Yes. And I always have. Now, I'd like to do things for someone else. I want to serve you, princess. I want you to do whatever you want to do. Spend whatever you want, love whatever you want. You're mine now, little red."

The way he said *mine* made me shiver.

"Go to sleep, little red. My cock is still filling you as my body is made to prep you for my eggs. But don't worry, we won't do that."

"Eggs," I said, shaking my head.

Everything about this evening had turned crazy.

He chuckled, his hand sliding up to my stomach. "One day," he whispered.

Fucking hell. I'd mated a Basilisk prince with a breeding kink.

Lucas's hand slid down further and I couldn't fight the moan that left my lips as he neared my clit.

All thoughts flew out the window again.

I hated that my clit was like an off button for reality, but fuck...

Lucas drew in a deep breath, dragging in my scent. "I'm going to make you cum again for me. And then you'll sleep."

"I don't think I can," I gasped.

"Doesn't hurt to try," he said, slipping two of his fingers down further.

Fuck. I was still so wet from cumming and from his cum too. I cried out like I was being shocked as he found my clit, giving it a gentle rub.

"You're so sensitive, little red," he hissed. "My little princess wants to cum again, hmm?"

I started to tell him to fuck off but choked on the words as he started to rub my clit in circles. He worked the pressure harder, the end of his tail binding my legs before I could writhe away from him.

"Stay *put*," he growled, rubbing me faster.

My nipples hardened as a chill of need worked through me. I gasped, falling back down the tunnel of primal need. He was able to turn me on and make me cum so quickly, his fingers doing exactly what my body needed.

"Cum for me," he snarled.

He rubbed faster and harder and I screamed, my voice echoing through the room as another orgasm crashed into me. My entire body tightened around his cocks and knots, and he kept rubbing me even as I came, drawing out my orgasm as long as he could.

I was left gasping and panting, my eyes tearing up.

"I think you can cum again," he said.

"No," I gasped. "No. I can't. There's no way, Lucas."

He chuckled as his fingers circled me, gentle again. Swirling our cum around me, little quakes of pleasure working through me.

"I'm going to make you cum until you start crying. I want to see you beg. Really beg."

"No," I rasped, even though there was a dark part of me that wanted him to.

I wanted him to make me cum until I begged him to stop.

Remember your safeword, he reminded me.

"No," I cried. "You can't make me cum again. Let me go!"

"No," he snarled. "I'm never letting you go. You're mine to fuck and to use over and over again."

I felt a tremor through my body as he started to circle my clit faster, the pressure still easy. I moaned against him, still recovering from the last one but the bastard didn't care.

He would make me cum over and over until he decided it was time to stop.

This was some sort of torture. It was hell and heaven and fucking everything that I needed.

"Your cunt is mine," he growled, thrusting his hips.

Fuck. He was still hard inside of me, I realized. A little cry broke from me as he started to rub me harder again, focusing on my clit. He moved his fingers back and forth, driving me straight back to the edge. It almost hurt, the pleasure sharper than a knife.

But fuck.

Fuck. I couldn't ask him to stop.

I had my safeword and yet...

I screamed, my head falling back against his chest. "Stop!" I screamed.

"Never," he sneered.

I'd never been fucked like this. My ass and pussy were full of cum and knotted, and he was forcing me to cum with just his finger on my clit.

"Cum for me, little red," he growled. "Cum for me. Be my dirty little princess."

I was falling deeper and deeper into sub-space now. I cried out, another orgasm crashing into me. Drowning me. My blood burned with heat, and I stopped hearing my own screams as he kept going. Relentless release, sending another orgasm through me.

FUCK.

I couldn't catch my breath, didn't have a moment to recover. I was his and his alone, to use and fuck and force to release.

I was begging, I realized. Words were coming from my lips, my voice almost broken.

"Please, please, please," I cried. "Please."

"Please what, little red? You want me to stop?"

Tears streamed down my cheeks and I let out a little sob.

I didn't want him to stop.

"One more," he growled.

"No!" I cried. "Please!"

His fingers started to work me over again despite my begging.

One final orgasm overcame me and his fingers pulled free. My entire body trembled against him, my mind shattered from the number of orgasms I'd just endured.

I gasped as I felt his knots pull free. I was immediately

turned over and he leaned down, cradling my face and kissing me.

"My little princess," he praised. "Look at me, baby."

I could barely fucking see but I still looked up at him. He wiped away my tears, kissing me again.

"Hold on to me," he whispered. "I'm yours, love."

I was crying again. I felt part of me unlock, a flood of emotions washing through me.

"I don't know why I'm crying," I sobbed. "I'm sorry. I'm sorry."

He shook his head, pulling me in for a hug again. "You can always cry, little red. You can always cry on me. I'm yours, baby. Don't ever be sorry for crying."

I sniffled, burying my face against his chest. His skin was covered in scales, but it felt comforting.

I finally started to calm down. It was as if the raging waves inside of me had turned serene and now I was just a puddle of need. His hand slipped up, rubbing the back of my head.

"That was intense," he whispered. "It's normal to have a drop after. Take a little rest, love. I'm right here. When you wake up, we'll have some food and chocolate and cuddles."

"Okay," I whispered, my eyes slowly closing.

I felt that comfort again. It was like a warm blanket covering me, keeping me safe.

With a happy sigh, I let myself fall asleep.

CHAPTER 6
Banana Pancakes

L ucas

LITTLE RED WAS STILL fast asleep in my bed.

The sky outside was still covered with snow clouds, and the threat of the storm still wasn't over. The massive windows gave us a snow-filled view of the forest surrounding my home.

I had shifted into my human form and was in the kitchen, trying to be quiet as I started breakfast.

Everything that had happened last night had changed our lives.

But....

Wasn't that what I had planned?

I'd seen her and known.

But I also knew humans had a difficult time with the suddenness of our bonds, and that their courting practices weren't as intense. Still, she had known she was going to date a monster.

There was a part of me that was constantly fighting the manipulative part of me. It was a battle and I lost often. Like last night, if she wouldn't have been so willing...would I have taken her car out?

Perhaps it was wrong and obsessive.

Well, it *was* wrong and obsessive.

I had felt her worries last night after she had realized what we had done. She felt out of place, scared and worried that I didn't want her. Humans were absurd in that way. There was a part of me that wanted to tell her I was so obsessed with her that I had nearly disabled her car battery so that I could keep her.

But also, maybe I shouldn't show her just how possessive I could be.

I was a Prince. Set to be King. I always got what I wanted. I always won.

This was no different.

But, I wanted her to be happy. Her happiness and well-being were now more important than what I wanted.

I thought about everything as I started to cook, making banana pancakes with fresh fruit and sausage. I wasn't sure exactly what she liked, but pancakes always seemed to be a safe bet.

All humans liked pancakes right?

I shook my head as I made them, grumbling to myself.

"You talk a lot to yourself."

I looked up at the doorway, surprised to see Sam.

She was standing naked with a blanket wrapped around her, her red hair tumbling down her freckled shoulders. She was a fucking goddess and I felt my knees go weak for a moment.

"I talk when I think," I whispered.

Sam smiled, her expression warming. "Cute."

"How are you feeling?" I asked, flipping a pancake onto a plate.

I turned off the stove quickly and then went to her, pulling her into a big hug. Her head fell back as she looked at me.

"Sore," she said, grinning. "But good. A little worried. A little scared. Also, I'm pretty certain we're snowed in. I looked at the weather on my phone and we got a lot."

"We're snowed in but we have plenty of food and water and power," I said.

"If I didn't know any better, I'd say you caused this storm."

I smirked. "If I could, then I definitely would have. I'm a little...devious sometimes."

"A monster," she teased, leaning up on her tiptoes to kiss me.

"Your monster," I said. "A monster who made you pancakes. I hope you like them."

"I love pancakes. Food, in general, sounds good right now."

"Mhmm. Maybe a hot bath. And a massage."

She arched a brow. "Are you telling me you'll give me a massage?"

"Anything you want," I whispered, swallowing hard. "But first, let me check your bite wound."

Her hazel eyes flickered but she nodded, turning around. She let the blanket slide off her and I swept her hair to the side.

It had already mostly healed, although I could see her skin was tender around the puncture wounds. I needed to nurse it some and it would help ease the pain.

I leaned down, kissing her shoulder wound. She let out a little breath and then a moan, her skin flushing.

A possessive growl left me and I tugged her closer, running my hands over her curves. She was so fucking gorgeous, from her thighs to her stomach and breasts.

Fuck. I just wanted to devour her.

"Oh," she gasped.

I sucked the mark, nursing it. I swirled my tongue over her

skin with a grunt, my cock starting to harden. My skin itched, the urge to shift growing stronger.

I drew back with a hum, sighing. "Eat, little red, before I eat you."

Sam pulled the blanket back around her with a little giggle. I went back to the stove, grabbing the plate of pancakes next to it.

"Go sit," I commanded, nodding at the bar.

This house was definitely less opulent than what I was used to. In no other home would I feed someone at a kitchen bar. Instead, there would be a massive dining table, one fit for hosting dinner parties with creatures of all kinds.

I thought about the two of us for a moment sitting at a massive table. Dressed as a King, her as my Queen. Her red hair would tumble down her pale shoulders, her expression warm like it had been since we'd met.

It was a thought I would hold on to for a while.

With a little hum, I grabbed the food and took the plates over to her. I had started a pot of coffee as well and went back, pouring us two mugs.

"Thank you," she said, beaming as I handed it to her.

"Of course, princess," I said, smiling as I took the seat next to her.

There were times that it was uncomfortable to be in my human form, but at this moment, it felt right. Sitting next to her, eating pancakes for breakfast after a glorious night together reminded me that I wasn't as monsterly as I believed.

Well, I *was* a monster. But perhaps I wasn't as bad as I thought.

"Did you sleep okay?" I asked as she bit into her breakfast.

She gave a nod, covering her mouth as she swallowed before sipping her coffee. "I did. I passed out. Did I snore?"

"No," I chuckled.

The idea of little red snoring made me stupidly happy for some reason.

"Good. Sometimes I do. So, what...what do we do now?"

"Well," I said, glancing behind us at the windows that showed us the snowy world outside. "Breakfast and then a hot bath. Maybe at some point, I will show you my fully shifted form.

I pulled my gaze from the windows. It was like being trapped in a snow globe, one that I would happily stay in forever.

I looked at Sam, giving her a soft grin. "Only if you want. We're quite frightening like that."

"I don't think you will frighten me," she snorted. "No. You're not as much of an asshole as you think you are."

"Easy to say when you're wearing rose-colored glasses," I teased. "It was the double cocks."

This time, she gave me a full laugh, her head tilting back for a moment. She was so fucking beautiful and I found myself wishing I could take her all over again.

Maybe in the bath...

My cock hardened at the thought of washing her body, imagining sliding my fingers inside her pussy again.

Her cheeks blushed and she looked at me, her eyes darkening. "You want me again," she whispered.

Her tone almost made it sound like it was a question.

"Of course I do," I said. "I want you more than anyone I've ever wanted in this world, little red."

"Why do you want to be with a human? I thought most monsters liked to date monsters," she said, frowning.

"It depends on the creature," I said, taking a sip of my coffee. The warmth felt good as my body didn't heat the same way that hers did. "Most monsters do like to date monsters. But some monsters' soulmates are human. Sometimes humans love monsters. I've always loved humans, even though my family hasn't been the kindest to them. My father used to hunt them..."

I trailed off, trying not to wince. Perhaps breakfast wasn't the time to tell her about how dangerous my family could be.

"That sounds terrifying," Sam whispered. "I'm still very new to this part of the world. It's like...I love it. But I am a little scared sometimes. I know how strong monsters are. A lot of them have talons and fangs and the type of strength I won't ever have. But...I've met creatures that have big hearts. That love harder than they bite."

I nodded, thinking about my friend, Naomi. Naomi was Naga royalty and had chosen a human mate, Ella. I'd known Naomi for ages and had never seen her this happy. The two of them had settled down in a home not too far from here. I'd heard the stories about Naomi winning over a cat and even caring for some goldfish.

It was nice to think about.

Maybe that would be me one day.

"Do you have any pets?" I asked.

Sam laughed, shaking her head. "So random. No, I don't. I'd like to get a dog at some point but sometimes I forget to water my plants, so..."

"Plants can't remind you," I said, smirking.

"Are you telling me that you want a puppy, Lucas?" Sam teased.

"Maybe," I admitted.

"Children and a dog," she said. "You want a white picket fence too?"

I snorted this time, but I didn't deny it. "Maybe not the picket fence, but I do already have a gate."

Her laughter rang again, making me smile. I liked making her laugh like this.

Fuck. How in the hell had I met a human that could make

me want to bend her over and mate her again and again, while also being someone I wanted to make laugh? I loved her already, even though I'd just met her.

The two of us fell into a rhythm of chatting while eating. Breakfast took longer than it ever did when I ate alone, and I loved it.

Once the two of us finished, I snagged her plate and the others— taking them to the sink.

"Would you like some help, Your Majesty?" Sam snickered.

I arched a brow, turning to look at her.

"I'd like for us to go to my bath so I can devour you, little red," I said.

"Oh, will we both fit?" she asked.

I nodded. "It's large enough to hold me if I'm half shifted. Sometimes I like to have my scales polished. It feels nice."

"Oh," she whispered. "I'd like to do that sometimes."

I paused, my heart skipping a beat.

"Would you?" I asked.

"Yes," she said, beaming. "Maybe brush your hair too. If you'd let me. Although I'm sure someone professional would do it better."

"I don't think anyone could make me feel better than you, little red," I said.

I walked around the kitchen bar to her, now determined to get her wet.

In more ways than one.

"Alright," I said, reaching for her.

I scooped her up, throwing her over my shoulder despite her squeal.

"Lucas!" she yelled, the blanket sliding off her.

Perfect. I smacked her ass, my cocks now hard. I let my form shift halfway, which felt as good as shedding a second skin. Now both of my cocks could be hard and ready for her.

"Bath time, princess. I need to get you wet."

CHAPTER 7
Tears

S ^{am}

LUCAS GLIDED down the hall and I realized just how big his house was. I was carried to another room and then through an arched doorway.

"Hey," I said, slapping at him. "Put me down!"

"Nope," he chuckled.

I scoffed but it was hard to fight a monster that had just made me banana pancakes.

"What kind of scents do you like?" Lucas asked, still keeping me over his shoulder as he slithered over to a cabinet.

I tried to look back behind me but he slapped my ass again, drawing out a squeal from me.

"I like jasmine and gardenia," I hissed, trying to writhe away from him.

That earned me another ass pat and a little growl.

It would take me a while to get used to being treated like

this. He simultaneously was sweet and an ass and I wasn't sure what to make of it.

I heard him select a couple of things and then I was promptly let down. Lucas towered over me, his hand snaking up and gripping my face.

I fought off a smile.

I really liked being a brat towards him. I liked to give him trouble, to push him.

He was a prince and he needed someone to tell him no every now and then.

His tongue flicked out over his fangs, his golden eyes glinting with hunger. "Kneel and wait, little red."

"No," I said, arching a brow.

The pressure of his gaze was almost enough to send me to my knees, but I fought it. I fought the pressure I felt.

Fucking hell.

I wanted to be on my knees for him, but...

I thought about last night. About the safeword we had set and how...

Even when I'd said no, I'd still wanted him.

It was like I was finally getting to live out my fantasies for the first time in my life. Finally getting a taste of the dark desires that had been living in my head for years.

"Little red," he said, his voice deadly calm. "You will kneel for me. Now."

I tipped my chin up, looking straight at him. Challenging him.

A low growl worked out from him and he leaned in close, his face only an inch from mine.

"Do you want me to bathe you and rub you with body oil or do you want me to fuck your throat so hard that you cry again?"

"Both?" I whispered.

His eyes flashed and within a moment, I was shoved

down to the hard floor. I cried out as my knees hit and his tail immediately curled around me, the tip working through my thighs.

Lucas's hand shot out and he grabbed my throat, gripping it hard enough to keep me in place.

"I wanted to treat you like a princess but you just want to be my little slut right now, hmm?"

"Yes," I choked out, and gasped in air.

He chuckled and his hand moved back, fisting my hair. I was presented with the full glory of both of his cocks in the morning light.

Last night, I'd felt them. But I hadn't truly gotten to see them, to worship them the way that I wanted. Each of them was so big that I wondered how I'd taken one let alone two. They were bright red like his scales, and the knots at the base both throbbed with need.

"Fuck," I whispered, swallowing hard.

"Open your mouth," he said.

"No," I said, looking up at him.

His forehead ticked, his fangs baring. "You really want me to make you, princess? Such a naughty fucking thing."

I started to talk back again but he grabbed my jaw, forcing my mouth open. I gasped just as he thrust forward, fitting one of his cock inside. He gripped my hair with a snarl, hitting the back of my throat.

I choked, tears filling my eyes.

Fuck, it felt so good to be used. To be worshipped and abused. I wanted him to fuck me however he wanted, to make me beg him to stop and keep going.

The tip of his tail rattled and then brushed over my pussy, making me moan loudly in alarm. He held me tighter, pumping in and out of my mouth faster. I started to choke again but he pulled out, allowing me to drag in air.

"Fuck," I gasped, my entire body throbbing. My head was swimming, my blood rushing.

I was so fucking wet. Every time he hit the back of my throat, I got more and more needy for him.

He growled, forcing the head of his other cock between my lips.

"Fuckin' take it, little red," he growled. "Take my fucking monster cock. I'm going to breed your tight little pussy and make you carry my eggs. Is that what you want?"

I sucked in a breath just as he started to fuck my throat again. The tip of his tail parted me, penetrating me just a couple of inches. I tried to writhe away but I was held in place, his tail starting to fuck me while tears streamed down my cheeks.

"Eyes on me, princess," he growled.

I looked up at him, and my vision blurred.

He *was* a monster, but he was mine now. Just as much as I was his. My mate— my Prince.

He chuckled. "Even taking my cock, you look so defiant. Such an angry little thing. And yet you suck me so eagerly."

I groaned as his hips thrust harder. His tail thrust up more, drawing a yelp from me.

He pulled his cock free, slapping my face with it. He then pulled his tail free of me, slithering it back. "Are you going to listen to me now?"

I was drawing in deep, ragged breaths. He wiped away my tears and I fought off a smile.

I was enjoying doing things like this with him too much. It was exhilarating.

"I want you to breed me," I whispered, my voice raw.

His eyes darkened, his diamond pupils growing larger. "Not until you're certain you want that."

"I want it," I whispered. "I want to know what it feels like. You keep bringing up your eggs..."

"Yes," he hissed. "Fucking hell, little red. I don't want to scare you away from me."

"If you haven't already, then are you really worried?" I asked.

We held each other's gazes, both of us thinking.

I was asking for more than I thought I would ever ask for.

But...I'd always wanted a family. I'd always wanted to have a life with someone, to grow old together. To be together.

We'd only met each other last night and already mated. I'd known that when the Barista matched me with someone, they might really be the one. Bianca had warned me of that much.

He had a reputation amongst Creatures and some humans.

Everything was moving fast, but...sometimes that was okay. I didn't have to fit my timeline into the same box as other people. And why would I want to? So what if I fell in love quickly? So what if I ended up committing to him fast? It didn't matter to anyone but me.

Would I have some questions to answer from people around me? Sure, but also, I couldn't find a shred of worry about it.

I wanted to say yes— I married a Basilisk Prince. Yes— I had children with him. Yes— I have a family now. A life now that isn't just getting up, going to work, and going home alone.

Lucas leaned down, brushing his lips over mine. His touch was gentle, his claws running over my skin softly.

I sighed happily, sinking against him.

"This is normal for my kind," he whispered. "This rush to mate. This need to be together, to commit and fuck each other until we're so happy we can forget the world. And I love it. This is what I wanted. But, I know it's not like that for humans. So I want to make sure you are happy, Sam. I want to make sure we're not fucking this up, which means I will knot you and take you— but we should wait a little longer for true breeding."

My eyes watered up some and I realized just how much I wanted that.

But, he was right.

I would wait.

"Little red," he murmured, kissing me again. "You were made for me. I don't know how I was so lucky. But, I love you as much as I possibly can already."

I closed my eyes for a moment, allowing his words to sink in. I'd done a lot of work with myself over the years of learning how to allow myself to receive things. From compliments to promotions to *love*.

It felt good to let him love me. To know that he meant what he said and not let the little doubt demons eat me up.

"Will you finally let me rub you and bathe you?" Lucas asked.

"Yes," I said, although my pussy was still throbbing and I wanted him inside of me.

He let out a little groan. "I'll knot you after."

"Promises," I teased.

He moved over to the massive bath and turned on the water. Steam immediately began to rise as he tossed a couple of bath bombs in.

Lucas came back over to me and this time, I didn't fight him when he picked me up. I was starting to get used to it and loved it more than I cared to admit.

He moved down a slope that I realized was made for when he was half shifted, lowering us into the water as it filled up. I immediately groaned, my body a lot more sore than I had realized.

Fuck, this felt good.

"Oh god," I sighed happily.

I wrapped my arms around his neck and he let me down

partially, but then tugged my legs around his waist. I held on to him as the water continued to fill, the heat making me moan.

He slipped both of his hands down to my ass, giving me a squeeze as he relaxed.

"What's it like being a Prince?" I asked, pressing my ear against his chest.

He let out a little sigh and the water turned off. I looked over my shoulder to see he'd turned the knob with his tail.

I fought off a smile. Perks of having a long tail.

"It's good sometimes," Lucas said. "I know I am lucky. I have had many experiences that others won't have. I think the hardest part is the way you are treated by those who have certain expectations."

I nodded.

There had been expectations of me growing up, but no one had ever been able to set higher ones than myself. That was also something I had worked on— undoing the 'everything about me has to be perfect all of the time' mindset.

"I enjoy it most of the time. Other times, I wish I could disappear."

"I understand that," I said. "I had to learn how to find the balance between going after what I wanted and not letting others stop me, while also being able to appreciate what I have. And sometimes that's hard. Some days I just want to stay home and never go outside again. But...I think that's how we all are to some extent."

Lucas hummed softly. "I imagine that sometimes you might overthink things."

"I do," I said, smiling. "Which is why this has been good for me. I haven't been able to overthink being with you. In fact, I've done quite the opposite."

"I've perhaps over thought it some. I was ready to have someone take out your car last night."

I arched a brow, moving to look up at him. "What?"

He made a face, wincing. "Sometimes... I am a little..."

"Crazy?" I said, trying not to laugh at him.

"Sure. Crazy."

"A brat."

He narrowed his eyes now. "Maybe. I like getting my way."

I stuck my tongue out at him, shaking my head. "You didn't have to do anything crazy to get me to come home with you."

"You're right," he chuckled. "I just...I didn't want to hide that I almost did that. Also, I definitely am an ass sometimes."

"Oh, I'm sure," I said. "A crazy Basilisk Prince."

He snorted and leaned to the side, grabbing a bottle of soap. "Yes. And you're my crazy little mate. Now, let me wash you and rub your muscles before I fuck you senseless again."

I was about to answer him when a sound echoed from the living room.

Lucas froze, his eyes widening.

I scowled and started to move, but he shook his head. "I'll be back."

"I'm sure it's fine," I said, reaching for him.

"No. All of my servants are gone right now. No one should be here but us."

"Maybe one of the pans fell or—"

"Sam," he growled. "Stay here."

I pressed my lips together as he shifted into his human form, getting out of the tub. I watched helplessly as he left, slamming the bedroom door.

I wanted to believe that it was just something falling in the living room, but the pounding in my chest told me otherwise.

CHAPTER 8
Stolen

L ucas

I SHIFTED BACK into my half form, moving down the hall and out into the living room.

"Brother."

Fuck.

His voice alone made me freeze.

I looked up across my living space to see my brother, the last person that should have been in my house. He was in his human form, dressed in a black suit. His hair was cut short, his deep brown skin glinting with his indigo scales.

We looked almost identical, except I preferred to keep my hair long and had crimson scales.

"What are you doing here, Liam?" I asked.

He cocked his head, crossing his arms. "I came to see if it was true. But, based on the scents, I would say that it is."

His rage was enough to make me wonder if I was going to fight my brother today.

"I don't know what you mean," I said cooly, taking on the air that I always had to take.

I was a Prince. I was royalty. My emotions didn't matter. I did what I had to, what was expected of me.

I fought his venom with venom, even if it was the kind that was so subtle, only we would notice.

"A human. I heard from one of your servants that you have taken a human to your bed for your little holiday getaway. *You*, a Prince. Next in line to the throne. When you have plenty of Basilisk women that would throw themselves at your feet."

"Get out of my house, Liam," I sneered. "I am off right now, and am—"

"Lucas?" Sam's voice called.

Fucking hell.

Liam stared at me for a moment and then he lunged, immediately changing into his half-shifted form.

I met him with full force, intercepting him just as Sam came out into the living room with a yelp.

"I told you to stay put!" I yelled, slamming into Liam.

Liam laughed as he shoved me to the side, slithering straight for her.

Sam screamed, backing up against the wall. She'd thrown on a robe but was still wet, and scared.

I grabbed Liam by his tail, dragging him back as he hissed at her.

"Stay away from her!" I roared.

Liam growled and swung back, hitting me hard in the head. I fell back, crashing into one of the side tables.

"You can't be with a human," he said. "I will end this for you!"

"No!" I snarled.

The two of us tumbled, fighting tooth and nail. His fangs ripped into me, his talons raking across my chest.

I looked up at Sam, seeing how she was frozen in place. "Run," I growled.

Her eyes widened and she took a step back just as Liam slammed into me again.

The bastard had always fought hard.

He twisted from my grip and then turned again, breaking off a leg from my coffee table.

"GODS DAMN IT LIAM!" I yelled. "You will pay for that!"

"A thousand times over if it means I can save you from a human," he growled, lunging for me again.

The two of us hit the floor, and I had forgotten that not only did he fight hard— he also fought dirty.

The leg of the coffee table hit me hard in the head— and my entire world went black.

I WOKE UP TO SILENCE.

My eyes cracked open and I blinked a few times, clearing my head. My temple throbbed with pain and I hissed as I touched it.

Fuck. What the fuck had happened?

I was in my living room and I looked at the wall of windows, seeing the heavy snow hitting the glass. The snowstorm had gotten worse and...

I felt a fierce tug of pain in my heart.

Sam.

Fuck.

Liam.

This was exactly why I didn't want my family to find out about Sam yet. Fuck, I should have been more careful.

I shouldn't have trusted anyone.

For Liam to come all the way here in the snowstorm meant that he was truly determined to stop my relationship with Sam.

But, I knew she was at least still alive.

For now.

Liam had always been the one to get his hands dirty and wasn't afraid of killing, especially if it was a human. He didn't like the world of humans, and he didn't believe that monsters and humans belonged together.

It was the old way, one that I had never truly believed in.

I wanted Sam more than anyone else I had wanted.

"Fuck," I whispered.

I sat up, swallowing hard. My mouth tasted like my venom, my muscles burning with need.

I had to get to her before the worst happened.

I had to stop Liam from hurting her.

I rose from the floor, looking around at all of the destruction.

She had to be close.

I looked out at the snowy forest, feeling a prick of fear.

She would die if he took her there.

Finally, I was able to work through the throbbing in my head. I rushed through the house, checking for Sam. Looking for Liam. I checked all of the rooms, desperate to see if he had fucked up and kept her here.

But I knew the truth.

The bastard had taken her out into the storm.

Rage burned through me.

Sam was mine. How fucking dare he lay a claw on her?

She was MINE. My mate, my princess. And now she was in danger, all because I had been betrayed.

A growl tore through me and I moved back towards the front door, bursting out into the frosty air.

313

I let him out.

The part of me that stayed caged up. That I kept from most of the world.

The beast inside of me.

The one that would find our mate.

With a heavy snarl, I turned into my full form.

Sam was ours.

CHAPTER 9
Snowflakes and Scales

S ^{am}

I HAD STOPPED FEELING my body despite the robe that was
wrapped around me.

I had stopped moving as the monster dragged me through
the snow, and stopped feeling the burn on my skin. My hair was
frozen to my face now, and I had stopped fighting him.

He had won, and now, I wasn't sure if I was going to
make it.

"Humans don't belong with monsters," he muttered.

This was probably the thousandth time he had said this
while taking me wherever the fuck he was going to take me. Part
of me wished I would black back out, but my mind still stayed
conscious.

He kept dragging me along, pulling me like a sled through
the drifting snow. The bright blue of his tail a stark contrast to
the white all around us.

Hang on.

It was his voice again. Floating through my head like a ghost.

I'm almost to you, princess.

I wanted that to be true.

Liam stopped dragging me, letting out a low growl. He dropped me and then turned, hovering over me.

"Still alive," he sighed, shaking his head. "Must be the mating bond keeping you from passing out. Your teeth aren't even chattering."

I glared at him even though I couldn't find the strength to move. I had never been one for murder, but I was rethinking it.

The difference between Lucas and Liam was that Liam was an actual monster. He was one that liked to hurt people.

There was a glint in his eyes as he studied me, shaking his head like it was such a pity that I was still alive.

Fuck you, I wanted to whisper, but my lips wouldn't move.

"He's a *Prince*," Liam scoffed. "He should be with someone worthy. No human is worthy."

Fuck you times two.

Liam shook his head, glaring. "I really don't get why monsters love humans. You're so weak compared to us. You live for such a short amount of time. Did he even tell you what would happen once the two of you were mated? Did he tell you that you'd live as long as him, and die when he dies? Did he tell you how soul bonds work and what the expectations are of someone who is mated to the Basilisk King?"

I felt a little tick of concern. He hadn't told me those things. I had no idea what some of the consequences could be for taking a mating bite.

Despite that, I knew I didn't care either. I willingly accepted Lucas' bite, and everything that came with it.

"I doubt he did because he's manipulative. He wants you to

believe you are safe and that you have nothing to worry about. Believe me, I know," he sneered. "I know how convincing Lucas can be. There's a reason he is next in line to the throne. But why am I even telling you? I'm just going to leave you here to—"

The sound of branches breaking and trees cracking interrupted his words. His head twisted and he growled.

He was met with a much larger growl, one that shook the snow from the tree branches.

"Of course, he would fully shift," Liam snarled.

Close your eyes.

I obeyed the voice, my heartbeat picking up as I closed them. The sound of trees crashing and hissing became louder. I listened as Liam cursed, shouting.

"She's just a human, brother!"

I sucked in a breath as I heard a scream, the sound of bones cracking making me flinch. I could hear them fighting, could hear the sound of flesh being torn by fangs.

I wanted to open my eyes, but I wouldn't. I didn't want to see what was happening. I didn't want to know.

Silence finally fell over the forest, the only sound the rattling of my breaths as they painfully squeezed from my lungs.

A new sound broke the silence—the sound of scales slithering across fresh snow.

Open your eyes.

I opened them.

Even if I could scream, I wouldn't have.

I should have. Anyone in their right mind would. Anyone who wasn't mated to a monster would.

I was faced with Lucas, and even in this form— I loved him. I knew him.

He reminded me of a massive dragon and snake together,

his scales the color of blood and glimmering. His eyes burned like golden suns, his tongue flicking out.

His tail immediately wrapped around me and I was lifted from the snow, and pulled against his body.

You will be okay, he told me. *You are safe, princess.*

I was safe and alive and back in the arms of my mate.

Finally, I let the darkness take me, falling into a deep sleep.

Confessions

L ucas

MY MATE HAD ALMOST BEEN TAKEN from me.

I'd left my brother alive, and knew that at some point I would have to deal with him again.

I had shown him mercy. I hadn't wanted to, but I did because I didn't want to start my relationship with Sam as a fresh murderer.

She was asleep in my nest, her cheeks bright red. She had been running a fever on and off.

If we hadn't been mated, then she *would* have died.

I had fucked up. As much as I wanted her, as much as I cared for her— I was still stupid enough to not think things through. I should have been more aware of how others might respond to me choosing a human.

I should have known that the monsters in my life would act like monsters.

Still...

She was safe and she was okay.

She had seen my full form, and she hadn't been scared. Not even a little, even though I could have swallowed her whole.

She has never been scared of me, and I never want her to be.

I let out a little sigh and picked up my phone, scrolling until I found Naomi in my contacts. I pressed the call button, not sure of what I was going to say.

"What's up?" she answered, sounding somewhat annoyed.

"I fucked up," I whispered.

"Oh hell no. Is the human okay? Fucking hell, the Barista is going to murder me—"

"No, no. She's alive. She's okay," I said, scowling.

I hadn't taken my eyes off of her for hours.

"What happened?" Naomi asked.

I heard a soft voice in the background followed by laughter. It sounded like there was a party. I frowned, checking the time on my phone.

Fuck. It was 11 at night.

"I met her on the date and she went home with me because of the storm," I said.

Naomi snorted. "I doubt she went with you because of the storm, but okay."

I narrowed my eyes, but she wasn't wrong. "I took her home and we immediately mated. Almost immediately, anyways."

"Okay?" Naomi asked. "That's fast but it's not unheard of. We do fall pretty fast."

"Yes, and not everyone can hold out as you can."

"Well, it's a matter of willpower and I've always had more of that than you."

I hissed but smiled a little. "Rude bitch."

"Not rude. Realistic. Get to the fucking point though, my

mate is mad that we are at a party and I'm now on the phone. It's New Year's Eve, Lucas."

"My brother found out and attacked us."

"Which one?"

"Liam," I whispered.

"Oh. The little shit. Did he hurt her?"

"He did but...she seems to be okay. She took my venom well and I think it kept her alive. He took her out in the snow storm to leave her for dead."

"How's her pulse?"

"It's good," I said, swallowing hard.

I'd been listening to it for hours, too.

"I guess what I'm trying to ask— is this my fault? Should I... save her from me?"

"As in— leave her?" Naomi asked.

I was silent. I couldn't leave her, even if I thought that was the right thing.

"The answer, if it were me, would be no. I could never leave my Ella. Ella is my mate and we chose each other, even if the world was against us. I know this is all new to you, but you chose her. You have the rest of your lives to figure out all of the other shit. Does that help?"

Oddly enough, it did.

I'd been thinking about everything that had happened for hours and had wondered— would she be better if she didn't have me? Would she be safer? Would she be happier?

"If you're concerned that she might do better without you, then perhaps you should ask her when she wakes up. You have to remember that she is your equal and that she can answer for herself. You're not her Prince in shining armor. You're not her King, Lucas. You're just her mate. Act like it."

I opened my mouth to answer, but Naomi cut me off.

"If she is in danger and you need help, call the Barista and ask him nicely. Don't tell him. Ask him. But, if you're both okay — I think you really should just talk. I need to go."

"Okay," I said, nodding. "You know I appreciate you, Naomi. I know we don't talk often and our fathers don't get along sometimes, but I'm glad we moved past that."

"I am too. I'm glad that you found your mate. But, if you don't do good by her—"

"I will," I promised. "She's mine."

Naomi chuckled. "Good luck, Lucas."

With that, we ended the call.

Sometimes, when I least expected it, I was reminded why having friends was important. Why having someone to call could help ease back from the edge.

Sam was safe. Unless she wanted to leave, she was mine.

If she wanted to, I would let her.

My chest ached at the thought.

I loved her. I loved her more than I had loved anyone else. We would learn about each other, and grow old together. Raise a family together. We could do everything we both wanted and more.

If she wanted to.

I let out a little sigh and crept closer, moving down into the nest where she was still asleep. Her body had recovered quickly, and at the very least— I was still thankful we had fully mated with each other for that reason.

Sam let out a little moan, her breath catching. I moved next to her, looking down at her perfect face.

I wanted her to still want me. But how could I expect her to if she had just survived an absolute nightmare?

"Sam," I whispered. "Princess. My love."

I could feel her again, the emotions in our bond growing stronger.

Both of us were scared for different reasons.

When she had been trapped with Liam, I had felt her help-lessness. Her rage. She had been so brave.

"I'm here with you, princess," I murmured, sliding my hand beneath the blankets to rub her softy.

She let out a little sigh, her eyes finally opening.

I gave her a few moments and then she turned her head, looking at me.

Tears filled her eyes and I felt like my heart was being ripped open at the sight of them.

"Princess," I crooned. "I'm here."

"I thought you died," she whispered. "I thought I was going to die."

"No, my love. I'd never let that happen. Ever," I said, reaching up to cradle her face.

I knelt my forehead to hers, squeezing my eyes shut.

"I've never been so scared," I said. "Fuck. I'm still scared."

"Me too," she whispered.

I frowned, holding her a little tighter. "Why are you scared, my love?"

"I'm scared you won't want me now. He made it sound like I was the worst thing for you and if I am—"

"He's wrong," I growled. "He's never been more wrong in his life. You are the best thing for me. The best thing that has ever happened to me, Sam."

She let out a little breath and her arms moved, wrapping around my neck. I nuzzled her, breathing in her scent.

A laugh escaped me, and I shook my head as tears filled my eyes. "And here I am, scared that I am bad for you. That you'll want to leave after facing such a nightmare because of me. I wouldn't blame you if you did."

"Never," Sam whispered, holding me tighter. "Never. I meant it when I said I'm yours. We can do this together. We can face any nightmare, any monster... *together*."

My breath was shaky, I realized. I'd never felt like this before— this type of vulnerability. I was used to always being the strong one, guarding my emotions against prying eyes.

I wanted what I felt with her. I wanted her to know just how much she meant to me already.

"Mistakes can be good," Sam said, kissing my cheek. "They happen. And god knows I've made my fair share. But sometimes they lead to good things. And I can't help but think this is one of those things. I'm alive. I'm okay," she said, "Perhaps a little more scared of monsters, but...also not."

"What he did was unacceptable," I sighed. "But I didn't kill him."

"Well, I wouldn't want you to," she snorted. She leaned back, studying me. "He is your brother."

"He is. And I hope one day he comes around and learns just how wonderful humans are for us monsters. But, we are safe. And I don't think anyone else will try to harm us. If they do, I will call the Barista."

Sam nodded, relaxing.

"I called Naomi earlier. She's the one who put me in touch with him. She told me something that I think helped me."

"What was that?" Sam asked.

"She told me that I have to remember that I'm not your Prince nor will I be your King. She reminded me that I'm your mate. I'm used to telling people what I want and getting it. I'm used to demanding things, to winning. But... I want you to know that, if you do decide you don't want to be in the world of monsters— all you have to do is say so."

Sam gave me a soft smile, rubbing my jaw with her palm. "I'm telling you that I do want to be, Lucas."

I closed my eyes again, and this time I accepted what she was telling me.

"Okay," I said, looking down at her. "Happy New Year's Eve, baby."

Her eyes lit up, her brows rising. "Is it already?"

"It is," I said. "It took you some time to recover."

She nodded and then relaxed. We both stared for a moment and then broke out into stupid grins. I leaned down and kissed her, surprised to hear a little moan from her.

I wanted her so bad.

Her hand slid down my body, her fingertips gliding over my slit. I broke the kiss, groaning. "Princess..."

"I want you," she gasped. "Please. I want you in your full form."

"I want you," I snarled, my cocks already hardening.

Her eyes brightened and she leaned up, kissing me. "Please," she said.

"We have all the time in the world, princess. I'm going to fuck you every which way, breed that pretty pussy over and over again."

"I want to carry your eggs," she whispered.

I moaned, the thought alone making both of my cocks emerge from their pocket.

"Please," she begged, grinding her hips up.

Fuck, she was really begging. She really wanted this, her face shining with need.

I couldn't say no. Didn't want to say no.

I loved her. We would build a life together— one filled with lust and passion and love.

"Please," she rasped.

"Okay, princess," I growled. "I'll breed you. I'll give you those eggs on the New Year's countdown and we will start our new year right. You're pretty pussy is *mine*."

"Yours," she rasped.

MINE.

CHAPTER 11
Loving the Basilisk

S ^{am}

I was begging him to breed me.

I wanted Lucas so bad. I fucking *needed* him.

His brother had turned my life into a nightmare and I was sure that I was going to die.

But, I didn't. I survived and was rescued by my monstrous mate.

Now, more than anything, I was sure that I was his.

I loved him, even if our relationship was new and still finding its place in our now shared world.

I pushed my hips up against both of his cocks, grinding against him. He let out a dark snarl, pulling the blankets back.

I was naked, my nipples immediately hardening.

He traced a claw across my skin, down my chest and stomach to my clit. He let out a dark moan, tipping his head back for a moment.

"Your scent," he rasped. "Fucking hell. Your scent of need alone could drive me crazy. I have to fill you."

"Please," I gasped.

It was the last time I had to say it. He gave me one last dark look and then moved off of me, his body shifting. I gasped as he became at least four times larger than he already was, the size of his bedroom making sense.

I hadn't thought much of it until now, but I realized that this was his nest. Large enough to hold him in his fully shifted form.

His heavy head moved, hovering over me as he parted his jaws. I gasped as his two massive fangs were revealed, dripping with a bright green substance.

My pussy clenched, my body aching.

I needed him. I wanted to bathe in his venom, to coat myself in it.

Drink my venom, mate. It will ready your body for my eggs.

I sat up, my head spinning as I leaned forward and licked his fang. A low growl rumbled from his long crimson body and I gasped as his tongue flicked out, the forked end brushing over my breasts.

The taste of his venom spread through my mouth and the effect was almost immediate. I was so fucking wet, so ready to take both of his cocks if that was what he wanted.

I licked up more, coating my hands with it before sliding my hand down to my pussy. I parted my legs, gasping as I touched my clit.

Pleasure immediately burst through me, enough to curl my toes.

That's it, princess. Get yourself ready for me, he said.

I groaned as his body moved, his tail wrapping around me. It was long enough to easily wind around my torso and each of my legs, keeping them parted and unable to close.

The feeling of his scales made me gasp, smooth across my

skin. The sensation sent chills through my body, a moan leaving me as I kept rubbing myself.

I was already so close and now I could feel my muscles contracting.

My venom alone will make you orgasm. You will lose yourself to me, but when we are finished, you will be safe.

"Okay," I gasped, moaning as his massive jaws moved between my legs.

His tongue replaced my fingers and I cried out as it licked over my clit, playing with me. Driving me to the edge.

The tips of his fangs rubbed against my hips, but then he moved closer and I stared in shock— realizing that he was able to fit his mouth around me between my legs.

"Oh god," I gasped.

His golden eyes burned with lust as his tongue pressed against me, pushing inside of me. It was easy too, given how wet I was.

I arched in his grip, screaming out as he started to fuck me with it. We were both filled with the need to mate, the need to breed. His venom dripped down my body, stinging with the same pleasure as hot wax did.

"Lucas," I cried, tears filling my eyes.

He was fucking me deep, hitting against my cervix.

He was driving me crazy, driving me closer and closer—

I screamed, my voice ringing as I came around his tongue. I writhed against him but he kept me still, forcing me to stay in his mouth and wrapped in his tail.

My entire body was singing with the aftermath of cumming so hard, but he wasn't done. He was far from being finished with me.

His tongue kept moving, kept fucking me. Over and over again.

I gasped as I felt him shove into me even more.

My body was his to use. I was his mate and love.

I loved the feeling of him fucking me like this, primal and carnal.

He growled and his tongue pulled back, his head moving.

I cried out, feeling empty without something inside of me. I needed to be filled.

"Please," I rasped. "I need you to fill me!"

Relax, princess. I'm about to fuck you in places you've never been fucked before.

His dark chuckle filled my mind and I groaned as the very tip of his tail moved, the sound of the rattle coming again.

My eggs stay in my tail. They've been there for so long, waiting for our mate. Waiting to find the one we'd breed. You're ours, princess. There are eight of them. I'm going to shove them so deep inside of you and then fuck you with my cocks, knotting you and filling you with my cum.

A choked sob left me as another wave of pleasure racked my body. There had been a time when I wouldn't have believed that even the tip of his tail would fit inside of me, but now I knew it would.

The tip pushed in, every ridge marking an inch more that I took from him. He worked it in slow, and I moaned as he began to lap at my clit and shove his tail further in.

"Fuck," I cried, my entire body lighting up with more need.

I couldn't stop *needing*. It was an unquenchable thirst, the desire to be bred so thoroughly by him.

My pussy. My mate. My future, he snarled, shoving his tail in more.

I pulsed around him and gasped as he hit my cervix.

Open your mouth.

I obeyed him and was immediately met with his venom dripping into my mouth.

I swallowed every drop.

Good girl, that's my princess, he praised, a low hum coming from him.

I tipped my head back, allowing my body to completely give in to him.

This was the closest to heaven I'd ever been. I could feel his tail pulsing inside of me, the tip opening and allowing something to start pushing even further up.

My breath hitched as an orgasm hit me out of nowhere, my entire body taking waves of pleasure. My voice was raw from crying out, but I still did— not caring if the entire world heard me.

Only ten more seconds until the New Year, princess. Ten, nine, eight...

I gasped as I felt it go inside of me, filling me. It was a bizarre feeling for his tail to push something further in, but fuck.

Fuck.

My body shivered with delight, and my breathing evened out as I relaxed.

Seven...

I gasped as I felt it again, even fuller this time. Another egg was pushed inside of me.

I raised my head, meeting his golden gaze. He watched me with such pride and love, a soft growl leaving him

Six...

I groaned.

Five...

Another..

Four...

My nipples were hard, my body vibrating. Shivering with this uncontrollable pleasure. Every second that went by was torture, but it was the best kind of torture.

Three...

I moaned. There was less and less room inside of me. I looked down, seeing how my body was starting to swell.

Two...

"Yes," I cried, tears filling my eyes.

His tail pulsed inside of me, sending little thumps through me.

Oh god. Fuck. I was already swollen with his eggs, filled as much as I thought I could be. But, we had one more.

One more egg.

One...

His tail pushed it forward and I groaned as it kept going until it was inside of me. I gasped, sliding my hand over his tail that wrapped around me to my stomach.

I was full of his eggs now.

Happy New Year, my perfect little princess.

With a low groan, he pulled his tail free. My clit ached, my pussy still needy.

He shifted, moving back into his half form. He leaned down, brushing his lips over mine.

"You did so well," he whispered. "So, so good."

"Thank you," I gasped. "Now fill me with your cock and let's start the year off with a bang."

He chuckled and kissed me once more before leaning back, positioning the head of both of his cocks at my opening.

"You're going to take them both," he said. "Your pussy was made for me and I know how much you ache for this."

"I do," I moaned. "Lucas, I need you. I love you."

"I love you too," he said, smiling at me.

He began to push inside of me, the feeling of his two cocks together making me cry out. They were thick, stretching me wide.

He thrust forward and the two of us groaned together, our bodies joined. He pulled back and then pumped forward again, his eyes locking with mine as he started to fuck me.

His hand settled right over where he'd just put the eggs, rubbing the swollen mound gently.

"Mine," he said. "My mate."

"Yours," I agreed, thrusting my hips up to meet his eager thrusts.

The two of us fell into a wild rhythm as he fucked me. His knots both pressed against me and I reached up, pulling his face in for a kiss.

We both groaned and he broke it, gasping.

"Knot me," I whispered. "Please."

He growled and nodded. With one final thrust, both of his knots filled me. The heat started to spread through me as he came, both of his cocks shooting out ropes of cum.

"Fuck," we both gasped, melting against each other.

He was knotted to me now and I was full of our eggs. I groaned, my entire body relaxing. I was euphoric and happy and exactly where I wanted to be.

Lucas rested his head on my chest, sighing with contentment. "I love you, Sam."

"I love you too," I whispered, running my fingers through his hair. "I never thought this would be where I would end up, but I am glad that it is."

Lucas smiled softly against me. "I have wanted this for a long time. To find someone to be with and share a life with. I know there will be a lot to handle, but I'm glad that I will have you by my side to do it."

"Together," I said, smiling.

"Together," Lucas said.

I intertwined my fingers with his and couldn't stop smiling as I closed my eyes.

I couldn't wait to spend the rest of my life with my Basilisk Prince.

Thank you

Thank you so much to Maida and April for all of your help! This anthology could not have happened without you. You're both amazing!

Also— thank you to all of my readers! I loved revisiting Creature Cafe for the holidays and had a lot of fun writing these shorts. It was exciting to see glimpses of their lives five years after, along with what the future holds.

Clio's Creatures

Hello Creatures,

My name is Clio Evans and I am so excited to introduce myself to you! I'm a lover of all things that go bump in the night, fancy peens, coffee, and chocolate.

IF you had the chance to be matched with a monster- what kind would you choose?!

Let me know by joining me on FB and Instagram. I'm a sucker for werewolves to this day.

Made in the USA
Las Vegas, NV
14 December 2023

82361795R00193